SAINTS
& SINNERS

SAINTS & SINNERS

SAINTS & SPIES SERIES
VOLUME THREE

JORDAN McCOLLUM

DURHAM CREST BOOKS

First printing, 2018

Published by Durham Crest Books
Pleasant Grove, Utah
Set in Linux Libertine

ISBN 978-1-940096-29-2

PRINTED IN THE UNITED STATES OF AMERICA

M OLLY ROLLED OVER IN BED, turning away from the clock on her nightstand, pounding her pillow to refluff it. She should be sleeping, not staring at the minutes ticking past.

In eighteen hours, they would be married. Her heart quickened at the thought. She drew a deep breath to clear the nerves—but it was more than nerves. A lead weight filled the pit of her stomach as it had every night for the last fortnight. She kicked off her sheets and got up to pace her bedroom.

She stopped at her closet door and the white garment bag hanging there. Her fidgeting fingers moved to the zipper, but she pulled her hand back. Her gown would look the same as when she'd checked it the last four nights. Nothing in there would soothe this nagging foreboding.

Molly sighed and wheeled away, clasping her hands to keep from fiddling with anything else. Everything would be all right tomorrow. Perfect, even. Wouldn't it?

The tension still tugged at her middle. Her fingers returned to the garment bag zipper of their own accord. Her gown was perfectly fine, from the ruched bodice to the beaded filigree at the waist to the flowing skirt. Molly took care not to snag the glossy satin as she zipped the garment bag back up.

All that had done nothing for the worry. She couldn't drive herself mad like this. She had to ring Zachary. He'd understand. Wouldn't he?

Molly marched over to her nightstand where her mobile phone and her engagement ring waited. Zachary would tell her how silly she was being, remind her how much he loved her, promise not to let anything ruin their wedding. She tapped the icon to ring Zachary, but a knock at the door stopped her before the call even rang.

At the mere possibility it was him, Molly broke into a grin. She ended the call, tossed the phone on her bed and practically jogged to her front door. She'd hoped to save him from her most comfortable, tatty, lose-their-drawstring-every-fortnight yoga pants until after their honeymoon. At the moment, though, she didn't care.

She did, however, check the peephole. The stout blond man standing in the corridor was Zachary's exact opposite. But . . . she recognized this man. From—

Miles Hennessy? Molly jerked back from the peephole. Why would a member of her old parish appear on her doorstep in the middle of the night, the night before her wedding?

And not just any member of the parish. One of their resident mobsters. The only one who'd somehow escaped the battery of arrests eighteen months ago when Zachary and a penitent mobster brought the rest of Doyle Murphy's crew to justice.

But Miles didn't know her fiancé was behind that. Not even the prosecutors knew Zachary had gone undercover as a priest. The man's own parents didn't know he was a covert FBI agent. Sure, the judge had declared a mistrial and Doyle was free while they waited for a second shot, but Doyle couldn't have tracked Zachary down.

"Please, I know you're there, Molly," Hennessy called through the door.

She held her breath.

"I need your help."

Though he couldn't see her, Molly turned a skeptical eye on the door.

"Please, just look."

Molly dared to peek out again. Hennessy held a men's wristwatch up to the peephole glass. A nice watch, silver band, pearly background to the digital face.

Her heart tripped. Just like the early wedding present she'd given Zachary yesterday.

Hennessy flipped the watch over to show her the back. From here, she could only tell it had an inscription.

Her hand hit the doorknob, but Molly hesitated, suddenly very aware that her gun and her badge were safely locked away.

Hennessy examined the watch's inscription. "Gray go dee yo?"

He gave up, but Molly's mind filled in the Irish inscription, even after Hennessy's butchering: *Grá go deo.*

Zachary's watch. Only that afternoon, she'd sat on the couch behind her, bouncing with nerves. She'd searched for weeks to find a gift for Zachary, and settled on a wristwatch. She'd never known him to wear a watch, and for a long moment as he tore off the wrapping paper, she'd been sure he'd hate it.

At the sight of the watch, his azure eyes lit up. When she explained the inscription meant "love forever," he'd kissed her until she was dizzy.

Then he'd strapped on the watch and figured out how to program a countdown clock. "Twenty-five hours," he'd murmured, pulling her close again. For a moment, she'd almost let herself believe everything would be perfect.

Eighteen hours left on that timer now. He couldn't be in danger. Sure, she'd worried something would go wrong, but Zachary, kidnapped? She tried, but couldn't swallow.

"I don't know what this means," Hennessy finished, "but I'm hoping you do."

She turned to run to her room and fetch her gun, but Hennessy's voice through the door cut her off.

"Sorry, I just . . . I thought you would be the one to help your fiancé." His voice faded on the last syllables. A quick check of the peephole showed no one.

"Wait." Molly flung the door open. Hennessy stopped in the hallway and whirled back to her.

"What do you mean, help my fiancé?" she demanded. "How did you get that?"

Hennessy opened his mouth as if to answer, but cut himself off with a wave. "I have to get back. Doyle's lost his mind, and if he thinks for a minute that I—do you know what he'd do to me?" He pivoted and headed down the corridor again.

If she'd doubted Doyle was involved, she didn't have to anymore. If Zachary could be in trouble, she had to act. Molly marched after Miles. "Doyle's lost his mind?"

Miles glanced over his shoulder. "Doyle has him."

Gooseflesh covered her arms. Doyle Murphy, accused mobster and murderer, had Zachary? She needed to ring the Bureau.

But as she turned back into her apartment, fingers closed on her wrist.

"You do want to help him, don't you?" Hennessy whispered urgently.

"I'm callin' this in."

"If you're going to help him, we've gotta go. We can call from the car, use my phone."

Molly flinched. It was one thing for Miles to try to be decent for once, but Doyle Murphy's henchman wanted to contact the FBI? That didn't feel right. "Have you gone mad?"

"Try straight. Now Doyle's trying to drag me back in." Hennessy's shoulders fell, the image of defeat. "Kidnapping a Fed? This is way too much, even for him."

Kidnapping? Molly's mind reeled, but she scrutinized Hennessy. Could he be telling the truth? He certainly seemed skittish enough.

Could this change be why he hadn't gone to jail with the rest of them? "If that's the case, tell me where he is."

"I don't know. Doyle didn't exactly drop a pin. He's got him in a warehouse or something. That's why I came to you."

She mentally shook off the panic threatening to take over her mind. Zachary needed her, and she would be there for him. "Right, we'll call it in."

Miles tugged on her wrist. "Please, from the car. We gotta get moving."

"Then I'll drive."

"I can't navigate you there at night. I can barely make it myself."

Molly's pulse climbed as a mental debate raged. Zachary was in danger. They had to call it in; she knew it. But Miles released her and strode down the hallway without her. "I gotta go. If I'm not back before he gets suspicious, it'll be my neck instead of Saint's."

The best lead—the best chance she might have of helping Zachary—was walking away.

She took only a second to lock her door handle before she chased after him. "Give me your mobile."

Hennessy patted his pockets, then groaned. "Seriously? Must be in the car. Come on."

Waiting for the elevator, Molly asked for Zachary's watch. Hennessy handed it over, and Molly examined it. Definitely his.

The ride down was filled with heavy, cottony silence while Molly's memory dredged up the most harrowing moments of her life: Zachary bludgeoned and bloodied at the hands of terrorists. Zachary passing out when they thought the coast was clear. Zachary lying in a hospital bed, unconscious.

Molly watched the display count down the floors, rubbing her thumb over the watch's inscription. Whatever Doyle Murphy had planned could be a thousand times worse. He had shot and tortured delivery men for being late. He'd ordered hits on nuns, if the old parish rumors were true. What would he do to the FBI agent who'd finally caught him?

Once they reached the underground car park, emotion finally subsided enough for reason to rear its head. "Wait, Miles," Molly said.

"Evening, Molly." A voice carried from behind her, bouncing off

9

the concrete walls.

She turned at the sound. Mr. Petrowski stood by his boxy Ford. What could her kindly old neighbor be doing out after eleven?

Mr. Petrowski looked from Molly to Hennessy and back again. "Everything okay?"

"Everything's fine," Hennessy insisted, a hard glint in his green eyes. "Tell him, Molly."

The alarm at the back of her mind sounded a warning chime. She watched Hennessy a minute longer. And then she saw it: a rectangle of light glowing through his pants pocket.

A phone. One he'd had all along. Molly backed up a few steps, trying to get between Hennessy and Mr. Petrowski. "Call 9-1-1," she said to Mr. Petrowski. "Your man here says my fiancé's been kidnapped by Doyle Murphy."

For an agonizing second, only Molly's heartbeat echoed in the underground. Then Mr. Petrowski shuffled as fast as he could for the elevator.

Molly turned to run after him, but before she made it three steps, a thunderclap reverberated through the garage. Mr. Petrowski tumbled to the ground. He'd hardly made it two meters from his car. She stopped short, glancing back at Hennessy.

He held a gun. With a suppressor.

Energy charged through her. Statistics said it was only luck he'd hit Mr. Petrowski. She could make it. His life depended on her.

But her hesitation had already cost her. As she reached Mr. Petrowski, something hard plowed into her back and Molly vaulted forward.

Was she hit?

In eleven hours, they'd be married—but right now, they were only going for a run. Zach exited the freeway, a mix of anxiety and adrenaline humming through his system. He ran through his mental checklist again: they'd have enough time for a short run before he'd have to turn around and head home to shower. Then there was the brunch, cleanup, prep time—though for him that only meant getting dressed—and then the real crunch set in. At least they'd start with the ceremony first, the important part, before the photos and reception.

All right, marrying Molly was worth enduring ten photo sessions and receptions. Still, his mom was sure to be on his case all day to make sure he was on time. At a red light, Zach reached for the glove box to retrieve the watch Molly had given him yesterday.

It wasn't there.

What? He was sure he'd put it there last night before the temple.

The light changed. On automatic, Zach made the left onto Molly's street.

And then he saw the squad cars in front of her building. His lungs froze. That couldn't mean—

It could be a traffic stop. It could be the building next door. It could be anyone.

Anyone who required three sets of flashing lights.

Zach lowered the radio's volume, another news report on the heat wave, to concentrate on parking. He'd missed Molly's call last night thanks to his dad and his dreaded pre-wedding lecture. Molly hadn't left a message. She hadn't responded to his text before he left this morning.

No, couldn't be related. She was probably asleep. Or hadn't seen her messages.

He pulled behind one of the squad cars and grabbed his phone. Molly's number rang to voicemail. Zach pocketed his cell, got his badge from the glove box and sprinted to the nearest uniformed officer.

"You'll have to move along, sir," the cop said automatically.

"My fiancée lives here." Zach held out his badge. "Please."

The officer looked back toward the ramp down into the parking garage beneath Molly's building. "There's been a murder."

The last word hit like a punch to the gut. "Who?"

"I dunno. Heard the guy who called it in couldn't ID the body."

"I know some people in the building. Maybe I can help."

The officer checked the garage entrance again. "Let me ask." He radioed the officer in charge and explained. With the supervising officer's permission, the uni pointed Zach to the sign-in sheet. Once his presence was logged, Zach started down the ramp. Each step tightened the invisible grip on his chest. He reached the bottom level at a sprint.

He'd come here for an early morning run, but this wasn't what he planned.

Cops, crime scene techs, and two plainclothes detectives clustered near a blood pool on the asphalt. A black body bag—full—sat on a gurney, waiting to be loaded into the coroner's van. Zach stopped short. The metallic smell of blood hit him harder than a cement wall.

This couldn't happen. Not today.

"You the one they just let in?" one of the detectives asked.

Zach kept his focus on the body bag as he approached and pulled out his badge. "FBI." Normally, he said it with force—he didn't get to say it often—but today, his voice was a hollow echo ringing in his ears.

The man who'd addressed him—white, fifties maybe, gray hair, suit—threw up his hands in mock celebration. "Tell me the Feds want this one. I've got three hours till my shift's supposed to start."

"Have you IDed the body?"

"Not yet," the graying detective said. "You live here?"

"My fiancée does." The weight of his own words hit him, and he stared at the body bag.

"Is your fiancée an eighty-year-old man?"

Zach looked at the younger detective, a Hispanic man with dark, wavy hair. "Huh?"

At the detective's tiny nod, the coroner unzipped the body bag. He pulled back the flap before Zach could brace himself. Not her.

Zach's shoulders relaxed instantly, and he tried to ignore the twinge of guilt at his relief at finding the old man who lived down the hall, the whole front of his plaid shirt coated in dried blood. "Victor Petrowski."

"Shot from behind." The younger detective gestured toward the exit wound.

Zach scanned the crime scene and spotted Molly's green Jetta. She was okay, then. Even if she hadn't answered the phone. He tried to clamp down on the disturbing murmur at the back of his mind. "Not sure which car is his."

One of the detectives pointed at a Ford. "Found his keys."

Unless Petrowski had fallen in with mobsters or terrorists, Zach couldn't do much more for him. And after that type of scare, he wanted to check on Molly as fast as possible. "I can take you up to Petrowski's apartment."

The detective turned to the coroner. "You done?"

"Yep. Load 'em up and move 'em out." The coroner and his assistant pushed the gurney toward the back of the open van. The older detective conferred with the crime scene team a minute before Zach led the detectives to the elevator.

"Any theories?" Zach asked once they were halfway to Molly's floor.

The dark-haired detective smirked. "Yeah, we think Victor Petrowski was shot in the back."

The graying cop filled in the rest of the evidence they'd found. "Maybe a robbery. No wallet on the body." The elevator slowed to a stop and the doors slid open. Zach led them to Petrowski's apartment.

The younger detective knocked. No answer.

"He's a widower," Zach said. "I got it." He pulled out the key he'd filed into a series of even peaks for Molly's apartment. Luckily, the

13

whole building used the same basic key pattern.

"That what they're teaching at Quantico these days?" The older detective folded his arms.

"Nah, I learned this on TV."

The dark-haired detective pulled out a baggie with keys in it—bloodstained keys. Zach backed off. Probably better that way.

The detectives started in, but the graying one paused at the door. "Any chance you know his next of kin?"

"Think he's got kids somewhere. Let me check with Molly." Zach headed down the hall. He couldn't help a little thrill: breaking into one another's apartments had become a running joke between them.

He'd guarded his keys jealously for the last couple months, and she didn't know he'd filed an old key into the fastest lock picking tool either of them had tried.

Zach slid the bump key into the deadbolt, applied tension and hit the key, forcing the pins to jump long enough to trick the tumbler into twisting. The lock flipped a quarter turn too easily. Unlocked.

Definitely not like Molly.

He repeated the procedure on the handle and let himself in. The lights were on in the living room, but an eerie quiet pervaded the air.

"Molly?" His voice bounced off the exposed brick of the far wall. "I have bad news."

He waited. No response. "Molly?"

Maybe she forgot their morning run.

Right. They'd only done this three times a week for the last four months. He started down the hall and called her name again.

Her bedroom door was open, the light on there, too. Her dress hung from the closet door in its plastic garment bag. The bathroom door stood ajar, the light off, but he checked anyway. Empty.

Back in the bedroom, the bedsheets were shoved to one side. Zach felt the striped sheets. Cold.

Not answering her phone. Apartment unlocked. She hadn't been here for a while.

No. This couldn't be what it looked like. Not today. But his carefully constructed denial was foundering on the facts.

He pulled out his phone again and called her. After a few seconds' delay, he heard her phone ringing, its screen lighting up amid the crumpled sheets. He ended the call and grabbed her phone, quickly bypassing the lock screen.

Her phone showed the last call she'd made: to him, at 11:14 p.m. No incoming calls or texts from anyone else since yesterday afternoon, and then, nothing revealing—her mother, Lucy, Zach.

He set her phone down on the nightstand by her ring. Her car was here. Where were her keys?

Back in the living room, Zach checked her purse in its spot on the side table, wallet and keys still inside.

Nothing else in the room was amiss, from the Swedish-designed sectional to the sleek dining table to the atmospheric photographs of Ireland.

None of it added up, and a couple obvious answers stared him in the face. If this was supposed to be a game, she would've left him some sort of clue. She couldn't have cold feet. Right?

He almost wished it were that simple.

Zach grabbed the brown leather wallet from her purse, holding on like he clutched a lifeline. It felt like he was plunging through Lake Michigan's shelf ice.

Something was very, very wrong.

Would they be married in eleven hours?

ZACH PACED AROUND MOLLY'S GRAY SECTIONAL as the phone rang once again. There had to be something more productive than playing phone jockey, but he hadn't found it yet. So far, he'd called his supervisor, and the Special Agent in Charge, and now Lucy.

It took five rings for his sister to answer. "What is it?" Lucy croaked, her voice hoarse from sleep.

"Are you staying with Mom and Dad?" He should probably know that. Ever since she'd left town in the world's most dramatic ghosting a couple months ago, it'd gotten harder to keep track of her.

She yawned, but kept her volume down. "Yeah, why?"

"Did Molly . . . say anything to you?" he barely dared to ask. She definitely hadn't called or texted Lucy, but *I'm thinking about skipping out on marrying your brother* was the kind of thing you probably told your best friend in person.

And he almost hoped she'd said it. At least it would mean she was okay.

"We went over the details for, like, two hours yesterday. The dress, the jewelry, the reception site. You know, only enough to kill my soul halfway."

He did not have time to deal with Lucy's freshly broken heart today. "Focus, Luce."

"Zach, why'd you wake me at—?"

"Did she say anything about having cold feet?" he asked before she could check the time. He needed Lucy calm, and seeing that it was 6 a.m. and he didn't know where his fiancée was would not help.

Lucy hesitated. Zach could almost hear the wheels spinning in her brain over the phone line. Lucy would know if Molly wanted to back out. She'd know if Molly was thinking about running away.

Or maybe she wouldn't. Molly might not want to burden his sister with those kinds of doubts, especially not after the way her relationship with Paul flamed out the second time.

A shuffle and a clatter carried from Lucy's end. "What's the matter?" Lucy finally asked in full voice. "What did she say?"

"Nothing." He'd love to hear Molly say almost anything right now, even if it was *I can't go through with this*. As long as she was okay.

But he couldn't tell his sister that. "Don't worry about it, Luce. We're just not going to make it to wedding stuff for a bit."

"Let me talk to her."

Her bossy tone triggered his instinct to deflect the truth—and tease his sister. "Are you kidding? You'd probably tell her to make a break for it while she still can."

Lucy didn't laugh, and Zach kicked himself. Lucy had done exactly that to her boyfriend.

He tried again. "Could you run interference for us?"

"I guess." She yawned again. "How long?"

"Until I say stop."

She fell silent once more. "Is everything okay? Let me talk to her—promise I won't talk her out of marrying you."

"Pass. Tell Mom and Dad we got called into work. Gotta go." He hung up before Lucy could object again.

Zach tried to shake off his own nagging doubts. Molly hadn't run away. She was in danger and she wanted him to come looking for her.

Zach tucked his phone in his pocket and gave the apartment another once-over. The new bookshelf, empty and waiting for him to unpack his books, seemed to stare back at him blankly. Waiting. Still not a single thing to show why she'd left, who'd taken her, where she was. Not one clue to indicate anything was wrong.

He went back to check her room, like she'd been hiding under the bed this whole time, waiting to jump out at him. The second dresser and nightstand they'd gotten to match hers stood empty. He flipped on the bathroom light. She'd made room on the towel rack for him.

Somehow, instead of feeling like she'd made room for him, she'd left so many holes in her own apartment. Spaces that weren't supposed to be empty.

He turned to leave again, but the bathroom light caught something on Molly's nightstand. He rounded the bed and picked up her ring. Wherever she was, she'd left her ring.

Zach paced in the hallway. This couldn't be cold feet. She'd left her phone. She'd left her wallet. She'd left her keys. She'd left the deadbolt unlocked.

But if it wasn't cold feet . . . she could be hurt. She could be lost. She could be in danger, in the street, in a human trafficking racket.

Zach's circuit grew tighter and tighter, his thoughts circling faster and faster.

He could get to her. He could stop it, save her. He had to. But he didn't know where to start.

He always knew where to start. There had to be something he could do. He'd never been good at handling the weird, unanchored feeling of grasping at straws.

He didn't want to start, to investigate—he wanted to skip straight to solving and saving.

The knock finally came at quarter past six, interrupting the irrational—he hoped—train of thought that had Molly being sold across the border. Zach answered the door to both of the men he'd called. He wasn't surprised to find his direct boss, Supervisory Special Agent Xavier Mason, but he wasn't anticipating the man in charge of the entire FBI in Chicago. Special Agent in Charge Rod Evans stood a couple inches shorter than Zach, his hair shifting from a sandy blond to white around the edges. Evans nodded a greeting.

"Wasn't expecting you to come down personally, sir," Zach said.

"A missing agent—and on your wedding day?" Evans clapped Zach on the shoulder, but Zach was mostly surprised he remembered. They'd worked together a little at church, and Evans was invited to the ceremony, but Zach didn't actually think he'd be able to make it to the temple with them. He was in charge of the whole Chicago FBI, after all.

Evans gestured toward the tall, thin African-American man next to him. "Are we the cavalry?" Xavier asked.

"What we've got so far."

The SAC and Xavier stepped into Molly's apartment. Zach had to make it seem like he was in control, or Evans could chain him to a desk during the investigation. He mentally steeled himself, shut the door and joined the other two men, forming a circle in Molly's living room.

Evans drew himself to his full height, making this huddle seem official. "So Special Agent Malone might be missing?"

Zach gestured at her purse on the side table. "Her keys, wallet and phone are here."

"Her door was unlocked when you got here?"

"Yeah."

"Okay," Evans drew out the word. "What do we know about the murder downstairs?"

Zach gave a quick report—not that he could go into much detail on Petrowski's murder.

"Obviously, we've got three scenarios here." Xavier ticked them off on his fingers. "Two unrelated cases and an incredible coincidence, Molly got involved in her neighbor's problem, or her neighbor got involved in her problem."

Problem sounded bad, but it could be a very mild way of putting it.

"Not cold feet, huh?"

"Wish it were that simple," Zach said. "But probably not without her car, keys, wallet or phone."

Evans acknowledged his point, his expression grim. "What do we know about Petrowski?"

Zach ran through his mental file on Molly's neighbor. "Retired. Postal worker, I think. Lives alone. Likes plants."

X smirked. "You know, the type who lives in constant fear of his many enemies. And this would fall under the incredible coincidence category."

"Yep," Evans said. "I'll follow up and see what Chicago PD finds on Petrowski."

"They're not going to want to share," Xavier interjected.

"Oh, I think we'll work something out." Evans shot him a look that was somewhere between confident and confiding. "I'm friends with the chief."

"Do we go through Malone's cases to see who might be carrying a grudge?" Xavier asked.

She probably hadn't made many enemies in six months of working with European embassies. And if she had, the Belgians were more likely to withhold chocolate than kidnap an agent. "Check up on Moskovitz and Relyea." Molly had contributed to one big criminal case in her first office last year, too. "She contributed to the Favera case in Arizona."

"We'll start there. And talk to her friends," Evans continued. "Just in case."

"Already did."

Another knock at the door. Hope filled his chest—but Molly wouldn't knock at her own door.

Zach answered. Three Evidence Response Team techs in FBI shirts stood on the doorstep. Crime scene investigators. "Hope we have the right place?" one asked.

Zach stepped aside to show Evans—the Special Agent in Charge was kind of a big deal—and the techs instantly straightened. Zach waved them in.

Evans looked from Xavier to Zach. "Let's move. She's waiting for us." He headed for Zach and the still-open door. "Time is ticking, people."

At the door, Evans paused and turned to Zach. "Right now, I want to keep you working on this case actively. You know her better than anyone—but we'll get her squad digging through her cases too."

"Good call. Thanks."

Evans turned to go, but looked to Zach again. "Four thirty, right?"

Their ceremony. He kept thinking of it as five, but guests were supposed to be half an hour early. "Yeah."

"We'll find her." Evans gave him a sure nod and headed out.

Xavier moved close enough to talk under his breath, watching the Evidence Response techs. "What do you think?"

"I think ERT is going to make a mess of my fiancée's apartment," Zach muttered. Not a single thing was out of place. ERT couldn't do much good here. "None of it makes sense."

He had to find her. He would.

Xavier tapped a fist on his shoulder. "Evans didn't seem worried. We'll find her."

He was right; Evans wasn't worried. But the SAC's confidence wasn't going to find Molly.

One tech started down the hall for the bedroom. "Hey!" Zach called.

All the techs jumped and stared at him.

"Get anything on her wedding dress and she'll personally murder you."

The techs exchanged a glance but saluted, though none of them could be sure Molly would be using that dress.

She'd been driving herself nuts for weeks, convinced something would go horribly wrong today.

And she was right.

"Hey." Xavier backhanded Zach's arm. "Any cameras in the

garage?"

"No, only the entrance. And the lobby." Of course. He'd been so busy thinking about finding her that he'd forgotten the obvious place to start. Zach and Xavier pivoted for the door in unison.

A heavy metal clang snapped Molly to attention. Had she dozed off?

In the sliver of light from the far end of the room, she could barely make out the metal frame of the bed she was on—correction, shackled to, a steel handcuff on her ankle.

Molly took stock of her dim, narrow cell. Corrugated walls. A shipping container, perhaps. She sat up in the dark, a metaphorical ice pick stabbing behind her eyes. And in her shoulders. Around her wrists. Exhaustion and heat must have overcome her at some point. She'd never got used to the nights not cooling off in a Chicago July, but this room was stifling.

Was she alone? She didn't dare speak. Instead, she listened in the stuffy heat, but her ears were still recovering from the gunshot last night.

The image of Mr. Petrowski flashed through her mind. Not for the first time, she prayed help had come for the old man.

She hadn't made it far in trying to help him before Miles Hennessy tackled her. Her aching knuckles reminded her she'd given as good as she'd got, but the man outweighed her a fair bit. He'd restrained her, wrestled her into his car and tied her wrists behind her to the headrest. She'd barely managed to maneuver herself to see the neighborhood where he'd taken her: an industrial part of town she knew a little too well, after she and Zachary had made an arrest not far away.

Ignoring the bite of the PlastiCuff straps in her wrists, Molly pushed herself to sitting. The sliver of light in the container's entry flickered and disappeared, as though a shadow passed in front of it.

Someone *was* here.

A lamp clicked on. It wasn't all that bright, but after the dark, she flinched away from the naked bulb.

She blinked twice to see her captor. Miles Hennessy.

She hadn't allowed herself to acknowledge the flash a second ago, but she had to admit she'd hoped—well, it didn't matter. She certainly didn't have to wait around to be rescued.

Molly took stock of at her prison. No sign of Zachary anywhere. Definitely a shipping container. Cardboard boxes occupied most of the perimeter. At the far end of the container, a worn wooden table supported the sad lamp and an electric fan. Hennessy switched that on next, and it buzzed to life.

"Sleep well?" he asked.

Molly grunted. She'd only meant to rest for a minute, but she must have dropped right off.

"Breakfast." Hennessy held up a McDonald's sack.

Molly glared at him. This man had likely murdered someone in front of her, and apparently thought kidnapping her was also funny. At least he didn't have his gun out. As if he needed it to stop a woman from running or resisting when she was cuffed and shackled.

"Hope you like hash browns." He tossed the greasy sack onto the bed next to her as if she were perfectly capable of feeding herself— and as if anyone could eat a hot breakfast when the temperature had to be in the nineties already.

Where was Doyle holding Zachary? Not that she could do anything to help Zachary yet.

"What, don't like McDonald's?" Hennessy settled into a metal folding chair across the room. "Or—wait, English isn't your first language, is it? You want me to put that in Irish for you?

24

O'McDonald's?"

Molly refused to rise to the bait or follow the distraction. She had something more pressing to worry about. "Where is Zachary?"

Hennessy cocked his head. "Who?"

"My fiancé." What was Hennessy playing at?

"Tucked in his nice, warm bed, I guess."

Ice seemed to crystallize in her veins. Zachary had never been in danger at all? She'd trusted Hennessy for half a second when it looked as though he had the person who mattered most to her, and it was all a setup.

"Really shouldn't leave valuables in your car," Hennessy mused. He pulled something out of his pocket that glinted silver in the light. "Even if you're in church."

The watch. Zachary's father made him leave it in his glove box at the temple last night.

Hennessy slipped Zachary's watch back into his pocket. "Eat your breakfast."

Molly eyed the sack. "I amn't hungry," she murmured.

"And you amn't very good with grammar."

She tamped down an internal groan. Hadn't she endured enough "correction" on her Irishisms yet?

"Y'know, I liked you, kid. You seemed sweet enough. Almost felt sorry for you when you went off the deep end over Father Tim."

Molly mentally flinched. So this *was* about Zachary. Or, rather, the priest cover Zachary had used to help catch Doyle's gang.

Not his whole gang. Hennessy had gone free. He couldn't hold a grudge against Zachary, could he?

Unless he was still loyal to Doyle Murphy. She'd testified against Doyle, after all. She wasn't exactly his favorite person, either.

If Doyle was roaming free, why wouldn't Doyle have taken her himself? Why would he kidnap her at all? Legally, tampering with a witness was evidence of the underlying crime.

Most of all, what was in this scheme for Hennessy?

She cast a hooded glance at him. He was here, and he could be the key to getting out. She'd have to figure out what he wanted and how she could use that against him.

3

Z ACH LET XAVIER TAKE THE LEAD in waking up the building superintendent, Jim Planter. Banging down the super's door shouting, "FBI!" didn't seem like the most covert way to introduce himself.

"We need to see your security tapes," Xavier said as soon as the office door opened.

Planter, balding and squinty, stepped back to let them in. "Only got the lobby. Garage ramp camera's broken."

Of course. "One tenant was murdered and another's missing," Zach snapped, "and the best you've got is a broken security camera?"

"Well, I mean . . ." Planter rubbed a hand over what was left of his brown hair. "What do you want me to do, go back in time and fix it?"

"You know Mr. Petrowski was shot here last night, right?"

At the mention of the victim's name, Planter's gaze fell for a long moment. "I could show you the lobby footage if it'd help."

Xavier managed a patient tone. "We'll take what you've got."

Planter beckoned for them to follow back into his office. Could the man stroll any slower? Didn't he know what today was supposed to be?

Humming—the man was *humming*—Planter flipped on the lights. "Let's see." At his desk, his fingers danced above the keyboard until he tapped the touchpad and angled the laptop to Zach. "Here you go. Should go back to about midnight."

Zach checked with Xavier. "Did we get Petrowski's TOD?"

"Not that I heard."

If Petrowski's murder was related to Molly's disappearance, that might not be enough. "Do you have the footage before this?"

"Oh, uh . . . sure." Planter bit his lip and pulled the computer back to himself for a moment. "Here you go."

Zach and Xavier leaned in to watch, but Zach glanced up at the super again. "Thanks, we've got it."

"Oh, uh—"

"Go. Now." Zach didn't bother hiding his irritation.

"We'll call if we need anything." Xavier's tone was more polite but allowed no argument.

Planter skittered away and Zach hit play. The grainy image flickered to life on the screen. No timestamp. He clicked the fast-forward button. Stragglers filed through the frame, one here, two there, traversing the tiles between the front door and the elevators or stairs.

After half a dozen tenants passed through, one lone man entered only the bottom of the frame. He walked in from the doors, his head and shoulders making the tape. His back to the camera, he ambled to the mailboxes.

He paused in the middle of the row of boxes. From his back, they could see one arm move in front of him. Then he spun away and left, moving past the camera so quickly he was gone before Zach had time to recognize him.

Zach startled. Doyle Murphy? It couldn't be. He hit rewind.

The highest-ranking member of the mob he'd taken down as his first assignment in Chicago. The man was on trial. He wouldn't dare—

Zach hit play. In real time again, Doyle ambled onto the screen, dallied at the mailboxes—Molly's box had to be right where he was standing—and turned back to leave. Zach paused the tape, then grabbed his phone. He took a picture of the still.

"Who's that?"

Zach looked up once he'd sent the picture to ASAC Sellars, his supervisor from Doyle's case. "That's a breakthrough." He tapped the computer screen. "Doyle Murphy. My very first case in Chicago. Molly testified against him—and I think he's at her mailbox."

Xavier studied the computer screen, memorizing Murphy's face, then nodded. Zach closed the browser window.

On the desktop, a giant red banner read *Weather Warning: Excessive Heat* above the day's forecast: a record-breaking high of 109°. He didn't want to think what that would feel like with humidity.

He closed the laptop, but the number stuck in his mind. What if Molly was somewhere outside? What if she was hurt and stranded? Locked in a trunk?

How long could someone survive in that kind of heat?

He'd been worrying about not finding her in time for the wedding. He might not even have that long.

He really could lose her today.

He reeled from the realization a moment before he came to his senses. He wasn't going to let her die today. And he'd just gotten the first solid lead in the case. Now he could act.

"Come on," he said. "Let's go see what Murphy left her."

Zach had seen Molly's mail key enough to know regular old lock picks would do. Xavier stood guard against anybody who got suspicious, but it took less than a minute to open the gold box.

The box was empty inside except for a small, folded piece of paper. Zach pulled it out.

This isn't basketball, kid. Welcome to the pros.

The echo of Doyle's voice rang through his memory. He'd said that to Zach. When he thought Zach was a priest.

No way could he know Zach was marrying Molly. The Bureau had kept any mention of Father Tim out of the case file, and Zach had only made one brief appearance at the trial—in disguise—to hear Molly testify.

Was this about him or her?

Zach showed the note to Xavier, then closed up her box.

"Let's take this up to ERT."

Zach led the way to the elevators, snapping a picture of the note to send to ASAC Sellars.

"Obviously Murphy's not in prison," Xavier said on the way up.

"The judge declared a mistrial, and now he's out on bail." The facts still rankled worse than that clerical collar ever had. "One holdout juror. Heard it wasn't totally aboveboard—but not enough evidence to go on."

Zach had been so sure Doyle would go away this time, but Sellars had known better. At the last second, Murphy had managed to twist and slither out of the airtight case. A case that might be less airtight without Molly around.

Eliminating a witness would be a clumsy move. Could be worse for his case than letting her testify again.

Whatever his endgame, it seemed worst for Molly.

Xavier led the way to Molly's apartment. The door was unlocked and the crime scene crew was still there when they walked in. "Got something for you," Zach called. One tech left his spot to collect the note from Zach.

"Just have to finish up in the bedroom," another tech announced.

"Great." Zach glanced around at the dark smudges on half the room's surfaces. The missing rug. The rearranged knickknacks. If she ever saw this—

Wait, *if*? He was thinking in terms of *if* they could find her? He'd bested Doyle Murphy before. He'd gone toe-to-toe with the man with lives on the line. He'd *shot* the guy.

Murphy didn't know Zach was marrying Molly. He didn't even know Zach was *Zach*.

Zach was going to get her back.

He turned to Xavier. "We've got a comprehensive list of Murphy's assets from the trial. Including properties."

X started for the door but paused at the last second. "Hey, man, I'm not saying—just, keep your head on straight."

"What?"

"With the super." Xavier leveled with him. "All I'm saying is that you're . . . you know, *involved.*"

"Are you saying I shouldn't do my job because I care about a victim?"

"I'm saying to keep your head on straight because you care about the victim. We're going to get her back. Don't make our job any harder than it has to be."

He hadn't jumped down the super's throat or anything—but Zach simply nodded. He'd focus on Molly. And they'd find her.

Sighing, Miles folded his newspaper and stood up from his hard chair. It'd been over an hour in this heat, and that stubborn woman hadn't looked at him or at the McDonald's he'd brought her. He would've fed her if she asked. They weren't trying to torture her. He might be a cheat, a murderer and a two-timer, but he wasn't a sadist.

"Fine, don't eat." He crossed the room and snatched the bag from the bed.

Molly still said nothing.

"I was doing this for you, you know." He shook the brown paper sack in her direction. She continued to stare impassively at a blank wall. "This passive-aggressive crap isn't going to do you any favors."

She slowly focused on him, her expression calm. As if they were having this conversation in their old lives, him a member of the parish, her the secretary. But now she was too good to talk to him.

"You're going to wish you'd worked with me. You're going to regret throwing this back in my face." He stalked from the container and into the main warehouse.

At his car, Miles stuffed the bag and the newspaper into his trunk. He should've run this whole thing the way he'd wanted to from the beginning—but no, he had to go and make sure Doyle was on board. And to do that, he'd had to convince Doyle that this scheme was about "justice" for him.

Like Miles really cared about making things right for his old boss. Like he cared if Doyle got even. But Doyle had taken the bait—he probably thought he'd come up with the idea himself by the time Miles was through with him. And Miles was stuck in this waiting game so Doyle could make his justice feel "poetic."

His phone rang. Miles checked the caller ID. Doyle. "Yeah?"

"Everything good?"

"Yep."

"She ready for a visit?"

Miles glanced back at the weak light spilling from the container. "Don't expect a welcome mat."

"Be there in twenty."

More waiting. Great. As if Miles was still Doyle's little peon, and Doyle still the number two guy in the South Side crew.

Doyle needed to think that, though. "Hey, can you bring another fan when you come? And an extension cord? Don't know if this is going to be enough"

Doyle laughed before hanging up.

Let him laugh. For now.

Ignoring the sweat trickling down her back, Molly strained to hear the voices echoing outside her corrugated metal prison over the fan's tinny buzz. Couldn't be Zachary—he certainly wouldn't be wasting time arguing with Hennessy. And if he did speak to Hennessy, it would be shouting to demand he take Zachary to her, not the murmuring carrying from outside.

She hadn't figured out how to play Hennessy yet, and now someone else was here. The standings were shifting, juggling her priorities and objectives too.

A shadow crossed the patch of light at the far end of the container. Hennessy walked in. "You've got a visitor."

She straightened her shoulders and turned up her nose, as if she had any choice in the matter.

The man who followed Hennessy in was a good deal taller with a stocky build and dark hair silvering at the temples. He bore a newspaper tucked under his arm and a wicked grin on his face.

Doyle Murphy.

She'd known he was involved, and still, her heart fell at the sight of him. The mobster she'd helped to bring down. She hadn't seen him since she'd testified at his trial four months ago.

"Good golly, Miss Molly. Fancy meeting you here."

Molly answered his attempt at humor with a single, slow blink. "What are you hopin' to get from me, Doyle?"

"I'm hoping you're enjoying your stay."

"Can't imagine I'll be stayin' much longer."

"Why? Someone coming to rescue you?"

Molly tried keep her expression neutral, to keep from betraying herself. He couldn't know who Zachary really was.

"Oh, I know," he said, as if he'd read her mind. The gleam in Doyle's eye grew more sinister. "I'm counting on it. On him."

ACH PULLED INTO THE PARKING LOT of Doyle's apartment building and left the car running to keep the A/C going a minute longer. They'd tried every known number for Doyle— no answer—so the next step was to come here. He hadn't expected the sight of the white stucco building to make his stomach lurch. This was where Molly had lived when they met. This was where he'd helped a mobster find Christ—and the FBI.

And this was where he'd shot Doyle Murphy.

Zach had never thought he'd regret *not* killing a man.

Zach's phone rang: an FBI office number he didn't have saved in his phone. "Agent Saint," he answered.

"Hi, the SAC said you'd want an update on a Chicago PD case as soon as it came in?"

The murder at Molly's. "Yep, what have you got?"

"Victor Petrowski's wife died ten years ago. Had two kids. The younger one couldn't think of anyone who didn't like him, except for Petrowski's sister."

Zach signaled to Xavier and they climbed out of the car. "And is his sister violent?"

"Sister's dead. The other kid hadn't talked to Petrowski in six years."

"Bet he took the news well."

"Yeah, *she* was pretty shook up apparently. Report says they fought the last time they spoke."

Zach grimaced—and instinctively searched his memory for his

last conversation with Molly. After the temple last night, maybe. Did he tell her he loved her?

Yes. Definitely. And she'd said it back, no hesitation, no fear.

"One altercation in his work history," the FBI clerk continued. "Petrowski kicked somebody out of the post office for swearing and using racial slurs."

Xavier opened the building's door for Zach. "They track the other guy down?" Zach asked the clerk.

"Alive and well in Oregon."

"That everything?"

Zach could hear a keyboard click in the background. "Um, Petrowski's TOD was about eleven thirty."

Just over six hours before Zach arrived at Molly's.

"And the SAC wanted a report from you."

"Have him talk to ASAC Sellars. He's got the evidence so far from his department."

"Will do." The clerk hung up.

The way to the elevator was too familiar, and the old feelings—apprehension at confronting Doyle, guilt at seeing Molly—nagged at him.

Again, Xavier took the lead to knock on Doyle's door. Hard to believe Zach had only been in Doyle's apartment twice before—once with another undercover FBI agent and once to save a hostage.

"Do you think it's a good idea?" Xavier nodded at the door, finishing the question with his eyebrows: *for you to go in?*

These people knew him as Father Tim. They didn't know anything about who he was or why he'd come today, but Zach left the parish abruptly the same night as half a dozen mobsters. At least a few people had to think those two were related.

A slight woman with dishwater-blonde hair answered the door. Claire Murphy. At the sight of Zach, she gasped. "Fa—"

"We need to speak to Doyle Murphy," Xavier said.

She gaped at Zach's chest as if his faded William & Mary T-shirt had her response printed on it. Maybe he should've tracked down a clerical collar to wear. "'s not here," Claire finally said.

"He's not here?" Zach folded his arms across his chest. "Where else would he be at seven in the morning?"

"Um." She shrank back into the apartment. "His lawyer's. About the retrial."

"Pretty dedicated legal team."

"They're wonderful," she murmured. "Who are you?"

Xavier pointed at himself. "Supervisory Special Agent Xavier Mason, FBI."

Claire stared at Zach.

"You know who he is," Xavier said. "When will Mr. Murphy be back, ma'am?"

She lifted one shoulder.

"Why don't you call and ask him?"

Half-turning back into the apartment, Claire cast her gaze around as if she were lost. Maybe Doyle really was there.

"Why don't we come in?" Zach ignored an eyeball from X, pushed the door open and stepped in.

Claire retreated past the kitchen island. "I don't think . . ." She wrung her hands.

Xavier finally followed Zach in. "You think this is going to help?" he murmured too low for Claire Murphy to hear.

Zach merely glared back. Xavier shot him a grim glance and shut the door behind him. "Have you called your husband yet?" he asked gently.

Claire shook her head fast, like she was afraid of the consequences.

"Do it," Zach insisted.

She scurried toward the phone on the white tile counter. "But . . . I mean, you shouldn't . . . be talking to him."

"He's not currently on trial." Zach tried to keep his tone reasonable but authoritative. She was partly right. "And this is unrelated."

Sort of.

Xavier stepped up next to Zach, both of them closer to Claire than comfortable. "Call him. Now."

She bowed her head, then lifted the receiver.

Zach scanned the apartment, trying to ignore the memories of the hostage situation here over a year and a half ago. The couch where Claire and her son cowered. The spot on the floor where Zach's sister sat bawling. Even the kitchen tile's grout lines still seemed to be stained with blood.

He sank into the couch and fixed Claire with an intent gaze. She fidgeted with the phone cord while she waited for someone to answer.

Doyle flashed an evil grin at Molly, ready to twist the knife and reveal how much he knew about her little boyfriend.

And then his phone rang.

He nearly flinched. Who could be calling him now? With a scowl, he wheeled from Molly and caught a glimpse of Miles's concerned frown.

Miles was right. They were in the middle of working on Molly.

This had better be an emergency. He checked the caller ID. Claire. With a sigh, he strode from the container.

"What is it?" he demanded.

"Um, Doyle?" Claire murmured.

He swore under his breath. Of course she had to interrupt him now. "If you're calling to remind me about Lizzie's softball game, so help me—"

"No, Doyle."

"Then what? I told you not to bother me."

"I know, I'm sorry—it's just that—" Claire stumbled over her words.

"It's just that what? You can't follow directions?"

"The FBI is here."

Already? Doyle clenched his jaw. "You know they can't touch me with the case pending."

"They say it's not related."

Better to intercept the Feds while he could before they went and ruined his timeline. Claire should have given the standard answer when they asked where he was. "Tell them I'll be home in a while. As soon as I'm done."

"I'll tell them."

Doyle ended the call. The Feds couldn't possibly know already. They couldn't have tracked this back to him yet. They wouldn't check the mail first thing in the morning, before mailmen were even out. The guy had to twist in the wind at least a little first.

Footsteps approached from behind him and he checked his back—Miles. But before either of them could say anything, Doyle's phone rang again. Claire. Again.

"What?"

"They say they're going to wait until you get here." Her words were little more than a whisper.

They must have intimidated her into calling. Nobody treated his wife that way. "Fine. I'll meet them at the FBI offices with my lawyer. Call Lehrman and tell him, too." He hung up and turned around to find Miles stepping out of the container. "Feds already," Doyle muttered.

Miles grunted. "So go home and tell whoever's there to bring the Father to you."

"Not time yet. Come on, he's supposed to suffer." Not to mention they hadn't forced Molly to admit the truth yet about who her fiancé really was.

Miles glanced back at Molly's cell. "If the FBI's already narrowed it down to you, the Father must've started suffering pretty early this morning."

"It's only quarter after." Doyle tapped his watch. He had a plan to punish Molly and the Father, and he wasn't ready to change it. "I want him to pay."

"He's going to. Like waiting until tonight was going to make him feel worse."

"Can't do it yet. We have to wait until tonight."

Miles gave him a look that said he wasn't so sure about this. "And how are we going put the FBI off for the rest of the day?"

"You don't get it, do you?" Doyle scoffed. "The whole point is to make the Father squirm. That's why we've got to wait until after they would've gotten married. Then we finally let him get his hopes up—and *then* we crush him. Like he tried to crush me."

Miles made a *go ahead* gesture. "It's your thing."

Doyle pounded Miles on the shoulder. "Couldn't do it without you."

Then again, Miles's help wasn't doing a whole lot. He might've even done something to tip the Feds off.

If Doyle wanted something done right, he'd have to do it himself—and he would. He had one thing to take care of first.

"Did you bring a fan?" Miles asked. "I'm going to need it before long."

Doyle pointed to the box fan he'd set beside his car, along with the extension cord. Miles saluted and turned back to Molly's prison.

Before Doyle could follow, his phone rang yet again. "What?" he barked into it.

"Um—uh—" a man's voice replied.

Who could be calling him? Doyle checked the caller ID. Didn't recognize it. "Who is this?"

"Eddie—Eddie Becker."

This time, Doyle did flinch. "You're not supposed to call me.

Ever."

"I know, but—my wife—the treatments aren't working and we need more."

More money? Was this schmuck seriously asking him for more? "I told you not to contact me."

"Yeah, but my wife—and what if I come forward?"

Doyle rubbed his temples. "You won't."

"I could."

He didn't bother to cover up a grumble. This guy could barely hold a phone conversation. Him blackmailing someone like Doyle? Not exactly a real threat. "I might let this slide one time, Becker. But if you ever think about contacting me again, you won't live to regret it."

Doyle ended the call and finally followed Miles in to see Molly.

Molly sat up, fighting against the pain, as Hennessy and then Doyle returned from their discussion.

Her objective with Doyle was very different than with Miles. When it was only her and Hennessy, she might have a hope of getting him on her side, getting out of here.

But Doyle had to have ordered this kidnapping. He was the one in charge. With Doyle, the best she could hope for was to get more information about his shady mistrial.

Doyle pulled out the newspaper he'd carried under his arm, opening it in front of her face with a snap.

The picture didn't require explanation: Zachary and her, smiling out at her. Their engagement photo. Their engagement announcement.

How—? Zachary and his mother had gone over and over this. He couldn't tell her he was a covert agent, so Debbie didn't understand why he didn't want a picture in the paper. Finally, he'd given in and let her place an announcement in their paper in Virginia.

"And what about Molly's parents?" Debbie had asked.

"Yeah, get one for them," Zachary had said.

How had she not understood that meant a copy of the paper?

Molly swallowed against the nausea threatening.

Doyle flipped the paper back to himself and read it to her. "'Colm and Katie (Ruain)—'"

"It's pronounced 'ruin,'" Molly murmured.

He waved her off and continued his dramatically mocking presentation. "'Malone of Oak Park, Illinois, are pleased to announce the engagement of their daughter, Mary Margaret (Molly) Malone, to Zachary Tyler Saint, son of James and Deborah of Hampton, Virginia.'"

She closed her eyes, the rest of the life history on the page playing through her mind as he read. *Miss Malone has an undergraduate degree from Garda Síochána College in Ireland and a graduate degree from DePaul University. She is a special agent with the Federal Bureau of Investigation. Mr. Saint is a graduate of the College of William and Mary and is employed by the government.*

A July 21 wedding will take place at the Chicago LDS temple, with a reception to follow.

The words danced in her mind until one phrase alone echoed: "employed by the government."

Doyle didn't know who Zachary was. Obviously, he favored Father Tim pretty strongly in the looks department, but they didn't know what he'd done to bring them down.

Unfortunately, Doyle did know exactly what she'd done to bring him down. Sending evidence to the FBI and testifying against him surely hadn't endeared her to Doyle.

But she could still protect Zachary. "What do you want from

42

me?"

He laughed. "I've already got it. All you have to do is sit and wait."

"Doyle," Hennessy broke in. "You can't keep them waiting long if you don't want them suspicious yet."

Doyle cut his eyes at Hennessy but refocused on Molly. "Sure. Be seeing ya."

"I sincerely hope not."

Doyle scoffed and turned for the exit.

"You and me again, kid," Hennessy said once Doyle's shadow was out of sight.

Molly met his gaze. "What did you mean, 'If you don't want them suspicious yet'?"

He downplayed the importance of his words with a flick of his wrist. "Doyle's got some Feds waiting for him. He'll be on trial again soon, you know."

She did know—and she knew Hennessy knew more than he was saying.

Doyle was willing to tamper with her, a witness. He was practically throwing away that pending case.

If he had half a brain, he wouldn't let her live long enough to testify again. No, if he had half a brain, he wouldn't have risked kidnapping a witness and an FBI agent.

She'd danced around the truth long enough: there was no way Doyle Murphy would let her walk out of here alive.

Molly studied the man across the room from her. Hennessy might be her only hope to survive.

Z ACH WAS HALFWAY ACROSS THE SQUAD FLOOR before it hit him that every desk was empty.

Because this was Molly's squad. They were all out searching for her, running down leads on cases she'd closed, talking to contacts.

And Zach was stuck here. Doyle and his lawyer were waiting in a conference room, like this was a regular old meeting.

He checked the time. Two hours. Over two hours since he'd found her apartment empty, and he didn't feel one step closer to finding her.

No, that wasn't true. He was one step closer: he knew Doyle was involved.

He'd already had to surprise one former parishioner today. It was too late to avoid Doyle altogether, and even that was too little to protect his old cover. Doyle easily could have targeted Molly for her testimony at his trial, but leaving a note addressed to Zach in her mailbox? He had to have some clue who she was marrying. Today.

Xavier, back from checking in with the agents tracking down Doyle's remaining holdings, reached the door to the conference room. He waited for Zach's nod to open it.

When Zach stepped in, an exaggerated gasp came from Doyle's quadrant.

"What?" Zach said. "The note in the mailbox was a coincidence?"

Xavier sat at the table and opened a manila folder. He slid the screenshot from Molly's lobby surveillance video and a photocopy of the note across the table. Murphy barely acknowledged them.

His lawyer laughed and smoothed his hair where it was graying at the temples. "What are you charging him with? Tampering with the mail?"

"You're copping to that?"

"Nice try."

"Let me get this straight," Zach said. "Molly Malone—remember her? Parish secretary?"

Doyle thought about that one, drumming his fingers on the table. "Maybe. . . . Is she the gossipy one?"

Zach tried to keep the irritation out of his tone—and failed. "You said you were going to lie to the archbishop and say I was sleeping with her."

"Oh, right. Molly. The cute one." Doyle's brow wrinkled. "Remind me who you're supposed to be now?"

"Molly is an FBI agent these days," Zach didn't answer. "But I'm guessing you picked up on that at the trial." He shot the lawyer a look that had scared lesser criminals into confessions. The guy had made it sound like Molly had done something unethical by delivering evidence and later getting a job with the FBI.

"And it just so happens that she goes missing and you leave a note for Father Tim in her mailbox, right about the same time?"

"Wow, crazy coincidence."

The lawyer placed a *shut up* hand on Murphy's forearm. "I need a moment with my client."

Before Zach could protest, Xavier stood and nailed Zach with a raised eyebrow laden with meaning. Zach followed him out of the interview room.

"We shouldn't have let him have a lawyer," Zach muttered.

"We don't have a choice. When this case goes to court, do you really think a judge would believe we don't consider him a suspect?"

"You think taking this to court is my top priority?"

"I know," Xavier said. "But we *are* going to find her, and then we'll make this dude pay—if we do this right. For the moment, you can't let him get to you."

How many times and ways had he heard that over the years? Don't let it get personal—and yet, time after time, he ended up on cases where there was no avoiding the personal aspect. "If you figure out how to not take kidnapping my fiancée personally, let me know."

The lawyer opened the door behind them and they both fell silent. Xavier led the way back into the room.

The lawyer gestured at the chairs as if inviting them to take a seat in their own interview room. "My client would like to cooperate with you."

Zach spared a glance at Xavier. As much as they both wanted to hope this would all be over in a minute, he wasn't about to trust Doyle Murphy or his lawyer.

The lawyer gave Murphy a subtle wave. Murphy ran his fingers through his graying hair and visibly steeled himself. "The word came down from the top."

"The top?" Xavier sent a silent warning to Zach. Months in the parish hadn't brought him anywhere near Doyle's superior, the don of the entire South Side mob.

"The boss."

"Sullivan," Zach concluded. "What did he want with Special Agent Malone?"

"Got me." Murphy held out his hands for an exaggerated shrug. "I hardly know the guy. Didn't even hear it directly."

His plausible-deniability act wasn't halfway convincing. Zach bit back a sarcastic reply and looked to Xavier.

Murphy shifted in his chair, setting his shoulders at a defiant angle. "Listen, 'Father' Whoever You Are, do you think Sullivan's running his plans by me with the Feds breathing down my back? He probably knew you people would drag me down here, since I seem to be your favorite punching bag—"

"Since you seem to be on tape in her building."

"You should be grateful!" Murphy rose. His lawyer took his arm, but Murphy shook him off. "You wouldn't have a clue what was going on if I hadn't stepped in. I might not know what they're doing or why, but at least I gave you a sporting chance—"

Zach did his best to keep his gaze—and temper—level. "I don't believe for a minute that you don't know where she is."

"If I was the one doing this, don't you think I'd be there myself? You think I'd be so stupid to get caught on film at the scene of the crime?"

"Oh, I'd bet on it."

The door swung open, and Assistant Special Agent in Charge Reginald Sellars leaned into the room. The heavyset African American scowled at Zach, as always. The guy had never liked Zach. "Need to speak with you," Sellars said in obviously measured tones. "Now."

In the hall, Zach focused on Sellars's black eyebrows.

"What are you trying to do?" Sellars asked.

"Uh, find my fiancée?"

Sellars grimaced. "I know. We've got people all over the city, searching every property that ever had one of his shell companies' names on it. But messing with Murphy himself? What about his trial?"

"How's the case going to go without Molly's testimony?"

Sellars shook his head with a heavy exhale. "We all want to find her, Saint."

Some of them more than others. "Is that why you dragged me out of there?"

"We also want to bring him to justice for what he's done—what he's doing. And that means treading carefully. Especially you, 'Father.' What's going to happen if Murphy goes to the press saying who you really are?"

Before Zach could reach for the doorknob, the door swung open.

Murphy and his lawyer walked out. Zach's jaw dropped—they were letting him go? What was Xavier smoking?

"Here." Xavier pulled out a business card and offered it to Murphy. "In case you 'hear' anything."

Murphy took the card, then turned to Zach. "What about you? You got a card?"

"Fresh out, sorry."

Murphy smirked. "I'm sure. Not like you'd lie to me. You're a regular saint, Father."

Chills trailed icy fingers down Zach's back. Murphy knew who he was. Maybe not that he was with the FBI, but definitely his real name.

Was this about Molly's testimony, or Zach's role in Doyle's arrest?

Either way, Zach snapped his mouth shut and watched Murphy walk away free.

And Molly was trapped somewhere. If she was still alive.

Past the sea of empty desks, Murphy and his lawyer rounded the corner, out of sight.

Zach was supposed to be getting closer to her, not further away.

Xavier started the other direction down the hall, pulling Zach with him. Sellars followed. "We got him," Xavier murmured.

Sellars almost laughed. "You're joking, right?"

X shot him a look that said he was definitely not joking.

"Did he say something after I—" Zach stopped short of snarking with Sellars standing there. "—left?"

Xavier looked from Zach to Sellars. "You missed it?"

"What?"

They reached the elevators and Xavier hit the down button. "He said he wasn't so stupid to get caught on film *at the scene of the crime*." Xavier checked their reactions again, but Zach just waited for the punch line. A smile tugged at the corners of Xavier's lips. "We only said Molly was missing. We never said her place was the scene of the crime."

"We don't know if it is." Sellars rubbed his mouth, mentally rolling the problem over. "Wouldn't he assume that after we showed him the picture?"

Zach could barely detect the sly smile X was holding back. "All the evidence showed was that he was in a building lobby delivering the note. He's the one who made that leap. Sounds to me like he knows more than he says."

The elevator arrived and the three of them boarded. Xavier turned to Sellars. "How are the searches going?"

"Made it through maybe a third of the places."

Zach leaned back against the elevator wall. Murphy might have made an admission or just an assumption. He was gambling the next hour or two of Molly's life on the difference. "Then we let him go because . . . ?"

"Because he isn't going to lead us to her while he's sitting in a conference room."

Zach pushed off the wall. "Even Doyle Murphy isn't stupid enough to lead us straight from the FBI offices to her."

"Of course not—but don't you think he's going to have to get back to her pretty quick here?"

Zach studied the faux wood grain in the elevator paneling. Maybe Murphy would be itching to get back to Molly, rub it in Zach's face that he'd had her all along—or maybe he would let her languish alone.

Or maybe she didn't need tending at all by now. Maybe she was already dead.

The elevator stopped at their floor, and the doors slid open, but none of them moved. "Z," Xavier started. "I know it's a long shot, but it's all we've got. Even if he has someone else guarding her, he can't leave whoever it is alone there all day—they've got to eat. Molly does, too."

"Oh, I'm sure her wellbeing is his top concern." Zach stopped the elevator doors from shutting.

"I don't see you coming up with any better ideas."

The doors' second attempt at closing—and Zach pushing them back—was the only sound for a long moment.

"All right," Zach finally agreed. "But if we're going to do this, we have to have at least two cars on them at all times. Do we know if Murphy came in with his lawyer, or if they drove separate?"

"Separate, I think." Sellars pulled his phone from his pocket. "I'll double-check."

"Hurry. They're probably already on their way out."

Sellars nodded and lifted the phone to his ear. Zach and Xavier stepped off the elevator, Xavier making his own call.

They were staking Molly's life on anything but a sure bet.

Molly blew a single breath toward her hairline, but it did even less to cool her off than the obnoxious fan. "Miles," she started. "I don't think you really want to do this. I'm with the FBI, you know yourself, and I'm sure we can—"

Hennessy huffed out a silent laugh. "You're a persistent little—"

A generic ringtone interrupted him. Hennessy checked his phone, then stood and stepped out.

Forty-five minutes alone with him and she hadn't found an opening yet. Hennessy had seemed only content to attempt small talk and feeble efforts at making her feel comfortable. Without, of course, undoing the shackle or the PlastiCuffs.

She tried to concentrate on the murmurs carrying through the door, but she couldn't even discern the tone of voice.

She couldn't resign herself to fate that easily, though. Hours remained before the ceremony—

Molly's mind stumbled over her own thought. Did some part of her really believe she might make it to the temple this afternoon?

Ridiculous as it seemed, she couldn't she give up that wild hope. She had to believe she could get out of here. Or Zachary would find her and save her.

Unless that was exactly what Doyle Murphy wanted.

Hennessy returned, apparently finished with his phone call. "Looks like it's you and me for a little longer. Doyle has another engagement."

"Did the FBI arrest him?"

"No, he's cooperating—just not without his lawyer."

Time to try another tack. "I have to say, I'm a bit surprised you're still this loyal to him."

"Oh?" Hennessy's single syllable carried a symphony of skepticism. "Because he's getting some . . . negative attention, I'm gonna turn on him?"

"I'm sure plenty of others have."

"And? What's it to you?" He took a step forward.

Molly lifted her shoulders in a defensive gesture, scooting back on the bed. "Nothin', nothin' at all—I was only thinkin' perhaps this plan isn't the best option for either of you, since Doyle will be goin' to jail."

"Oh yeah?" Laughter danced behind Hennessy's eyes. "Maybe you should quit thinking, then."

All right, she'd try a different tactic. "Are you doin' this for the money? I'd gladly pay you."

His eyes laughed again, and he shook his head. "No, kid."

"What, then? Safe passage? Get out of jail free card?"

"You can't give me what I'm getting out of this."

Molly scoured her memories of the morning so far. Doyle had said he was counting on someone coming for her, and he'd gloated over her wedding announcement. She was the bait to lure Zachary here, but surely if the plan was to make Zachary suffer, her life was ransom.

She'd have to get out of here before Zachary could find her. Until Hennessy left, she couldn't attack her restraints.

What was Hennessy getting out of this? Certainly he didn't care that much about ripping Zachary's heart out. Could his loyalty to Doyle really run that deep?

Not unless Hennessy was benefiting somehow. She could find his weakness and get out of here. She'd have to wait until he wasn't suspecting it.

6

ZACH HAD TO HAND IT TO XAVIER. He'd gone all out for this idea. In the last ten minutes, they'd watched Doyle and his lawyer leave on the security cameras to figure out where they'd parked, ordered a roadblock set up, and positioned themselves in Xavier's car, watching the parking garage's only exit. The one thing they didn't have was another car, but Zach didn't have time to get a Bureau car and couldn't risk Murphy seeing his car.

A red minivan pulled up to the garage exit and out onto the side street. Not Murphy.

Zach's phone rang. "Hello?"

"This is Kent, from Molly's squad, calling to report on my searches."

Zach sat up straighter. Of course he knew Kent—he'd become Molly's closest coworker. "Good news?"

"Afraid not."

Zach puffed out all his enthusiasm in one breath.

"I'm on my way back to the office," Kent continued, "just checking to see if there's anything else I can do first."

"Actually, yeah." The guy could use a spotter in his car, but a second car pursuing Doyle was better than nothing. "You good at tailing people?"

"My hidden talent."

"Okay, great," Zach said. "We're tailing Murphy from the parking garage across the street. Should be leaving any minute."

"I'll be there."

Xavier signaled for Zach's attention, and nodded toward the garage exit. They both craned their necks for a better view. A vintage gold coupe was waiting to pull onto the road.

"What does Murphy drive?" Kent said over the phone, as if he had a telepathic connection to their car.

Xavier offered Zach a piece of paper, but Zach hardly needed the reminder. "Black Audi, sedan." He read off the plate number.

The gold coupe roared onto the roadway, going left. With the roadblock in place, that was the only option.

"I'm at Ashland and Roosevelt," Kent reported.

Zach glanced at the gold coupe, turning onto the main road—Roosevelt. Ashland was a couple lights to the east. "Great," he said. "Hold tight."

As if on cue, a black Audi pulled up to the garage exit.

"That him?" Xavier asked.

"Yep." How could he forget the windows, as dark as they could make them?

"Who tints the windows on an Audi?" Xavier muttered.

Murphy pulled onto the road, away from their barricade. He paused at the main road and then took another left.

"He's coming your way," Zach informed Kent.

Xavier pulled out, sneaking around the barricade, to follow Murphy onto the main road. They spotted the black Audi a few cars ahead of them and hung back to remain unnoticeable.

Kent's voice cut in. "He's taking a left at the light on Ashland."

"Yeah, we see. You got him?" Zach asked.

"I'm headed the wrong way. I'll catch up."

Zach tried to project where Murphy might be going. Ashland fed right into the Eisenhower Expressway, which might not be a mess with morning traffic yet. Still, the road hit four other interstates in the city, plus the nightmare Circle Interchange. "If he gets on the Eisenhower—"

"I know." Xavier swung into the turn lane, barely making the same light Murphy had gone through.

Doyle changed to the right-hand lane. Only a few lights between them and the Eisenhower on-ramp. Zach silently prayed Murphy would make a right turn before the freeway.

Doyle continued straight through two green lights. He slowed as he came up to a cross street, the last before the Eisenhower on-ramp.

"Better catch up if he's getting on the Eisenhower," Zach said.

"He's getting on the Eisenhower?" Kent's voice carried on the phone.

"Sorry, thinking out loud. Keep you posted."

The on-ramp was off the next right for Doyle. Xavier maneuvered past two slower-moving cars.

Doyle went right.

"Kent, what's your twenty?" Zach asked.

Kent read off the cross street, only a block behind them. Zach updated him in return. "Murphy's making a right."

Xavier pulled into the right lane to follow him. Zach involuntarily checked the bank sign on the corner. The light board showed the time and temperature: 8:13 AM. 92° F.

How hot was Molly right now? Was she somewhere safe and cool—or out in the sun? Or—

Xavier made the turn. Ahead of them, Zach could just see Murphy bearing left onto the on-ramp. "Getting on the Eisenhower," he told Kent, then spoke to Xavier. "Stay back, okay? If Doyle Murphy makes us, there's no way he's going straight back to Molly."

X shot him the side-eye. Of course he knew that. Xavier picked up speed to merge onto the Eisenhower. Shockingly, traffic was moving along well for this time of day. X pulled into the third lane from the right, one lane further over than Doyle.

"I'm getting on the Eisenhower," Kent announced.

"He's in the second lane from the right. Hurry up."

The car in front of them braked. Doyle's lane continued forward while they stopped short. Zach searched behind them for a break in the next lane's traffic. Instead, he spotted Kent's white coupe shooting past them in the merge lane.

"You got him?" Zach asked.

"Gimme a sec." Kent's car zipped to the left just before his lane became an exit ramp. "This lane?" he asked.

"That's the one."

Xavier finally spotted a break in traffic and pulled into the left-most lane. Tense silence reigned as Xavier leapfrogged his way between the two lanes to try to catch up with Doyle. Zach watched the skyscrapers on the horizon grow bigger the closer they got.

"At the Circle," Kent said. "He's taking 90/94."

"North or south?" They had to get in the correct lanes to follow him, and guessing would not cut it today.

"He's headed . . . um, the sign says east—toward Indiana?"

"Outbound." Zach pointed for Xavier to merge right. "We're coming up on the split."

Kent made a *hm* that sounded like approval. "You're catching up quick."

Zach resisted the urge to snort. The tables had turned. "Have you merged with the interstate yet?"

"Not yet, still on the little feeder road, two cars back from Murphy. Passing a UIC building."

Xavier took the exit ramp, following the curve around to the Ryan Expressway.

Another kick to the chest: Ryan was the cover name Molly had used in the case they'd worked together five months ago. The case that brought them back together.

"Coming up on the merge," Kent said.

"Passing that UIC building," Zach replied. How long ago had Kent mentioned it? A minute? Less? He glanced at Xavier.

"I know, I know," he murmured. "Pick it up." He moved to the left lane, passed a truck, and slid back into the right lane to pass a minivan.

"Murphy is on 90/94, moving to the middle lane," Kent broke the silence. "Picking up speed. I'm a couple cars ahead of him."

Zach bit back the reminder to stay on his tail. Three cars was good enough—he had to keep some cover if he didn't want Murphy to spot him.

They slowed down as traffic narrowed to a single lane. "Coming up on the merge with 90/94," Zach said.

"You're like half a mile back. Hurry and you'll get us. Murphy's in the left lane."

They finally passed the bottleneck and reached the freeway proper. Xavier swung into the left lane and floored it. "Now that's how I roll," he muttered. He passed a big rig on the right, then moved back into the left lane to pass an SUV.

"What's the speed limit?" Xavier asked.

"Forty-five. And it's a construction zone." Zach checked the speedometer—almost seventy.

X didn't slow down. "It's always a construction zone. The state flower of Illinois is the orange and white construction cone."

"What's Murphy doing?" Zach asked Kent.

"Same as he was a minute ago."

Zach suddenly remembered why Kent had been such a problem for Molly when she'd first transferred here. "I mean, how fast is he going?"

"Oh. Probably fifty-five or sixty. He's moving to the middle lane."

"Well, we're catching up." Another ten seconds, and Zach updated their twenty. "We're on the overpass above the Metra tracks."

"I'm just past that. He's changing to the right lane."

Zach scanned the cars ahead of them—four cars up, a little white car zoomed down one of the middle lanes. "We see you."

Xavier reined in his speed, matching traffic as they fell in behind a flashy red convertible in the middle lane. Doyle's black Audi was in the right lane, two cars up. Further ahead, Kent's car merged into the right lane one car in front of Doyle.

An on-ramp joined the freeway. The new right-most lane was marked Exit Only—and Doyle shifted into it.

"He's in the exit-only lane," Zach said. "Take the exit."

Kent signaled and moved into the exit lane across two solid white lines.

"Follow?" Xavier asked.

"Yeah."

Xavier did as he was told. "Where does this go?"

"Across the river?" Zach shrugged. "I was too busy watching Doyle." They passed under another sign—they were headed to I-55.

"Great." X's voice filled with sarcasm. "Another interchange."

"Don't get too far ahead," Zach warned Kent.

"Don't get too far back," Kent replied.

The ramp expanded to two lanes. Xavier stayed one car behind Murphy in the left lane and Kent held his position two cars ahead in the right lane. The road curved around, hugging the expressway tight. They crossed the river, still separated from the main interstate by concrete barriers.

"Split ahead," Kent announced. "Is he signaling?"

"No, holding steady in the left lane."

Kent signaled and moved into the left lane. "Here we go again," Kent muttered.

Their lane veered off, passing over an on-ramp, another interstate—I-55—and another bridge, curving back again to dip under the interstate they'd just left and another off-ramp.

After the tension of racing to catch up, cruising along the freeway with no way of leaving their single lane was anticlimactic. "Nice, man," Zach said to X.

"Good thing we had Kent with us."

"Nice job, Kent," Zach told the other car. "Easy riding from here."

Kent laughed. "Famous last words, Zach. But let's hope so."

Finally, their feeder road met with I-55. Another complex interchange snaked overhead, casting shadows across the four lanes.

Murphy slid into the fast lane.

"Nice while it lasted," Xavier muttered.

"Murphy's in the left lane," Zach said to Kent. "We're taking the second lane from right."

"I'll take the other middle lane. This road ends pretty quick up here, so he'd better figure out where he's going fast."

Yep. The freeway terminus would dump them in the Near South Side right along Lake Michigan.

Not too far from where he and Molly had closed that case together.

They got less than a quarter mile before Murphy signaled and shifted into the middle lane in front of a van. Zach checked the left lane—there'd been no one in front of Murphy, so he wasn't passing someone.

"Heads up," Zach announced. "He's in your lane."

As soon as he'd said it, Murphy changed lanes again, shifting over two lanes. Another Exit Only lane joined the freeway.

"Now he's in the second from the right."

"That lane ends." A yellow road sign overhead confirmed Kent's announcement.

Murphy merged right again—into the exit-only lane.

"He's exiting again—293D. We're on him, you?"

Kent's white car cut across two lanes of traffic to exit. "Barely," Kent said.

"Which way?" Zach muttered. Murphy hadn't signaled yet.

"He's signaled every lane change," Xavier said. "What kind of mobster signals?"

"I'll go right." Kent moved into that lane.

Murphy moved from the right lane to the left lane of the off-ramp—and signaled left.

Zach angled his phone to speak into it again. "Bad luck, Kent. We're still on him."

"I'll move to intercept." Kent made his turn, the wrong direction.

"Wait, doesn't left slingshot you around, back onto 55 going the other way?"

Zach wasn't sure. He checked with his boss; X lifted his fingers from the steering wheel to say he didn't know either. "We'll let you know in a minute."

The ramp swung them around, cutting underneath the freeway they'd just left. A second curve brought them back to that same interstate, headed the opposite direction.

"What is he doing?" X's shoulders dropped. "Did he make us?"

"Couldn't have." They'd kept at least one car between them at all times, until they'd reached this last ramp. "We're on I-55 South, heading west," Zach announced to Kent. "What's your twenty?"

"MLK Drive, waiting to get on the on-ramp."

Zach tapped his fist on the car door. This was a lot easier with two vehicles.

Murphy stayed in the right lane, even after an overhead sign announced the lane was exit only.

"And again." Xavier groaned. "We're toast."

"He's exiting at 293B." Zach paused to check the sign for further directions—and sighed. "It's the exit for 90/94. East. Outbound. Toward Indiana." They were literally going in circles.

"I'm coming up on 55," Kent said in the same grim tone. "You burned?"

"Only thing that would explain dragging us all over the place like this, just to get back on the same road."

They followed the black Audi, keeping a car between them mostly out of habit and because the ramp was only one congested lane. The long line of cars wove under and over the two interstates before joining up with the expressway.

"We're on 90/94 again," Zach said. "Still on him."

Kent made a strangled noise of defeat. "Coming up on the exit to follow you."

Xavier scrunched up his mouth, frustrated. "Sorry, man. We did everything right."

"I know." Zach kept his eyes on the Audi. Other than the occasional update from Kent, they rode in silence for a mile, two cars behind Murphy in the right lane. Traffic slowed as construction cones narrowed the expressway to one lane. Murphy signaled to exit.

"Exiting at 35th Street," Zach announced.

"Copy," Kent said. "Catching up."

They merged onto a road, and followed Murphy for one, two, three right turns.

"Wait a minute," Xavier said.

Zach scanned the street ahead of the Audi. The road dead ended into a parking lot. Was this a trap?

No. The parking lot ahead—and the one to their right—was too full for Murphy to try something.

Zach squinted, but he'd need ESP to figure out Murphy's next move. "What is he doing?"

The black Audi pulled over. Xavier pulled into the parking lot. "Is Murphy a Sox fan?"

"Why?"

Xavier nodded to the stadium across the street. "We're at Comiskey Park. Or whatever it's called now."

If Murphy was coming here to a ball game—Zach glanced back at the street where Murphy had parked. His car door was open.

Zach lifted the phone. "We are stopped on 34th Street, across from the Guaranteed Rate—new Comiskey. Murphy has pulled over and opened his door. Get down here!"

"Getting ready to exit," Kent replied.

Xavier pulled even with Murphy's Audi, keeping a row of parked cars between them. Xavier stopped the car in the middle of the lot. He and Zach hopped out of the car, weapons drawn to approach Murphy.

He was still sitting in the car, the door open.

"What is he doing?"

Finally, slowly, Murphy started to stand.

"Hands in the air!" Zach barked. "Higher!"

Murphy complied. His hands were first past the car roof, then his dark hair, gray at the temples. Then his face—

The driver was Murphy's lawyer.

MOLLY SHIFTED ON THE BED, the frame clanking beneath her. She'd given up on wishing for relief from the heat. It was hard to gauge how long it had been—the weather was affecting her brain already—but it seemed as though enough time had passed to try again. "Miles," she started. He looked up before she continued. "You've always been kind to me." Kind of kind.

Hennessy raised the magazine he'd been pretending to read for half an hour and flipped a page.

"How would you feel if someone had Teresa?"

"It'd stop her nagging."

Clearly, he was a romantic. But they had children—two. What was his daughter's name? Molly racked her brain. "What about Megan?"

He sucked in a soft breath. She'd struck a nerve.

"Leave her out of this."

"Miles, what is this? Doyle's last trial went his way; why would he jeopardize all that today?"

Hennessy pinned her with an expression that might have worked to quiet Teresa or Megan. "How many times do you think Doyle's lawyer can manage a mistrial?"

That did quiet Molly. Was he saying that Doyle and his lawyer had arranged a mistrial?

Before she could ask anything else, an engine rumbled past. Hope—vicious, cruel hope—spread through her chest, a treacherous cancer.

The engine stopped and a car door slammed. She almost held her breath until she heard the approaching footsteps. Not nearly fast enough. No chance that Zachary—or any other federal agent—would be walking to get her.

Doyle Murphy strode into the room once more, gloating more than ever.

Of course. Just as it seemed like she was making progress with Hennessy.

"How was the meeting?" Hennessy asked, flipping through his magazine.

"Surprisingly productive." Doyle smiled, that wicked gleam in his eyes again. He turned to Molly. "He been treating you right?"

"Sure now." She scoffed. "Other than this entire scheme. But I suppose this was really your idea, so."

Doyle laughed. Hennessy, on the other hand, tightened his jaw, glaring lasers at his magazine.

Whatever troubled Hennessy aside, Doyle's laughter was good for Molly. Get in his good graces, flatter him, appeal to reason, bargain a bit, and she could be out of here. "Doyle. You're smarter than this. Havin' me here won't help anythin'. Witness tamperin' is evidence of the underlyin' crime. It only hurts your case."

"My case? Didn't you hear?" He mocked her, simpering. "Mistrial?"

Of course she'd heard. They'd already established that. "They'll only try you again."

"We'll see about that, now that we know the good 'Father' is with the Bureau."

Molly strained to keep her expression neutral. Zachary would never have confirmed that. Doyle was bluffing. He had to be. "Is he? Definitely not in my division."

Doyle snorted. "Yeah, we'll see what he has to say about that when I've got him where I want him."

A dozen razors stabbed into her heart at once, and her mind

dredged up the image of Zachary in a warehouse not far from this one—battered and bleeding. She couldn't let that happen again.

She checked Hennessy's reaction. His magazine dipped toward the floor, an intense stare focused on Doyle. A muscle in Hennessy's temple throbbed.

Molly lifted her chin. If she couldn't get Doyle to see reason, perhaps she could better divide and conquer when he left again. "You're a reasonable man, Doyle. You know this isn't helpin' your case. You'll not be gettin' away with this unless—"

"I can't get away with this?" Doyle exchanged a glance with Hennessy. "The FBI placed an agent undercover as a priest. *You* can't get away with *that*."

Doyle's wicked grin returned and he stepped toward Molly. "Tim O'Leary—Zach Saint—he's going to pay. He's going to suffer every inch as much as I have. Him and Cally both."

"Cally Lonegan, too? You're plannin' to track him down in witness protection?"

Doyle sneered. "You Feds think you're all so safe and secure. I got to the Father, didn't I? I can get to Cally." He pointed to Hennessy. "Got his brother-in-law sitting right there. You think Marie and Teresa could go two years without talking?"

Molly tried to remember any interaction she'd seen from the sisters in her old parish. They'd never struck her as particularly close, never making an effort to sit together on the rare occasions they were both at Mass.

No, he had to be bluffing. He'd gotten to her and Zachary because of an announcement in the paper. Cally wouldn't dare make that same mistake, and neither would his wife. The US Marshals had never lost someone in their program who was following the rules about breaking off all contact, and she couldn't imagine Marie taking that risk, even for her sister.

Doyle thrust his hands on his hips, the proud papa of his plan. "I'm getting away scot-free," he practically crowed. "Which is more than I can say for you."

"All because of your brilliant plan, so?" Molly said, sarcasm replete in her voice.

"So what?"

This was no time to explain the Irish tag word. Molly stole a glimpse of Hennessy, still holding his jaw as though he were barely biting back a response. Doyle was blissfully oblivious to Hennessy's sulking.

If she could get Doyle out of this room, perhaps Hennessy would finally yield to persuasion.

Zach didn't dare take his gun off the man, though he wanted to pound something. Murphy's *lawyer*? All this for nothing?

If the lawyer was here, driving Murphy's car as a decoy, that made him complicit in the kidnapping and anything else Murphy was planning today. They had to at least question him. "Hands on top of the car!"

The lawyer complied, although the set to his shoulders showed he clearly didn't want to. "Come on, boys. You've got nothing on my client so you're taking it out on me?"

Zach ignored him, his gun at the ready while Xavier frisked him. Nothing. X shook his head and Zach tucked his gun away.

Xavier whipped the lawyer around. "What are you doing?" X demanded.

"Doyle said he wanted to drive the Cougar. Can you blame him?" The lawyer lit up like a firework. "I mean, it's a pretty sweet ride—a '69 Cougar, totally rebuilt, real gold flake—"

"We don't care," Zach interrupted. "How stupid are you, giving your car to him in the middle of an active investigation?"

"What? The man practically paid for it anyway."

Xavier painted on a look that said *oh, really?* "Are you admitting to taking a bribe?"

The lawyer scoffed. "Nice try, boys, but *I'm* the lawyer here."

"What's your name again?" Zach asked.

"Frank Lehrman."

In one fluid motion, Xavier pulled out his cuffs and slapped one onto the lawyer's wrist. "Frank Lehrman, you're under arrest."

"On what charges?"

"Obstruction of justice," Zach began. "Interfering in a federal investigation. Criminal enterprise. Accepting a bribe. Take your pick."

Lehrman scowled as Zach cuffed his other wrist. "Ticking you off isn't a crime."

"Today it is." Zach and X each took hold of one of Lehrman's arms. Xavier *Mirandized* Lehrman as they approached Xavier's car.

"Wait, wait, I can explain all this," Lerhman interrupted.

They stopped. Waiving his right to counsel? Perfect. "Let's hear it then."

"Really, Doyle said he wanted to give the Cougar a test drive. He said we'd meet down at Comiskey, and he had the route all programmed in his GPS, just follow the directions. I didn't know we were going to run around like that, or that you'd follow me—him—"

"Relax." Xavier clapped him on the shoulder. "We believe you." Sort of.

"Then I can go?"

Zach opened the back door to X's car. "No." He pushed Lehrman into the back seat.

"I haven't done anything! You don't have any charges! You can't hold me!"

"Oh?" Zach didn't bother to hide the sarcasm in his voice. "Don't you know what 'you're under arrest' means? I thought you were the lawyer here."

"This is false arrest—"

Zach slammed the door shut. He and X turned around to keep Lehrman from eavesdropping. Or lipreading. "What are we going to do with him?" Xavier asked.

"He's under arrest. Come on, his client was in for questioning in an ongoing kidnapping, and he thinks it's a good time to play musical cars?" Zach scoffed. "We have to at least hold him to make sure he's not aiding and/or abetting anymore."

X rubbed the back of his neck, unconvinced. "How long are we going to keep him without evidence?"

"Until we trace his car—and Murphy."

"This dude's probably got LoJack or something. I'll find out."

Zach glanced back at Lehrman, slumped in their back seat, playing the part of the defiant teenager. Mob lawyers. Even worse than regular defense lawyers.

Zach looked back to where the Audi still stood with its driver door open. Showing the fancy interior panel.

He'd only been in the car once, for a few minutes, while receiving an extortion threat, so he didn't remember much about it, but he was pretty sure there was a built-in navigation system.

"Hang on." Zach pushed off Xavier's car and jogged to Doyle's Audi. Sure enough, the center console held a large screen. He climbed in the driver's seat. The air-conditioning hit him, and he realized how hot it was outside.

"Record-breaking heat continues today," the newscaster on the radio said. "The death toll has now topped eighty—"

He snapped off the radio and focused on the screen. He hadn't used one of these before, but it wasn't too difficult to find the GPS navigation and the Last Destinations icon. Zach scrolled through the addresses. No telling how long ago Murphy had programmed these in. They'd have to at least check to see what they were.

"Think we need a warrant?" Xavier muttered, suddenly at his

side. "Or should we ask the lawyer?"

"Seems to me that Murphy stole his lawyer's car. We're taking it in to impound, right?"

Xavier acknowledged the point. No warrant needed, and the keys were even in the ignition.

For a split second, Zach hesitated. If Murphy had transported Molly in this car, this was a crime scene, and Zach might be destroying evidence.

But if he had to choose between saving Molly and prosecuting Murphy, the choice was obvious.

"I'm going to run down these addresses." Zach shot Xavier a silent question to ask for permission.

X held out his hands, helpless. He couldn't say yes—but he also couldn't say no. "I'll let Lehrman stew for a while. If we can get ahold of the number Murphy's using right now, we should be able to pin down his location."

He was going to try to crack a mob lawyer? "Good luck."

"You too." Xavier's voice was sincere, but by the time Zach looked up to acknowledge him, his boss was walking away.

It was probably too good to be true, but Zach pulled up the most recent address in Doyle Murphy's GPS and clicked the button to navigate there.

The first address was Andorka's, a sandwich shop. The second address, backtracking past the ballpark, was Soluri Brothers. Another sandwich shop.

Odds seemed low that Doyle had programmed every sandwich shop on the South Side into his GPS to mess with Zach. Just in case, Zach pulled out his phone to search for the next address to make sure it wasn't another waste of time. Before he could enter it, the phone vibrated with an incoming call. He waited for the number to come up—his parents.

He gritted his teeth. Avoiding this conversation altogether felt right, but that might have just been years of hiding his job talking.

Today, he had even more to hide from them than usual. Not answering, however, was sure to raise more alarms.

Gripping the phone tighter to steel himself, Zach answered. "Hey."

"Where on earth are you?" his mother demanded in her thick Southern accent.

A direct question. Time for evasive maneuvers. "Didn't Lucy tell you?"

"She said you had an emergency at work—but it's your wedding day. I thought you had today off."

He feigned a sigh. "You know how it is. The government." Covering up with his mother was sometimes the hardest part of being a covert operative—especially after Lucy, Molly and Molly's parents had all discovered his real job while he was in the line of duty.

"Uh huh. How long is this gonna take?"

"Mom," he said, aiming for a calming tone. "If I knew, I'd tell you."

"I expect you told Molly."

"She knows where I am. Of course." He could hear the drawl creeping into his own voice and forced himself to focus. "Hey, I have to get back to this thing—crisis meeting, you know. Was there something specific you needed?"

"Aren't we supposed to be setting up for the brunch soon?"

Crap. Zach checked the time his phone. 8:47. They were supposed to be at the chapel at 9:30.

And "they" included Molly.

"Hold on a sec—I have another call. It's Molly." He hit the mute icon and stared at the phone.

He was too used to coming up with explanations that were *not* "I'm working for the FBI." His parents knew Molly was with the Bureau—she wasn't a covert operative. Her story would be even more believable than his, especially if he could get Kent to call Molly's mom to backstop the cover.

Zach unmuted his phone. "Hey, Mom, that was Molly. She said she's really sorry, but they had a major break in a case and she's the only French speaker they could get today."

"On her wedding day?"

"I know—can you believe the FBI?" Zach hoped his tone would convey an eye-roll. "Anyway, she's stuck out in Joliet and I'm afraid she'll probably miss the brunch."

"You're joking, right?"

"I wish."

Mom was silent a long moment. "Fine." Her voice clearly said it was *not* fine. "I take it you're missing it, too?"

"Sorry."

"It's only your own wedding." She sighed. "But if I find out you two are off doing something fun, so help me, Zachary Tyler Saint—if you're doing this to get out of brunch—"

"Mom," he cut her off. "You know I wouldn't do that to you. Neither would Molly."

"Okay." She drew out the reply as if she still doubted him.

"We'll be there as soon as possible. I promise."

She hmphed. "You'd better. Love you, Zachary."

"You too." Zach ended the call and rubbed his forehead. This was such a big deal to his mom—she was probably already brainstorming ways to make sure they still got their fill of the three-ring Saint family wedding circus, since Lucy insisted it'd be a long time before she could ever think about following suit.

If ever. He didn't get to talk to her much since she up and moved a couple months ago, but from what he could tell, she was very much in the "I will literally never love again" phase.

He knew that phase all too well. But then it had worked out with Molly after all—until today.

Zach's phone buzzed again. He checked the caller ID: an unfamiliar Chicago number.

With as many family members as he had in town this weekend, it could be anyone. If he was smart, he'd let it roll to voicemail.

But if he was *really* smart, he'd make sure the caller wouldn't suspect anything.

"Hello?"

"Zach?" Lucy gasped.

He sat up straight at the urgency in her tone. Was she in danger too?

He cranked the A/C. "You okay?"

"I just—I just—" She gulped for air. "I actually saw Paul. I think."

Zach stifled a groan, hitting the button on the console to navigate to the next address in Murphy's list. At this rate, it'd be faster to drive there than wait until he could search on his phone. The GPS announced it would be eleven minutes to his destination. "Where are you?"

"The hotel lobby."

"Why would Paul be on the North Side in the middle of the day on a Friday?" He checked that the way was clear and pulled into traffic.

Lucy hesitated a beat. "I don't know."

"Lucy, relax. He knows you left town. He doesn't have any reason to believe you'd be at that particular hotel." He'd never even been to Molly's ward there, only to Zach and Lucy's smaller branch on the South Side.

"Did you tell him I moved? Tell me you didn't actually say that."

Zach made a conscious effort to unclench his jaw. The one member of his family who had some idea what was going on today, and she was running to him for moral support.

"No, I followed your orders, ma'am. All he knows for sure is that you quit your job, changed your number and cleared out of your apartment in twelve hours. Considering what an idiot he is, you're probably right—he hasn't taken the hint."

"Don't call him an idiot."

Anyone who strung his sister along for a year and a half

definitely qualified, but Zach pressed on. "He probably saw the wedding announcement in the paper and tracked down one of our friends to find out about the brunch. Do you want me to get a Chicago PD unit down there to pick him up for stalking?"

"Thanks a lot, bro. I thought you of all people might understand what this would be like for me. Obviously, I was wrong."

"Lucy, I understand. You know I do." Though when Zach had been suffering six months ago, his sister was secretly double dating with Molly and her boyfriend.

Silence. He glanced at the call timer on his phone. Another ten seconds and he'd tell her he had to get off, and she wouldn't think he was enough of a jerk that she'd go running to Mom.

"Zach, I—" Lucy's voice caught. "I actually wanted it to be him, but I didn't, you know? I want to see him, but I don't want to see him when it hurts like this—and he's got to be furious with me."

So much for his ten-second countdown. "I know. But we've been through this. He wasn't angry when he came to me, just worried."

"Do you think it'd be bad if I called him?"

"Yes." He rubbed the back of his neck, trying to soften his own irritation. They had this specific discussion at least once a month. If she wanted to talk to the guy that bad, she should just do it.

"It's so hard not to. I do still want to see him. I do still think about him all the time. And then I get here and it's twice as hard not to remember . . . everything. Think about how it could have been. Could still be."

He understood all too well—and he was going to be in the same situation if they didn't find Molly soon. Today was supposed to be the one day he didn't have to talk Lucy off this cliff again. "Listen, Luce, I'm sorry, but I have to go."

"Zach, I know you're busy, but I—"

"Lucy." He dropped to a dangerous whisper. "I'm sorry you're upset, but this is supposed to be a big day for me, so if you don't mind, I'm going to have to focus on my relationships for one day of my life."

Lucy scoffed. "I was just trying to say thank you, you jerk."

No wedding day was perfect, but he couldn't seem to do anything right today. "Sorry."

"Let me talk to her."

His heart hit a sandbank and faltered. Of course—she could ramble on about Paul because she didn't know the whole truth. The GPS announced he'd arrived at his destination: an Indian restaurant.

How many restaurants did this guy have programmed into his GPS?

"Come on," Lucy pressed. "I promise I won't scare her off."

"She's not here."

She hesitated. "Who did I just hear then? Sounded like a woman?"

"GPS."

A longer pause. "What's going on?" Suspicion tinged her words.

Zach blew out a long breath.

"Zach," Lucy tried again, heat rising in her voice. "You woke me up at, like, six o'clock this morning to try to keep Mom and Dad busy on your own wedding day. Not even Molly's mom has heard from her today. What. Is. Going. On."

"I wish I knew," he snapped.

Lucy fell silent for almost a minute. "Could she have ghosted you?"

"Why would you say that?" His answer was too defensive, too quick.

"I don't—I don't think she did. Is she okay?"

This time, he couldn't answer at all.

"I'll pray for her," Lucy murmured. "And you."

"Thanks. We need it."

"If there's anything else we can do, call me right away. I'll keep Mom and Dad busy."

Zach thanked her and ended the call, then searched for the next address in the GPS on his phone. Nick's Gyros. Next address, down near Doyle's Place: Barraco's Pizza. Next address, not far from Zach's apartment: White Castle.

Seriously? They couldn't follow Doyle, couldn't use his car against him, couldn't find anything but restaurants?

Zach's phone vibrated. Again. Another unfamiliar Chicago number. If this was Lucy— "What?" he demanded.

"Temper, temper, Father. Get up on the wrong side of the bed?"

Doyle Murphy.

Zach's skin turned colder than the overworked A/C. He squeezed his reply through clenched teeth. "I want Molly back, Murphy."

"Wow, Father. You really might want to consider anger management."

"I'll tell you what—you take an anger management course during your twenty-five to life, and tell me all about it."

"You always were funny." Murphy didn't laugh. "But in case you've forgotten, this isn't basketball."

"Yeah, in basketball the losers seldom get jail time."

"We'll see who loses today."

Ice shot through his veins. "I swear, Murphy, if you hurt her—"

"Threats? I expected more from you. But if you want to try to bully your way through," Murphy continued, "see where that gets you."

Zach scanned the interior of Murphy's car. A car that might cost Zach a year's rent seemed like a worthless trade for Molly. "Then what do you want?"

"You're going to do everything that I say, all day. Starting with deleting any recording of any conversations we have today."

"Yeah, right."

"Then she's dead."

Zach hesitated. An FBI agent and covert operative running around at the beck and call of a mobster—what was he going to make him do?

But really, was there anything he *wouldn't* do to get Molly back? He didn't want to find out the answer to that question.

"Father?" Doyle prompted. "Can I call you Father, or is that weird?"

Weird, but not his biggest problem. "First, you prove she's alive."

Murphy scoffed. "I'm calling the shots today, Father."

"Prove she's alive and I'm yours. Let me talk to her."

"Dream on. Have a nice life."

For the first time all day, he was actually moving closer to finding her, and that was slipping away. His rib cage felt like it was trying to contain an angry cougar. "Just—just let me ask her something only she would know. Through you, if you want."

Murphy waited. Zach strained to pick up any background noise.

"What's your question?"

Now Zach was the one fumbling for time. He should have had a question already planned.

Something only Molly knew—a recent experience. Something that would let him know if she was okay. Something she could pass along a message with.

"Ask her who took her through the temple last night. Other than me."

Murphy's end was quiet for a moment. Maybe he was kidding himself, but Zach thought he could hear Molly in the background for a moment before Murphy returned. "Grace Canavan."

What? Zach sat back against the headrest. The right answer was Lucy—but only Molly would've given this answer, too. She was trying to tell him something with the name of the criminal in the case they'd worked together. And he wasn't getting the message.

"Happy?" Murphy asked.

"Very. I'm all yours."

"I'm ecstatic."

"I can tell." Zach tugged at his seatbelt, like that would help to relieve the tension. "So what am I doing?"

"Right now, you're going to sit tight at FBI headquarters."

"What?"

"That's right. You sit tight. I'll call you in an hour. You're going to go everywhere and do everything that I say. And you're going to start by not calling this number back. This phone rings, you'll regret it. Get it?"

"And after that?"

"Depends on you, kid. You want her back, then I'll need something in return."

Zach tried to think what he could offer. Murphy's car. Money—how much cash could he scrape together today or get from the Bureau? Did he know anyone with power or influence that Murphy might ask for?

Only the SAC. The head of the city's FBI. Not that he could promise a whole lot from Evans.

"You're not going to ask what?" Murphy sucked his teeth. "I'm disappointed. So is Molly."

"Then what do you want?"

The call ended.

8

MOLLY SHOOK HER ARMS, trying to relief the PlastiCuffs' bite. She watched Doyle end the call, not daring to breathe. Could they tell she'd lied?

Doyle tossed his phone to Hennessy. Hennessy busied himself with taking the battery off the phone—so it couldn't be tracked.

They didn't know. They didn't know who Grace Canavan was, or that Molly and Zachary had arrested her not half a mile from here. Molly exhaled at last.

Doyle had been too busy talking and plotting for her to try to reason with him. This was her chance. "Doyle, you're smarter than this. We can still walk away."

He snorted, barely acknowledging her. "You going to conveniently forget the last ten hours?"

She doubted he'd believe her if she said yes. She'd tried getting him to see reason now three times. He seemed dead set on this plan of his. "Then what're you doin'?" she asked. "What're you after?"

"Not for you to worry about."

"I deserve to know at least what you're askin' in return—what you think I'm worth to him."

Doyle lifted an eyebrow. "You don't want to know what he offered?"

"That's patently ridiculous."

Doyle smirked in a way that made her want to smack him. He pulled out a handkerchief and mopped his brow.

Molly regarded him in silence. Zachary wouldn't offer anything; Doyle would demand it. He already appeared to believe he could slither out of the charges against him because of the controversy Zachary's cover as a priest would doubtlessly generate. How else could Murphy use the man?

Perhaps he was after something specific. Getting the charges dismissed was even less likely than Molly erasing the day from her memory—unless Doyle believed Zachary's relationship with the Special Agent in Charge meant more than it did. If he knew about the SAC. Molly searched for a way to test the waters with a bluff. "Did he offer the undersecretary?"

Doyle cut his gaze toward Hennessy for a split second. "What do you know, Miles? She's smarter than she looks."

"Glad one of us is," Molly murmured.

Doyle scowled at her.

She didn't buy his lie for a moment. Zachary couldn't have offered something she'd made up. Guessing the same apocryphal administrator would have been too much of a coincidence—and she hoped she meant enough to him that he wouldn't stake her life on a poor bluff.

However, now Doyle must think this person was real. What if he turned around and demanded Zachary deliver something from the fictitious undersecretary she'd invented? She had better cover her back. "Be careful with that one. Last I heard, the undersecretary wasn't takin' Zachary's calls."

"Then your boyfriend's going to have to get creative."

Molly tried not to show her frustration. What was the best move for her here? For the second time in her life, Doyle was using her to try to extort Zachary—but this time, more than just her reputation was in danger.

Doyle would want to kill two birds with a single stone, but what could the other bird be? Surely nothing in his life was on par with making the charges against him disappear. "Come now, Doyle." What tack hadn't she tried? A line from her *Burn Notice* marathon with Zachary last week popped into her memory. "Blackmail is a gun with a single bullet. Use it up and you're finished. You didn't come into this without a plan."

Behind him, Hennessy flinched ever so slightly.

"That just isn't like you," Molly finished.

Doyle's grin felt more like a leer. "You know me too well."

Obviously not well enough.

"What do you want from him, so?"

Doyle slowly lifted his chin. "Everything. Every. Last. Drop."

Stepping back into the air-conditioned FBI building felt so good, Zach was hit with palpable guilt. He should be out in the heat looking for Molly if there was any chance she might be outside.

But Doyle Murphy wanted him here.

Zach found Xavier sitting guard outside a conference room. He'd already told him about Doyle Murphy's call—sort of. He'd left out the part where he'd agreed to do the guy's bidding.

Xavier acknowledged him. "Did you give Murphy's number to a tech?"

"Yeah. He tried to locate Murphy's GPS or triangulate the number, but the phone was off."

Xavier frowned. "What do you want to do, Z?"

"Anything but sit tight."

"Yeah, but—for all we know, he orchestrated this whole scheme to have us drag his lawyer in so he could keep an eye on you."

Zach glanced toward the interview room. "So, what, we cut Lehrman loose?"

"Of course not. But I do think you should stick around here, in case."

"While she's out there? I can't do that."

"We have to at least make it seem like you're cooperating."

Zach tried to ignore a spike of panic. X didn't know how much Zach had agreed to cooperate with. In fact, even Zach couldn't be sure what cooperating would entail. "Any word from her squad?" With that many people searching, they had to be done checking Doyle Murphy's properties.

"All dead ends."

"Let's comb through Murphy's lackeys' holdings."

His boss pulled out his phone. "Should we try talking to the lackeys in person?"

"Most of them are serving time out in Pekin." He couldn't afford a six-hour round trip.

Xavier looked up from his cell. "How many of them aren't in jail, then?"

"Off the top of my head, two. Miles Hennessy and Sam Fahey." They couldn't find anything to tie Hennessy to the bout of arrests Zach had hit off, and Fahey was already in jail at the time. Zach had never met the guy.

"We'll have Novak and Jackson run them down."

Great. Everyone else on their team got to do a heck of a lot more than sitting around, acting useless. Why did he have to be the only one who couldn't help his fiancée?

Xavier finished his last call and returned to Zach, shifting uneasily. "Did he give you any proof he has her?"

Oh, he'd forgotten that part, too. "Yeah, asked her a question for me—but she gave the wrong answer."

"Does that mean—?"

"She said Grace Canavan."

Xavier had worked that case too. He knew that had to be Molly as well as he did. He thought a minute. "Obviously she's not being held by an Irish terrorist."

"I dunno, Murphy's Irish. Irish American."

"He knows less about Ireland than I know about Africa," Xavier muttered.

Zach had to give him that one. "Maybe it's a trap, like when the Canavans called her?"

"Or maybe she's trying to tell us more people are involved than we thought."

"We need one more little thing to put the pieces together." Zach pulled out his phone, but immediately slid it back into his pocket. He didn't dare push Murphy yet, not with Molly's life in his hands.

He looked at the interview room door. He wasn't the only one here who could talk to Murphy. "Has Lehrman had enough time to sweat it out?"

Xavier understood his meaning immediately. He hopped up to get the door to the conference room. "Let me do the talking."

All they had to do was get Lehrman to call Doyle, try to get information out of him. If they could get Lehrman to cooperate. If not, they'd settle for Murphy's current main contact number.

When the door opened, Lehrman's head snapped up instantly.

"Sorry to keep you waiting," Xavier said. He took a seat behind the table and Zach joined him.

Lehrman shifted in his chair. "I've been polite. I've told you everything I know. Twice. You can't keep me here."

"Actually, we have some more questions for you." Xavier leaned back in his chair. "But mostly we're trying to track down your car."

That shut Lehrman up. He searched Xavier's and Zach's faces. "You still haven't found her?"

X grimaced. "The Cougar never showed at Comiskey—Cellular—Guaran—the ballpark. Wish you had—what's that service called?"

"OnStar?" Lehrman guessed. "LoJack?"

"Anything like that."

Lehrman sank back in his chair like he was wounded. "Knew it."

Zach slid the folder in front of himself, trying to make this appear official. He was allowed to lie to suspects, but right now, he'd be bluffing even if it weren't okay. "In the meantime, I'm afraid we have more bad news for you. New evidence has come into play, and we've got Murphy for witness tampering."

"What?" Lehrman said the word carefully, like his intonation could break the case for the FBI.

Zach schooled his features to hide a flash of triumph. They were getting to him. If he didn't know where Molly was, Lehrman could put pressure on Doyle, make him see this was the smart thing to do.

"Witness tampering."

Lehrman scrutinized Xavier for a long minute. "No. Don't think you can trick me like that. My client has no reason to confess when he's innocent."

Zach managed not to laugh. "Then he's not concerned about the retrial coming up?"

Lehrman snorted. "You people had nothing and then bungled the case the first time, and we have no doubt you'll do it again until you get tired of making fools of yourselves."

Xavier looked at Zach—that was it. Lehrman's real weakness: his ego. They should have seen it after the way he talked about his car.

Zach took over the questioning. "As it so happens, Special Agent Malone—I'm sure you remember her? We still can't seem to find her."

"Have you tried her cell?"

Zach didn't bother to answer him. "Strange coincidence, though: your client was able to ask her a question for me, something only she would know, and the answer was right."

Lehrman snorted again—but worry flashed behind his eyes.

Time to bring it home. Zach didn't always enjoy lying to extract evidence—but this time he definitely would. "And then he told us how he'd used the Cougar to transport her—with your permission."

Lehrman's heavy eyebrows shot up. "First I've heard of this."

"Yeah, that's not what Doyle's telling us."

The lawyer jumped to his feet. "You have my client here? He has a right to consult with me—you can't question him without me." He started for the door.

Zach leaned back in his chair, trying to act a lot more casual than he felt. "About that."

Lehrman turned back to him.

"You're the lawyer here."

The lawyer didn't respond.

"You know you can't consult with him if we think you're conspiring. Crime-fraud exception, et cetera, et cetera."

Lehrman scoffed louder than necessary. "Why on earth would you think that?"

"The AUSA's offering Doyle a deal to testify against you."

The lawyer drew a quiet gasp, but he reined himself in. "About what?"

So far, Zach hadn't really been risking anything with his bluffs. He knew Lehrman probably wasn't in on the kidnapping. But now he was taking a bigger risk. This was where his plan could backfire.

"He's willing to testify about your role in the mistrial."

"Representing him?"

Zach echoed Lehrman's sarcastic look and hoped Xavier was doing the same. "That what they're calling it these days?" X asked, playing the part perfectly.

Lehrman's gaze swung from Xavier to Zach and back. "You don't know anything."

X shrugged and stood. Zach followed suit. "AUSA'll be excited. Crooked lawyers are her favorite convictions."

"She always manages to get the maximum jail time," Xavier remarked, like he was really marveling to Zach.

"Jail?" The color drained from Lehrman's cheeks and he sunk back into his chair.

Zach laughed and Xavier joined in. "With the evidence Doyle's giving up, you'll never see the light of day again. How many counts are we up to?"

"I lost track after twenty-seven," Zach said. "And then we had to come see you. Felt like we owed you, since we can't find your car."

Lehrman took the reminder like a gut shot. He lowered his head onto his arms, folded on the table.

Xavier gave him a sad smile. "You won't get to drive her again anyway. As soon as Doyle's done with his statement, we'll be back with your silver bracelets."

He sat up. "I want my lawyer."

"Up to you. Unless—" Zach turned to Xavier. "Do you think the AUSA would give *him* the deal if he flipped on Murphy first?"

"He'd probably have to finish his statement before Murphy did. The guy's got enough for three life sentences already."

Zach nodded. "And then we could get him his car and he could go."

Lehrman beckoned for something. "Give me a piece of paper."

Zach glanced around as if checking with an imaginary audience to make sure he'd heard right. "Are you . . . waiving your right to counsel?"

"I'm the lawyer, aren't I?"

"Yes, you are," Xavier said.

Lehrman considered it one more minute. "I'll write a statement, but that's it."

Xavier ducked out to get pen and paper before Lehrman changed his mind.

"Oh, hey," Zach said, as if this had just occurred to him. "Let me get your number so I can keep you up-to-date on your Cougar."

Lehrman dug a business card from his pocket. Zach patted his chest, as if he were checking the pocket of a dress shirt instead of his old W&M T-shirt. "Sorry, still out of cards."

Xavier returned, offering paper and pen.

Lehrman regarded X for three seconds too long. "You're going to get her back, right?"

For a split second, Zach thought he was referring to Molly—but no, Lehrman had to mean his car.

"We'll keep looking."

Lehrman started on his statement.

Zach personally walked Lehrman's card down to the techs' lab. When he arrived, the closest analyst jerked up from her computer. Zach read the name tag on her cubicle: Reyes. "Can I help you?" she asked.

"Got a number to run down." He gave her the business card.

"Lawyer?" Reyes murmured.

"Yeah, I want a list of everybody who's called him."

Reyes looked up, her brown eyes wide. "Can we do that?"

"He's upstairs confessing to collusion. I need every number that's called him—and if any of today's calls are burner cells or a Murphy, get a location on them, too. Oh, and double-check this one, too." He read the number Murphy had used off his call history.

"You got it."

Maybe Zach wouldn't have to play stoolie for Doyle after all.

MILES SHUFFLED THE CARDS DOYLE HAD BROUGHT and cast a glance at Molly. "Should we deal you in?"

She turned away. "Go fish."

"Five-card draw," he corrected, though he doubted she'd see the humor.

She ignored him.

"That's all right." Doyle examined his nails, gloating though Molly wasn't watching. "I like playing one-on-one. Facing off. Showing who's really the best. Ante up."

Miles said nothing, and managed not to scoff as he tossed his two bucks into the pot. Molly made a big show of staring at a cardboard box—but he knew. She was watching him. He could feel it even stronger than the breeze from the annoying fan.

Nah, he had nothing to worry about. Wasn't like she could read his mind. Miles was in control here, and Doyle and Molly were both clueless.

"Cut." Miles passed the deck to Doyle.

Doyle split the deck near the middle and moved the top half to the bottom. He pushed the cards back across the table. Miles dealt and allowed himself half a smile. Doyle would never realize Miles was the one pulling the strings.

Miles examined his hand: two pair, queens over nines. He kept his expression impassive and watched Doyle assessing his own cards. Doyle's mouth hinted at a frown. He wasn't much of an actor.

After what he'd said to Molly, Doyle really did seem to think this scheme was his idea.

Doyle's version of the plan was the kind of clumsy melodrama the guy was known for. It had served him well—he'd made it to second-in-command—but his complete lack of finesse was exactly what had brought Doyle and his whole crew down eighteen months ago, with a little help from Molly, her fiancé and Cally Lonegan.

Blackmailing a priest. Wasn't like Doyle could've gotten away with that. Incredible they'd kept it up as long as they did.

"Your bet," Miles reminded him.

Doyle tossed in a ten. Miles eyed the bill. Apparently, his hand was better than he'd let on. Miles met the bet, then placed the lone seven from his cards face down. "I'll take one."

Doyle passed him a card. He didn't take any for his own hand.

Must be a lot better than he'd let on.

Miles picked up the new card: a nine. A full house. Only a straight flush or four of a kind could beat him. The odds were remote at best. He could beat Doyle easily.

"Raise." Doyle tossed a twenty on the pot.

Miles checked his cards again. Doyle only had a one-in-a-thousand chance of beating him based on the hands.

But Doyle seemed to think this wasn't about the cards. It was about—what did he say?—showing who was best.

And for now, Miles was letting Doyle think *he* was the best. No matter how wrong that was.

Miles tossed his cards on the table, face down. "Fold."

Doyle showed his hand. "Three jacks." He collected his money with a triumphant chuckle.

Three of a kind? Miles should knock that smug overconfidence right off his ugly mug.

And he would. In fact, he'd hardly have do to anything, just let Doyle dig his own grave. That was how things always went when Doyle was left to his own devices. His extortion ring had finally blown up, like Miles had expected all along.

But Miles would be the one making sure things blew up in Doyle's face. All it would take was time. Doyle was already doing half the job himself.

Typical Doyle. Sending Saint on some errand? Miles hadn't told him to go and do that. What had happened to Miles's careful plan once Doyle's weak little mind caught hold of it? Nothing good, that was for sure.

Miles collected the cards. Make it through today, and it would all be in the bag. He just had to let Doyle think he was the boss for a few more hours.

He shuffled the cards again but made no move to deal. "You ready to call him back?"

"Not before ten thirty." Doyle's gaze grew cold. "I said ten, but let him squirm for a while. See how he likes it when somebody starts pulling his strings."

Miles riffled the cards loudly. Six more hours, max. Felt like an eternity, though. He slapped the deck on the table in front of Doyle.

Miles scrutinized Doyle as he dealt another hand. Doyle checked his watch. He ran his fingers through his hair, bit his lip, stood.

"Folding?" Miles asked.

"Just done." He started to pace the narrow container.

This was Miles's chance to get Doyle back on track. Miles caught his attention and nodded for Doyle to step out with him. They both checked on Molly. She lay still on the bed, her back to them. Secure enough for a minute.

They stepped into the main warehouse. It had to be ten degrees cooler out here—and it was still hot. Miles turned back to Doyle. "What are you thinking?"

Doyle glanced back at the container. "What, am I not being nice enough to your little pet? That's half the benefit. The Father has to know we're tormenting her at least a little."

"Hurting her isn't going to make a difference to the kid if he doesn't know about it." Miles shook his head. "But that's not what I meant."

"What, then?"

Miles managed to hide his irritation. "What's the endgame here? Blackmailing Saint into doing your dirty work?"

Doyle speared him with a crusty look. "Of course not. That's another way to break him down before we deliver the final blow."

"Which is?"

Doyle blinked slowly, as if he couldn't believe Miles was this dense.

Miles was pretty sure he wasn't the dense one here. "If you kill Molly in front of him, he'll take you down, probably right then and there. We can't let her go."

Doyle continued to glare at him in a way that rivaled Miles's teenage daughter's disrespect.

Hopefully that was a good sign that Doyle hadn't forgotten their real objective—and the plan Miles had engineered to keep himself in the clear. But until Doyle said the words, Miles wouldn't dare relax. "Like she said, tampering with a witness is evidence of the underlying crime. It'd be as bad for you to kill her as for her to testify."

"What do you think we're going to do? Let Molly go so we can get charged with kidnapping?"

Miles swatted away that obviously stupid suggestion.

"We stick to the plan." Each of Doyle's words was a declaration.

Good. Now to handle Doyle's other unauthorized changes to the plan. "What are you going to make the Father do?"

"Becker has been after me for more money."

Miles couldn't help a single syllable of a laugh. Clearly the guy didn't understand how bribes worked.

"I wanted to send the Father down to shut him up." Doyle grinned. "Put the fear of God into him."

All right, that was funny. Miles had to give him that one.

But it would appear Miles would have to give him the rest of the plan, too. This was the part that took the most finesse—when Miles had the answer at the ready, and he had to make Doyle think he'd come up with it himself. "Hopefully that shuts him up. You know how those people are, back begging for a handout every month."

Doyle kept his eyes on the decrepit warehouse racks, his expression grim.

"If only there were some way to make this problem go away permanently."

Still, Doyle seemed stumped.

Come on, this was the only way to tie up the last loose end from the mistrial. Not that Miles really cared about the trial, but Miles had also been involved with this loose end, and he wanted a clean getaway. No witnesses.

If Miles suggested it, Doyle would reject the idea outright. Miles tried again. "Why don't you go get some air—get us some lunch or something—and think about it? I always get my best ideas while driving." Which wasn't true, but Doyle had once told him the same thing.

"Yeah, me too. What do you want for lunch? McDonald's?"

Miles shrugged. "Sure. But go to the one in Bridgeport, on Halsted. It's better than the ones around here. Plus, it'll give you more time to drive." Miles looked at the shipping container. The burner phone they'd designated for calling Saint was still inside, its battery off. "You got another phone you can use? A clean one?"

"'Course. Always got a spare for emergencies." Doyle led the way to the cars and Miles did a double take. Instead of Doyle's black Audi, he found a vintage gold muscle car.

"Where'd that come from?"

"It's Lehrman's. I thought the FBI might follow me from headquarters—"

"I thought you met at your place. You went downtown with them? Today?"

Doyle grunted, waving away Miles's concern. "They're all bent out of shape over the note I put in the mailbox."

Pressure began to build his behind his eyes. What had Doyle done? "What. Note."

"For the Father. In Molly's mailbox."

Miles clenched his jaw so hard his teeth groaned. No wonder the Feds had jumped on the case so early.

He needed Doyle out of here so he could work on damage control. "Get me two Big Macs."

Doyle hopped in the sports car.

Miles popped the trunk of his car and grabbed a bottle of water from his cooler, practically downing it in a single gulp. His plan was only designed to run for a few hours before he made his exit and let Doyle take the fall. What would he do if the Feds showed up earlier than expected because of Doyle's idiocy?

He needed another contingency plan.

As the sound of the engine faded, Molly counted the seconds. Her hearing was recovering, but not enough to detect Hennessy's shoes outside the shipping container with that irritating fan. She didn't dare hope that he had left too.

Twenty minutes alone and she could be out of here. She stole a deep, silent breath, trying to ignore her shirt clinging to the sweat on her back, her chest, everywhere. Who had said she was crazy for getting married in the dead of summer? Bridie? She hated when her sister was right.

The arc of light at the other end of the container flickered, a shadow passing by. Miles stepped into view.

Molly's heart deflated. She didn't realize she'd held out hope, still, again.

Hennessy slumped back into his chair. His cheeks were flushed—perhaps more so than when he'd left?—and dark splotches stained his shirt. He was suffering too.

Small comfort. But if guarding her was wearing on him, she might be able to crack him a bit more easily. The chain on her shackle jangled as she drew her knees to her chest to hold against the sick feeling beginning to roil inside her.

Hennessy picked up the deck of cards, concern etching canyons in his face.

Every time Doyle gloated, Hennessy had stared daggers at his back. Clearly, he wasn't totally on board with this scheme. If Doyle was gone, this was her chance to sow more seeds of division.

"You don't have to do this, you know," she ventured.

Hennessy looked up, with what appeared to be mild interest.

"There's still time to go back. Take this back." She didn't dare name his crimes. Keeping it vague made them seem smaller. Easier to walk away from.

"Your neighbor would probably beg to differ."

Guilt stabbed at her chest and Molly flinched. She couldn't tell Hennessy he'd get away with Mr. Petrowski's shooting. Hennessy would never buy that line, and they both knew she couldn't deliver on that promise. "All right, but if you let me go, I don't have to tell anyone you were involved."

"Right." He undid the top button on his polo. "An FBI agent is just going to look the other way when a known mobster shoots someone in front of her and then kidnaps her."

"Of course not." She met his gaze and leaned forward, lowering her voice to an urgent whisper. "Clearly Doyle's the one I want punished. The Bureau would blame Mr. Petrowski on Doyle, too. We don't have to come down on both of you."

Hennessy studied her for a long moment, his mouth taking on a skeptical set. "I'll take that under advisement."

Molly scooted to the edge of the bed. "Miles, listen. We both know you don't want to be doin' this, under Doyle's thumb. And you don't have to. All we have to do is walk away."

He narrowed his eyes. As though he were considering her offer?

Before he said anything, his phone rang. He checked it and stood. "I'll be right back. Don't go anywhere." With a smirk at her shackle, Hennessy strode out.

Molly tried to block out everything else to concentrate on listening, but once again, only murmurs carried back to her. He hadn't gone far enough for her to try to escape, still too close for her to relax.

She scanned the area around her for the fifth time. Nothing new had cropped up. Not that she could reach anything.

Perhaps she wouldn't get twenty minutes alone. If she wanted to escape, she'd have to be ready for the next phone call.

MILES PACED A NARROW CIRCUIT IN THE WAREHOUSE. He couldn't even be grateful for the respite from the stifling container.

He couldn't believe his caller ID. Doyle was using his regular phone to call the number Miles had gotten for today and today only, to keep it completely untraceable. Surely the FBI was keeping tabs on Doyle's phones, and that meant Miles's burner cell was on their radar.

What. An. Idiot.

"What?" he answered.

Doyle sighed. "I got a family thing today."

"Are you serious?" And he'd thought Doyle's IQ couldn't drop any lower.

"Just letting you know I'll be late with lunch."

"You called me from this number to tell me that?"

Doyle grumbled, like Miles was the one who was out of line. "Backup burner's dead."

"Charge it. I'll call you with my new number." Miles ended the call. At least one of them realized that even ancient technology required the occasional top up.

This phone was no good to him. He'd have to ditch it, far enough away to throw the Feds off the trail.

He frowned at the container. Doyle might see Molly as only the innocent parish secretary, but Miles knew better. They didn't let just anybody in the FBI, and she'd been law enforcement in Ireland, too. She was working hard to negotiate her way out of here, and she'd been watching him.

But neither of those were the same as escaping. Unless all that training came with hidden handcuff keys, that ankle shackle meant Molly wasn't going anywhere. He wouldn't be gone long.

Shaking his head, Miles got in the car and drove out of the warehouse, the A/C already on high. He knew exactly where to go.

Miles pushed his fingers through his hair, then thought better of leaving oils on the phone and wiped his hand on his pants as he drove under the bridge trusses. It was only a ten-minute drive. No need to worry. She wouldn't magically find a way to escape while he was gone, and he had to do this. He had to take care of this.

Molly strained to listen to the silence, a drop of sweat inching its way down her neck. The engine had faded at least a full minute ago, and she could hear no footsteps approaching. No shadows crossed the light in the door.

This could be a test, to see if she'd try to escape if he left her alone. For all she knew, he was sitting outside the door, waiting.

A risk she'd definitely take.

Once again, she scanned the room as if something might have appeared in the last thirty seconds that she could use to free herself.

The chair was too far away. The boxes were too far away. The table was too far away—and what would she have done with any of those? They held more promise of hurting her than helping her, especially with her wrists behind her back. Freeing her hands from the PlastiCuffs had to be her first priority.

Molly placed her free foot on the rough wooden floor of the container, slowly standing. She wasn't sure if it was lack of use or lack of food and water that made her leg weak, but standing alone took extra effort.

There had to be something sharp within reach that she could use to slice the plastic. It might cut her, too, but it would be worth it.

Molly sat on the bed again, this time sliding off to kneel on the hard particleboard, her shackled foot dangling in traction. She twisted around until the mattress hit her fingers. Once she had a good grip, she wrenched her body the other direction. The mattress followed.

Revealing no sharp edges or helpful bolts on the metal bed frame. Nothing to cut the straps with. Her sweaty fingers lost their grip on the mattress, and it slid onto her leg.

The small amount of exertion from pulling off the mattress suddenly caught up with her, a rush of heat as though someone cranked up the oven thermostat. She needed a full minute to regain her strength.

Was there anything else within reach with her hands behind her back? If she knee-hopped as far as her handcuffed ankle would let her, there was nothing within the range of her teeth. Nothing she could hook her hands over to try to pop off the plastic ratchet box holding her hands hostage. Nothing she could use, not even a cardboard box.

There had to be something.

It didn't have to be big. In fact, smaller could be better. Something very thin could fit inside the slot in the ratchet box and hold the ratchet itself open so she could loosen the straps. A thin flathead screwdriver. A straight pin. Perhaps a staple.

The floor wasn't exactly clean, but it didn't have the sort of dirt and debris that would yield the tool she needed. Still, Molly leaned down to make a very careful, inch-by-inch sweep.

She was running out of places she could reach to search when a sound echoed in the warehouse outside the shipping container.

Molly's lungs shrank. The only thing worse than breathing the stifling air was *not* breathing it.

An engine.

Miles was back? Or Doyle?

Molly scanned the room once more—the mattress. It was still off the bed. How would she get it back on the frame?

She twisted until her fingers felt the rough material again. She gripped of the fabric. Now she only needed to get up.

In the warehouse, the engine stopped. A car door slammed.

Molly moved her free foot to support her as she tried to balance the mattress. She didn't have much choice in how to go about this. All the dance training in the world couldn't give her the ability to stand from kneeling and move the mattress without weighting her shackled foot.

This was going to hurt.

Molly braced herself, then lifted. The metal bit into her ankle, screaming and searing against her skin. As soon as she had a halfway tenable position, she put all the weight she could into her free foot, but her ankle still strained against the metal.

In the corner of her vision, she saw a shadow flicker across the door's light. She had seconds left. Her pulse filled her ears.

She pushed and twisted. For an eternity, the mattress seemed to hover, debating which direction to fall.

Molly threw her weight onto the mattress, making the decision for it. The mattress fell onto the bed frame, landing a bit askew, and a bit loudly, but otherwise, not too discernibly different than it had been. She heaved two great breaths, her loose curls sticking to her neck and cheeks.

At least in the heat, Hennessy couldn't tell she'd just exerted herself.

Hennessy swept through the door, his thick lips curled into a simper. He actually seemed refreshed, the ruddiness of his cheeks a little less prominent. "Did you miss me?"

She gulped down air and didn't answer. Not that he expected her to.

Hennessy couldn't have been gone for twenty minutes. She definitely couldn't wait for that much time again—and she couldn't sit here and wait for Zachary to find her. If Hennessy or Doyle were here when Zachary arrived, they'd kill him too.

Her brain tripped on that last word: *too*. Had she already accepted that she was going to die today?

Perhaps so. Better her than both of them.

But that didn't mean she had to choose suicide by criminal quite yet. If there was any chance of making it out alive, she'd take it. Until Zachary found this container, she had nothing to lose.

Once again, Molly drew her knees to her chest, folding up to fight against the nausea curdling in her stomach.

And then she saw it. At the end of her pants' ratty drawstring, something silver glistened.

The safety pin she'd used to rethread the string last week.

Molly turned to Hennessy and set her jaw to hold back a telling smile. Now if she could only get him out of here again. "Where's my lunch?"

He'd put this off long enough. Zach gripped his phone tighter, pacing outside the conference room like that might help this call be less awkward.

It wasn't like they'd dated. He'd helped her out on a case once, over a working lunch one time. And he'd forgotten her name afterwards. And she found out.

She had no reason to like him, let alone help him, but he would call in every favor he could claim today.

"Hello?" AUSA Jill—oh, man, he hoped it was Jill—Hardt answered.

"Hi, Ms. Hardt? This is Special Agent Zach Saint."

"Jill," she supplied, and even that one syllable proved that she hadn't forgotten or forgiven him for forgetting her name.

"I know," he said, though the defenses in his voice didn't exactly make him sound believable. "Listen, are you busy right now?"

"Yes."

Of course. An Assistant US Attorney was always busy. "Because I've got Doyle Murphy's lawyer down here confessing to conspiracy—"

"I'll be there in three minutes." She hung up, as if saying goodbye would take too long.

Zach passed the time checking in with a couple agents from Molly's squad—no luck in searching all of Doyle Murphy's lackeys' properties so far. By now, the SAC had assigned four other squads to tracing and checking properties, and at least two more to canvassing Murphy's neighborhood on the South Side.

And still it didn't feel like enough. Not being out there himself chafed at Zach.

Murphy wanted him here, and that bothered him even more.

High heels clacked over the linoleum behind Zach. He finished his call and wheeled around.

A short woman in a purple blazer stood in front of him. Assistant US Attorney Jill Hardt. "Where is he?"

Zach knocked on the conference room door. "Thanks for coming. I know you're busy."

"If it means throwing the book at Doyle Murphy, I'd skip a meeting with the Attorney General." Jill considered that a millisecond. "Well, I'd do that anyway."

"We need him to get ahold of Murphy as soon as possible—"

Xavier poked his head out. "We've got Murphy's lawyer writing up a statement about collusion in his mistrial."

"This isn't a joke?" The AUSA broke her normally professional character with a gasp and then a gleeful grin. Sometimes Zach forgot she was about the same age as him. "I *knew* our case was better than that!"

Xavier showed her into the conference room. Zach stayed near the door, listening as Jill accepted the written statement.

"A juror," she murmured. How had they gotten to him?

A cell phone rang. Not Zach's and not a ringtone he knew from Xavier's. Zach leaned into the room. It had better not be Murphy calling his lawyer—not when the only reason Lehrman was co-operating was because they'd said Murphy was in the next room confessing.

The phone rang again. Frank Lehrman dug in his pockets.

It could be a call from anybody. Who had Lehrman's car. And who they'd lied about being in the next room.

As soon as Lehrman saw his phone, he scowled at Xavier. "He was confessing!"

Zach couldn't see his boss's expression, but Xavier's voice remained calm. "Put it on speaker."

"Attorney-client privilege!" His ringtone started over.

Jill waved the statement. "Not if you're conspiring."

"Your Cougar's slipping away, man."

Lehrman glared at them until his ringtone restarted again. "I'm rescinding that statement."

Jill practically giggled. "Too late. Book him."

Xavier stepped forward until Lehrman held up a hand, then answered the phone and put it on speaker. "Hey, Doyle," Lehrman said. "You got my baby?"

"Yeah, she's fine."

Lehrman blew out a sigh, like his precious car was his biggest concern. That car was going to be Lehrman's undoing one day.

Today, it seemed.

"Listen," Murphy continued, "we've got a problem."

"With the Cougar?"

"No, our friend called. Wants more money."

Lehrman glared at the paper in Jill's fingers. "I know. Can I call you back about that?"

Doyle grumbled. "Fine."

Jill snorted a silent laugh.

Lehrman turned away a little. "I really do need my car back."

"Right, right. I can meet you at Washington Park at eleven."

If they caught up with Doyle at Washington Park then, they'd at least have a chance at finding Molly.

"Park-park? Not the neighborhood?"

"Yeah."

"Eleven? That's—that's—" Lehrman pulled the phone away from his ear, checking the time. "I can't—"

Xavier waved him off, then signaled a thumbs-up. Lehrman glowered but said to Doyle, "Okay, fine."

Zach's phone buzzed, and he pulled back from the door before Lehrman finished his own call. Agent Jackson was calling. "What have you got?" Zach answered.

"Talked to Sam Fahey. Shady character."

Despite spending two months as a priest in Fahey's parish, Zach had never actually met the man. "Hm. And?"

"He was real evasive, but he didn't seem to know anything."

"You worked him good?"

The other agent's tone turned to laughter. "We scared him pretty good. Still didn't come up with anything. Going down to see Hennessy."

They ended the call, but before Zach could turn back to the conference room, the tech, Reyes, ran up to him. "There you are," she puffed. "We got a hit on that number you wanted—the first one." She held out a piece of paper.

Zach tried to ignore the spike of hope through his heart and read the paper's header—not Lehrman's number, the one Murphy had called Zach from. Murphy had made another call twenty minutes ago. He snatched the paper. "What took you so long to get this to me?"

"I couldn't find you." Reyes shrugged sheepishly. "I didn't have your number."

That was her excuse? "Did you at least get the name on the caller?"

"Not caller, recipient—your guy called him."

"Thanks for the correction." He didn't bother keeping the annoyance out of his tone.

Reyes bit her lip. "Sorry, it's a disposable phone, activated today."

Might be nothing, but on a day like today, he couldn't risk dismissing anything remotely suspicious. "GPS? Triangulation?"

She winced. "It's off, and we didn't get a fix on it fast enough."

Molly's life was on the line, and this tech had lost the best—only—lead they'd had yet? "What?"

"We're talking to the cell company."

"We're *talking* to them?" Zach scoffed. "Please, don't let us offend a great and powerful cell phone carrier." He tossed the paper into Reyes's face. "Get on the phone and yell at them until they give us the data! We have an agent out there and—" He broke off. He glanced around. A dozen agents who had been hurrying through on their way to help the hunt had all stopped. Every eye on the floor was on him, especially both wide eyes of the quavering tech in front of him, filling with tears.

"And we have to get her back," Xavier finished, walking up behind him. "They'll cooperate without a court order on a kidnapping in progress. This is the number they contacted us with."

Reyes's eyes grew even rounder. "I didn't know—they didn't tell me—"

"Do it." Xavier gave her a card and she scurried off.

Zach rubbed his forehead. He didn't mean to jump down her throat. Just today—

He'd buy the kid lunch or something, as long as they got through this day. As long as they got Molly back.

"Zach," Xavier ventured.

"I know."

"Watch yourself. Do not let your temper cost you this case."

This was a lot more than a case, and they both knew that. Zach couldn't seem to win today—but if he could get Molly back in the end, he'd take every knock along the way.

"Agent Mason?" AUSA Hardt called. "Ready for you."

Zach followed Xavier in to take Lehrman into custody.

He'd fantasized about arresting the guy while he was cross-examining Molly, but today that rang hollow.

They had Murphy's car and his lawyer and evidence he'd tampered with the jury. Maybe they were circling in on the man himself, but Zach didn't feel any closer to finding Molly.

Except that Murphy was supposed to call him back. He consulted the clock on his phone. In twenty minutes.

Xavier's phone rang right as he escorted Lehrman out in cuffs. He checked the number and handed it to Zach.

Zach recognized the number as an FBI extension. "Yeah?" he answered.

"Uh, hi? Agent Mason?"

"Close enough."

"This is Alejandra Reyes. The analyst? We just talked?"

Cut. To. The. Chase. He forced himself to bite back an impatient tone. "Did you get through to the carrier?"

"Yes, but they're having some troubles with data outages today. Dropped calls, spotty cells."

Of course. "If I didn't know better," Zach muttered, "I'd think Murphy was behind that."

"But that wasn't why I called. We pulled the caller info on the other number you gave me—Frank Lehrman's cell phone?"

"Okay."

"He's gotten calls today from Doyle Murphy, an unlisted number and Eddie and Laura Becker, a landline."

"Try to get a location on all the cell numbers." He ended the call.

Laura could be Lehrman's daughter for all they knew, or they could be some legit client. If Lehrman had any.

It had definitely not been long enough for Xavier to have taken care of Lehrman, but when Zach turned around, his boss was walking toward him—with the Special Agent in Charge in tow.

A thin thread of tension twisted around his stomach. Had word about how he'd treated Reyes already gotten back to the SAC? Was he about to be chained to a desk instead of doing everything he could to find Molly?

Best to tackle this straight on. Zach approached them, meeting in the middle of the empty desks of Molly's squad. He decided to preempt the possible reprimand. "I assume Agent Mason told you Murphy contacted me?"

"Yes. Looks like it was a good call to keep you involved. No demands yet?"

"Only that he wanted Saint to 'sit tight' until he called back," Xavier said.

"Said it'd be an hour," Zach added. "That was a little before nine."

All three men consulted the nearest clock on the wall. It read 9:46.

"Chief of Police said they still don't have any leads," Evans said. "Other than Special Agent Malone being gone, they've got nothing that ties her to Petrowski. Nothing that even remotely helps us."

Xavier took over the reporting. "We've run down every address we have a record of from Murphy's case, and we're working through his underlings' seized properties. Thanks for the manpower."

"Are you kidding? We've got an agent's life on the line. I want to throw twice as many people at this." Evans pressed his lips together, like the action would squeeze out a new lead. "Seized properties—from his guys we've arrested?"

Xavier confirmed his assumption.

"Anybody we missed in those arrests?"

"Two guys," Xavier said. "We've got agents talking to them. Covered everyone else we know of."

"Except—" Zach stopped when the SAC and Xavier both whirled on him. "Except Cally Lonegan."

"In witness protection," Xavier added.

Evans nodded. "Go through Sellars and talk to him."

"We might want to check on Lonegan, too," Zach said. "If I were Murphy, I'd blame Cally at least as much as Molly and me. And Murphy definitely wants something. He said when he calls he'll set a ransom."

Evans worked through that. "Does he want money?"

Zach willed himself not to look at Molly's empty desk. She was worth a lot more to Zach than everything in his bank account and then some—but Murphy couldn't be that hard up for cash.

"What's he playing at?" Evans wondered, as if he'd read Zach's mind. He clapped his shoulder. "You holding up okay?"

"I guess." He waited for Xavier to exchange a knowing glance with him, but his boss held an impassive expression.

Zach finally dared to check Evans's reaction. The SAC arched one eyebrow, but said nothing. "Let's be careful out there. We can't afford to risk this case—to risk Molly's life—on our emotions."

The words stung—again—but Zach nodded. Molly's life depended on him keeping his cool, and he'd lost it once.

"If there's anything we can do, say the word. I'm pulling in every agent we can find, but I can call in more from the resident agencies."

Their satellite offices? If only this were a case that could be solved with sheer manpower. "Thanks."

Zach's phone rang. Someone reporting in? Or—all three men read the wall clock. 9:50. A little early.

His veins buzzing with anticipation, Zach pulled out his phone. Caller ID said it was Kent from Molly's squad. He'd been checking on the last of the seized properties. Zach's letdown doubled when Kent had nothing to report, so Zach passed along a new assignment: to wait on standby while they figured out the next move.

"Let's get you more help." Evans pulled out his own phone and started off, hopefully to make that happen.

"Hey! Hey!" a woman's breathless voice called behind them.

Zach turned around and found Reyes, the skittish tech. She shrank back. "Sorry, Agent, uh—"

He realized she was trying to address him. "Saint," he supplied.

"Yeah. We got a hit on that phone. It's on."

What? Zach almost jumped toward Reyes; she jerked back. Zach held up two hands like he was trying to calm her down. "Which phone?"

The tech offered a piece of paper—the number Doyle Murphy had dialed half an hour ago, now at a street corner near the river. Xavier peered over Zach's shoulder.

"It's not as precise as we'd like," Reyes said. "The weather has done something to the closest cell tower, and they can't get out there and fix it until the heat wave lets up."

It wasn't Doyle's phone, but it meant something. Maybe he'd called someone who was guarding Molly for him.

"Good work," Zach said. "Thanks." He stared at the paper a moment longer. Finally, he could do something. He was ready. More than ready.

Murphy was supposed to call back any minute, but Zach couldn't sit around and wait any longer. Not when he knew where someone who could take him to Murphy was—maybe even where Molly was. Disobeying Murphy's orders to run this number down was taking a chance, but it seemed like *not* going would be the bigger risk.

Zach signaled Xavier. "Let's go." He looked to Reyes. "Call us if anything changes on this."

"Uh huh."

Zach took a step toward the elevators, but turned back to the tech. "Hey, um." He rubbed the back of his neck. "Sorry I, uh." He waved the paper. "Thanks for this."

"She's on your squad?"

"My fiancée."

Reyes punched Zach in the arm. "Go get her."

11

ACH WATCHED THE MINUTES INCH BY on his dash clock. Ridiculous that the fastest way to get there took him across the river, half a mile on the Expressway, then back across the river. Thirteen minutes to the intersection, Kedzie Avenue and 31st Street.

They couldn't have thrown her—no. They wanted something from him, and she was the only way they were going to get it. They had to keep her alive.

And he had to be sure she was alive.

The run-down and abandoned warehouses he passed, bleak and industrial, didn't exactly inspire hope.

And neither did the less-than-precise coordinates. Without a third cell tower, he wasn't going to a specific location. He was going to a search area. One that he couldn't possibly search in time before Murphy called.

He was already fifteen minutes late with his call. Zach couldn't let himself think about what that might mean for Molly.

Zach reached the intersection indicated on Reyes's map. The target location covered all four corners of the intersection. Xavier pulled into a tiny parking lot on one corner, in front of a closed restaurant with the menu painted on the front, amid graffiti. Zach, still driving Doyle's car, followed.

Two of the other corners of the intersection were empty fields—not what Zach expected to find in an industrial area. The fourth corner was a yellow-brick warehouse that appeared to be empty. On the far side, it abutted a red-brick warehouse.

The choice was obvious. Without a word, Xavier and Zach made a beeline for the warehouse. "How long till Roberts and Walker get here?" Zach asked. The closest search team from Molly's squad couldn't be far behind.

"Maybe five minutes."

The warehouse was well built but dingy, with most of its lower windows covered in translucent paper on that side, a few glass panes broken or missing. Below them, white paint awkwardly covered more graffiti. If it weren't for the faded For Lease sign flapping in the breeze—and the bright yellow self-storage signs on the red-brick side of the building—Zach might have assumed the place was abandoned too.

Hopefully there was at least one occupant.

Xavier nodded to the nearest side door. "Exigent circumstances."

Adrenaline rushed through him like a tidal wave. Zach managed to push past his shaking hands to pick the lock in record time. They silenced their phones and grabbed their guns. They slipped through the door, sweeping the dark warehouse with their weapons.

Dust swarmed thick in the sweltering air. What little light made it through the heavy film on the windows reflected off the bottles, cans and broken shards of glass below. Metal racks stood in the center of the floor, some of them leaning against one another as if they'd lost the will to remain upright. Decomposing cardboard boxes littered the floor and the racks.

No signs of life. Or at least not human life, as something—*things*—skittered away in the shadows.

He caught Xavier's eye and motioned for him to proceed counterclockwise.

"Remember the last time you searched a warehouse," Xavier whispered.

Zach didn't respond and started clockwise. The muffled echo of their footsteps added to the tension like the ticking of a countdown timer. He skimmed the center area with his gaze and his weapon, his back to the wall as he crept along the perimeter. He scanned the room for an enclosed area—a storage closet, a clean room, a break room—where they were keeping Molly.

Was he about to get her back?

Zach rounded the first corner. No enclosed area visible in the far corner, and there was nowhere between the rows of racks to hide her.

Nothing, nothing, nothing. He reached the far corner a second or two before Xavier arrived at the opposite corner. Xavier shook his head. Nothing. They continued to scan the warehouse until they met in the middle of the last wall.

"Now what do you want to do?" Xavier asked.

He couldn't give up this easily. He checked the time on his phone—what had he done with the watch Molly gave him yesterday?

Murphy was twenty minutes late calling.

"Let's search again," Zach said, shoving aside the worry, "then check the other buildings."

By the time Zach met Xavier again at the doors, he was convinced Molly wasn't here.

He wasn't convinced this was the end of the search. "What else is in the search area?"

Xavier pointed. "Next building over, I think."

They left the empty warehouse, locking the door behind them, and rounded the building. Immediately next to the warehouse, a yellow sign hung on the brick building next door: self-serve storage units. Kind of a cliché for hiding a captive, but always serviceable. Zach wasn't going to complain.

They found the manager in the office. "We're trying to find someone who might have rented a storage unit." Zach flashed his badge without identifying himself or letting the manager get a good look, then grabbed his phone to show him a picture of Murphy. "He's about six foot, stocky, more gray now."

The manager shrugged, no help. "Want me to check our records?"

he offered.

"Yeah, Doyle Murphy."

"Let's see." The manager grabbed his mouse. "Nope, no Murphy."

Zach pulled up a picture of Molly without him in it: the background on his phone, a cropped photo from the night he'd proposed outside the Biograph Theatre. "How about her?"

"Nope. What's this about?"

"Thanks for your help." Xavier led the way out.

Zach glanced down at his phone—the picture of Molly that came up when she called. Her dark curls, her deep blue eyes, the light smattering of freckles across her nose. When the backlight on the phone went dark, he dropped it in his pocket.

He was going to see her again. He couldn't let himself doubt that, even if the question was already tugging at the edges of his thoughts.

He couldn't lose hope. He had to believe he would find her. Zach offered yet another silent prayer as they headed back down the block, but no peace came. Doubt settled into his chest like a block of cement.

"I know the location isn't precise," he murmured as they waited at the corner. "But I'd like to think we don't have morons on our team."

"Do you want to call Reyes and double-check?"

Zach shook his head. "I'm going to call this phone."

As soon as he said it, Zach second-guessed himself. Murphy had expressly told him not to call, and while this obviously wasn't Murphy's number—unless the guy had called himself—word could get back to Murphy immediately.

Xavier gave him a look of *well, all right, if that's what you want to do.* As if Zach knew what to do next. He was making this up as he went along.

Zach dialed the number off the tech's paper. After a short delay, a faint musical tone carried down the sidewalk.

The phone was here? No. Could they have missed Molly?

Zach and Xavier glanced at each other and reached for their

weapons, not drawing yet, but wanting to be at the ready. Crouching and holding close to the building, they crept down the block toward the ringtone.

The music grew louder until they passed the second broken window on that side of the building. Zach stopped below the window, taking a split second to brace himself. The phone Doyle Murphy had called was right above him. Molly could be anywhere nearby.

Zach stood and pointed his weapon through the window.

Inside the windowsill, a phone flashed a red light and vibrated.

Just the phone. Nobody around. Nobody to answer.

This was a trick. Murphy had lured him here. Molly could be anywhere—and Zach might have put her in more danger by following this wild-goose chase.

He called for Xavier to come over. Xavier put on a latex glove and reached in the broken window to get the phone. Once he picked it up, it stopped ringing.

"Unbelievable." Zach turned away. "The car, the phone—he is not this smart!" When had Murphy grown this intelligent? Was this the same guy he'd taken down a year and a half ago?

Xavier slipped the phone into a plastic bag and they returned to the car.

Zach's phone vibrated. Fighting back the opposing forces of hope and dread, Zach pulled it out—Kent again.

Murphy was more than half an hour late. He'd planted this phone in his call history and in this warehouse to throw Zach off the scent, keeping him running around.

He wasn't getting any closer to Molly.

Zach finally answered the phone and gave Kent directions to their corner. They'd passed dozens of empty warehouses. They had to keep searching.

Even with all the agents in the city, they couldn't search every warehouse. And if Murphy was holding her somewhere else, then this was all wrong.

Why hadn't Murphy called?

Xavier scrutinized him for a moment. "Take a minute," he told Zach.

Yeah. Zach climbed in Doyle's car and switched his A/C to full blast. Wherever Molly was, he was willing to bet she wasn't cooling off in front of a fan.

Xavier directed their search teams: Walker and Roberts, Kent, Novak and Jackson. X signaled to Zach that he was going to search too and pulled out.

All the resources of the FBI might not be enough to help. And Zach was alone.

Half an hour ago, he was going crazy because he couldn't do anything. Now he had plenty to do. Too much to hope he could make a dent.

The weight of impossibility was bearing down on him worse than the heat. Zach drained his water bottle and tossed the empty in the back seat. He felt like he'd been wrung out and hung out to dry.

Murphy was half an hour late calling. He'd just talked to his lawyers. But something had to have gone wrong if Murphy was keeping Zach waiting this long.

Would Zach get her back okay?

Nothing was going to plan today. Doyle checked his watch again. He was supposed to have called the Father half an hour ago. Just enough time to wriggle. He wanted to make him suffer, not give the guy time to find his fiancée.

He shouldn't be able to. If they could track Doyle's phone, it'd only lead them to a McDonald's. A McDonald's with the world's longest drive-thru line.

And in another half hour, he had to be at Washington Park to give this car back to Lehrman and make an appearance at his kid's softball game.

His phone vibrated in his pocket.

Better not be the Father. Could be Claire trying to remind him about the game. He pulled out his phone—the one he'd used to call the Father. He checked the caller ID. Not the number he had for the Father. "Yeah?" he answered.

"Doyle Murphy?"

The voice sounded a little familiar. Not the Father, definitely. "Who's asking?"

"Listen, I don't need much, just enough for my wife's medical bills."

Becker. "No."

Doyle started to hang up, but Becker's pleading reached his ears first. "I'm going to talk to the police."

Rationally, Doyle knew this sounded like a desperate ploy, matched by an even more desperate tone. But more police attention was the last thing he needed today.

He'd have to take care of this problem permanently. Bluffing Becker would buy him the time he needed to fix this. "Go ahead," Doyle said. "Confess to what you've done. That'll definitely take care of your wife's medical bills. At least, any future ones. You've got life insurance, right?"

"Wha-what?" Becker stuttered. "You wouldn't—would you?"

"You don't know me, Becker," Doyle said. "I'd recommend you keep it that way." He ended the call.

This was ridiculous. The drive-thru line was getting nowhere, and probably all because of some stupid broken ice cream machine or something. Doyle pulled out of line and into a parking space, then turned up the Cougar's air-conditioning. Didn't help with the soaked spots where his back touched the seat, but better than nothing.

Doyle dialed the number. The Father answered on the second ring. "Hello?"

"Enjoyed your downtime, Father? 'Cause the fun's about to begin."

Doyle could almost hear the Father calculating over the phone line. "I have to know she's okay."

Murphy laughed. "In due time, Father. Don't be so impatient. Impatience . . ." He had to have something good to say on that topic, but proverbs failed him.

"Let me speak to her," the Father demanded. Like he was the one in charge here.

"Not a chance." What proof that she was alive could he offer when he was a good ten minutes away from her?

"Let me ask her something again. Through you if you want."

"Fine."

The Father was silent long enough that Doyle had to check to make sure the call was still connected. The call timer continued counting up into the silence.

"Who's giving her away?"

The obvious answer was Molly's old man, but if the Father was asking, that probably wasn't right.

"She won't say," Doyle finally said. "Seems like she's not interested in cooperating with us. Hope you're more willing than she is."

"Not if I don't know she's alive."

Great. As far as Doyle knew, she was still alive and kicking, but he didn't have a way to prove that right this second.

He couldn't tell the Father that.

Not good enough for the Father. "This is taking too long. I'm calling your bluff."

Doyle's phone beeped to signal the call had ended.

What? The Father was cutting Molly loose. That wasn't how this was supposed to go.

He couldn't go groveling back to the Father. The man had forgotten who was in charge today. And if he didn't crawl back to Doyle begging, the Father was going to regret this for the rest of his life.

However short that might be.

But what if he didn't call back?

Zach gripped his phone tighter, numb other than the static buzzing in his brain. What had he done? Playing hardball with Molly's life was idiotic.

But if Doyle couldn't show him she was okay, then there was no game to play.

He tried to find Reyes's number in his phone, but before he pulled up his call history, his phone rang again. Same number.

Oh, great, so Doyle could toy with him some more. But if there was any chance Molly was alive, he had to take it.

He tried to push down the heat building behind his thoughts, but failed. "What kind of game do you think this is?" Zach demanded.

"Fine, Father. Walk away. Molly will be disappointed, but you do what you want to do."

"Keep talking. We're tracking your phone, and we'll be there by the time you get around to asking for your ransom."

Doyle's tone grew condescending. "I see poker isn't your game. You're not a bluffer."

It wasn't a bluff, but if he wanted to think that, great. "Prove she's alive."

"She's not answering questions, kid."

Was he trying to cover up killing her?

No, Zach couldn't believe that. Not yet. "Give me something here."

Doyle scoffed. "What do you want? She thinks blackmail is a gun with—"

"One bullet," Zach murmured along with Doyle. Unless Doyle had watched the same season of *Burn Notice* as Molly and Zach had last week, that was Molly. Zach tapped a fist against the steering wheel. "What do you want?"

"I want a 'government employee' as an enforcer. You're going to go see a guy for me."

Dread filled Zach's gut. That couldn't mean what he was thinking. He needed to elicit more information. He'd have to play dumb. "You want me to go on a social call for you? How about this: you give me Molly back and you go visit your friends yourself?"

"I can hang up too, you know."

Zach bit his tongue.

"Good," Doyle said after a moment. "Now, listen this time. I want you to go visit him as an FBI agent."

Zach flinched. That had to be a guess. Doyle still didn't know who he really was, and he wasn't about to admit anything to Doyle. "Can't imagine you have a lot of friends who'd be happy to see a law enforcement officer on their doorstep."

"That's the idea."

Great. All he had to do was keep Doyle busy and complacent until they could find Molly. "What do you want me to do with this 'friend'?"

He could almost hear Doyle's smile. "Kill him."

"No," Zach said immediately.

"Okay." His tone was nonchalant, almost dismissive. "You won't kill him, I *will* kill her."

Zach froze. He'd have to choose between some random person's life and his fiancée's.

His fiancée was an FBI agent. She would willingly lay down her life to save a civilian.

This civilian was some sort of business associate of Doyle

Murphy. Killing him meant Zach was doing the country a favor—or the mob's dirty work.

But was there anything he wouldn't do to save Molly?

"'Kay." Zach wished his voice didn't break on that single syllable. "And then what? I pretend like this didn't happen?"

"If you know what's good for you. Or are you so high-and-mighty that 'the government' won't care about a little murder?"

Zach fell silent. Doyle might know his generic cover story, but he wasn't smart enough to blackmail him into providing his own blackmail. Zach could always tell the truth about this, about Doyle kidnapping Molly and extorting him—again—but none of that was an excuse for cold-blooded murder.

He wasn't going to do this. But he couldn't let Molly die.

Doyle started giving instructions: "You're going to go to his house alone. Alone, got it? Call me when you get there. Put it on speakerphone and put your phone in your pocket, and I'm going to listen to everything you say and do. Don't try any little tricks, notes, anything like that. I *will* find out. Got it?"

"Yeah." He couldn't go through with this. Zach checked the car's knobs and vents, obviously stalling, but the car's A/C was already running full blast. Finally, he found himself asking, "What's the address?"

Doyle rattled off a street address: Kilkenny Lane in a town called Hometown. Zach didn't know where Hometown was. He found a pen in the center console and wrote the address on his palm.

There had to be something he could do to help himself. Maybe the FBI had a file on the target. "What's the guy's name?"

"You don't need to know that."

"Come on. The first thing a real FBI agent would do at the door is ask if he's got the right person."

"This guy isn't intimately acquainted with police procedures. Yet."

Zach pounded on the center console. Doyle's plan wouldn't work, even if Zach were willing to go along.

But if he didn't at least pretend to go along with it? He didn't dare risk those consequences. "I do this and then you'll let her go. Safe. Immediately." It wasn't a question.

Doyle ended the call.

There had to be something Zach could do to get out of this.

Of course there was. All he had to do was catch up with Doyle at Washington Park. Zach entered the park in his navigation app. Twenty minutes to get there, and he had exactly twenty minutes.

This time, he had to catch Doyle.

12

MILES ONLY WANDERED A FEW FEET from the container doors. He barely dared to leave Molly alone, even for what he assumed would be a quick status report from Doyle. "Yeah?" he answered the phone.

"Found the perfect solution to our little problem."

They didn't share any problems, but Miles wasn't going to let that put a damper on Doyle. "Oh, really?"

"Remember how I was going to have the Father run a little 'errand' or two for me first? Yank his chain?"

An embellishment Miles hadn't actually allowed. "Yeah?"

"Let's just say our friend won't be calling me again."

"What makes you think he can handle Becker?"

Doyle gave a long, loud honk of laughter. "One of them is an accountant and the other one was the undercover cop who shot me. Doesn't take a genius."

"You're right there." So he finally figured out how to take care of Becker. What did the guy want, a sticker? If he screwed up Miles's timeline, he'd get a sucker punch and then some. What kind of schedule had Doyle put Saint on?

"Hold on." A musical tone carried from Doyle's end of the line— his other phone? "I know, Claire," Doyle answered. "She wants to— fine, just bring your keys." A slight shuffling and Doyle came on the line. "Ever regret getting your kid her license, Miles?"

"Only when she drives. So when is this hit supposed to happen?"

"Gave him our friend's address and sent him there now." Doyle sounded as giddy as a guy could get when ordering a murder.

"Nice work." Miles hoped Doyle didn't notice how tight his voice was around that compliment.

Apparently he didn't, because Doyle wished him luck and ended the call.

Miles poked his head in the container again. Molly immediately met his gaze. Had she been watching for him?

Of course she had. He could feel it. Watching. Wiling. Waiting.

Miles stepped out of her line of sight before he turned back to his phone. He had to keep tabs on Saint's location in case Miles needed to make an early exit. He needed somebody on the ground—somebody he could trust. Somebody who wouldn't go running to Doyle.

He didn't have many options, with most of his friends in jail. He'd be building up the South Side from scratch once Doyle was out of the way, but he'd rather have his own men. People he could trust.

Today, though, he'd settle for someone who was free. Like Sam Fahey. Miles scrolled through his contacts and dialed.

"Yeah?" Sam answered.

"Heard anything lately?"

Sam hemmed. "Two Feds came by this morning. Searching for Doyle. Wanted to know if I knew anything about him."

"Do you?"

"You think I'm interested in being seen with him these days? I done my time once; I ain't looking for another stay. Why'd you think we moved away when I got out?"

If he'd taken the same standoffish attitude with the FBI, they probably weren't following Sam. "Let's keep it that way," Miles said. "I got a job for you. You've got a camera phone, right?"

"You kidding?"

"How fast can you get out to Hometown?"

Zach was exiting the interstate when his phone rang. Murphy?

He was a mile from Washington Park still. Murphy might have seen him.

No. It shouldn't be Murphy. Zach hadn't had time to make the drive to Hometown from the FBI field office, where he was supposed to have been when he got Murphy's call. No way was Murphy calling back already.

Zach finally stopped at a light and pulled out his phone—his mother. Again. Not answering would only make things worse. Better act normal.

He hit the speakerphone button. "Yeah, Mom?"

"Zachary." One word from his mother and he felt like a total disappointment. "I wish you could be here."

He glanced at the time on the car dash. 10:54. "What, too much food? Not enough hands to clean up?"

"You know this was important to me, Zachary."

He was thirty years old and his mom could still make him feel like a little kid. "Sorry, Mom. Not exactly a picnic for me, either."

His mother paused. "I know, honey. I'm sorry you got called in. Any idea when you'll be through?"

"I wish. Everything's going wrong today."

She hesitated again. "Are you sure you're okay?"

Zach kicked himself. He was letting his emotions show. He sighed, trying to sound frustrated but not too much so. "Just a lot more stress than I anticipated today."

"Weddings are stressful—but if you would've told them you couldn't come in today, Zachary, this wouldn't be half the problem it is."

Man, she could twist the knife with the best of them. "I didn't have a choice. Please don't make this harder."

Zach came up to the last red light before the park, and suddenly he remembered why he knew this park so well: they came here all the time for church activities. Softball, swimming in the aquatic center, fishing in the lagoon, visiting the museum, even cricket.

This park was massive.

"Have you heard from Molly?" his mother asked.

He needed to end this call, fast, and without making her suspicious. "No. Guess it's the same for her."

"You know you have to be at the temple in five hours."

"Thank you, Madame Timekeeper."

"Are you in the car?" Mom asked.

"Yeah, I am—and I'm almost there. Gotta go. Love you." Mom echoed the goodbye and he hung up.

Five hours. He'd known all day they were supposed to be there an hour early, but he'd been counting down to the ceremony time. If they were going to make it there in time, he'd have to find her by . . . now.

Was it time to let go of that fantasy?

The only objective that mattered right this minute was finding Molly. As long as he found her alive, he could worry about the timing later. They could get married any day of the week. Rebook their tickets to Ireland. Finding her was all that mattered.

Either she was here or Murphy was.

Zach's phone chimed with a text, then a couple more. He cruised into the nearest parking lot, pausing at a stop sign to check the messages. Other agents arriving at the park.

The place had to be a mile long and half a mile wide. Even a full squad didn't seem like enough agents to search.

Xavier responded to the group text, doling out Zach's assignment: park Murphy's car and lie in wait.

Sitting around. Of course. Heaven forbid he have the chance to *do* something.

Zach pulled into the parking lot behind the armory, as far from the pool as he could get. This lot was pretty full, too. They were right by the softball fields. Surely nobody was playing today.

Murphy couldn't possibly have hidden Molly here. But he had to have her nearby. Zach texted Xavier to direct another squad his way, and Zach got out of the car to take his position. Murphy wasn't about to drive off without his keys.

Zach waited for the first squad. Once they pulled in, Zach assigned them to search in a grid pattern and refreshed their memories with pictures of Murphy and Molly. The other agents started out, leaving Zach to scan the parking lot for any stragglers.

Then he spotted it: a gold sports car that was all too familiar. A classic muscle car.

He crossed the lot to check. The cursive insignia glinted on the rear quarter: *Cougar.*

Doyle was here.

Zach turned back to the squad he'd sent off on the hunt, but they were already out of range.

Then he'd search too. Zach started off on his search track almost running, or as close as he could get in this heat. He scanned every face he passed, and within the first minute, people noticed him and watched him warily, especially the spectators filing out of the stands of a softball diamond.

No Doyle, no Doyle, no Doyle.

The crowd from the bleachers thinned, and so did his hope. Searching for Doyle like this was too much of a long shot. He should be waiting at the car. Zach wiped the sweat from his forehead and changed course for the parking lot.

He needed somewhere to wait and watch. Near the car, out of sight so he could maintain the advantage. Somewhere in the shade.

He spotted the best vantage point: a tree that would keep him hidden with a view of the lot. Zach situated himself in the shade and scoped out the parking lot again.

Murphy's Audi was gone.

Zach checked his pocket. He still had the keys. He'd locked it. It couldn't be stolen.

Maybe he'd forgotten where he parked. He scanned the whole lot, each row and around all the edges. No black Audi.

The Cougar was still there. Doyle was expecting to meet up and trade keys with his lawyer, right? One eye on the lot for Murphy, Zach headed over to check out the Cougar.

The Cougar's keys were in the ignition.

No. No way. Doyle couldn't have dropped off the Cougar and snuck the Audi out of here that fast. Even if he'd gotten lucky and carried an extra key. Doyle Murphy was not this good.

Did this mean he'd have to do what Doyle had told him to? Kill someone?

Zach ran his hands through his hair, clenching his fists a minute. He checked the lot one more time.

His phone rang and for a split second panic peaked in his system. This was Murphy calling him, and Zach was *not* where he said he'd be. Doing what he said he'd do. Murder.

He pulled out his phone—not Murphy's number, or at least not one Murphy had used with him yet. "Hello?"

"Agent Saint?" a woman answered. "It's Dawson-Maldonado."

Right, one of the agents searching the park. He didn't dare let himself hope. "Tell me you've got something."

"Did you say Murphy owns a black Audi?"

"Yeah." Zach managed not to thank her for bringing it up.

"I just saw one on its way out of here."

"Did you get a look at the driver? Which way did he go?"

Dawson-Maldonado paused. "The side windows were tinted, but I think it was a woman driving?"

Couldn't be that many black Audis here. "Got a description?"

"Two women actually. Blonde, an adult and a teenager."

Doyle's younger daughter had to be old enough to drive now. Claire Murphy was blonde. Could that be them?

"Thanks, Dawson-Maldonado," Zach said before hanging up.

If Claire Murphy and her daughter drove off with Murphy's car, he'd have to drive something out of here. His options seemed to be the Cougar, sitting with its keys in the ignition—and whatever Claire had driven.

Zach dialed Reyes. "Hey, Reyes, it's Agent Saint. I need to you run down a car registration for me. Need to know what Claire Murphy drives."

"One minute." A minute ended up being more like twenty seconds. "I've got seven Claire Murphys in Cook County—*is* this Cook County?"

"Yeah. How many in the Beverly area?"

"Just one: champagne Cadillac." Reyes read off the license plate and then the address.

That was the one. "Thanks." Zach lowered the phone to hang up, but Reyes said something else. "What was that?"

"I got a hit on one of the phones you have me tracking. Called this number about twenty minutes ago?"

Doyle's number. Zach sucked in a breath and braced himself. "Where was it?"

"Um, looks like he was at a McDonald's. All the towers were working for once."

He'd passed a McDonald's on his way into the park. "McDonald's where?"

"Oh, uh . . . 95th and St. Charles. By Beverly Boulevard?"

Zach groaned. That was closer to Doyle's house than Washington Park. Was he keeping Molly in that area?

"Sorry," Reyes murmured.

"Not your fault." Zach ended the call. He scanned the lot for Claire Murphy's champagne Caddy but nothing sprung out at him.

Doyle either parked somewhere else, or he was already gone.

He needed more options. He needed to be everywhere at once. He needed . . . help.

Zach texted X the update on Murphy's car and told him to send somebody to sit on Murphy's apartment, then tucked his phone back in his pocket.

Time to get to where he told Murphy he'd be.

He really should *not* do this, but there was only one car here that he could drive away and the owner wouldn't know.

Zach hurried over to the gold Cougar and hopped in.

Molly craned her neck, her shoulders twinging in response. She was sure Miles's shadow hadn't gone far, and it had only been a moment since he left. An excruciatingly long moment, while a lone drop of sweat slowly inched down her spine.

Was she alone?

Should she be worried that it was now only one drop of sweat? Surely it was only getting hotter. She should be sweating more than ever.

Molly thrust that thought away and focused on the container doors again.

An endless minute inched by until the arc of light in the door—getting shorter and shorter, as if the angle of the sun had changed—flickered with a shadow.

Molly shifted on the bed as Hennessy walked in with a larger fan connected to an extension cord under his arm and a peach in his other hand. He set the peach on the table and the fan on the floor next to him. She waited for him to switch it on, but none of the breeze reached her.

At least it meant more air was circulating. Those fans had to be the only things keeping her from roasting in this oven.

Her attempts at getting to Miles hadn't made much headway thus far, but she had to try again. Divide and conquer.

Her stomach gurgled, giving her the perfect topic to begin. "Will we ever eat?" As though anyone could think of food in this heat.

"We can only hope," Hennessy grumbled.

"I thought Doyle was bringin' lunch."

"You know what they say: if you want a job done right."

She sat back against the wall, trying to appear comfortable. Casual. As if she weren't trying to undermine a mob boss. "I bet he's eaten."

"And I guess he could stand to miss a meal." Hennessy picked up his magazine and used that to fan himself, too.

"I don't see Doyle in here swelterin' with us, either."

Hennessy flipped open the magazine. "What's your point?"

"Only that he's the one sayin' he wants vengeance, to make Zachary suffer, but he's off in an air-conditioned car or restaurant. Or home, I suppose. He's got you here to watch me, so he doesn't have to do any of the heavy liftin'."

"And, what, your sense of justice is offended for me? Please." He chuckled and flipped the page.

"Well, this wasn't your idea. No use shootin' the messenger—you're here roastin' along with me."

Hennessy loosened the last button of his shirt. "I guess."

Molly turned a dispassionate stare on the wall to give the conversation a calculated lull. If she pushed Hennessy too hard, her strategy would be obvious. "Do you have any other magazines?"

"Last week's *TV Guide*."

They still published that? She stretched her legs, rattling the shackle chain. "I'll bet he's off relaxin' at the pub."

"What, you're not relaxed here?"

"Oh, I am. If you see a cabana boy, would you flag him down for me? I'm runnin' low on daiquiris."

Hennessy laughed. "I could use a couple mojitos myself."

She joined in his laughter. Building rapport with him—reminding him she was as human as he—was easier than she'd thought. Granted, it hadn't done much to help her earlier, when she was trying to win his sympathy, but if she worked on a relationship of trust, reminding him of their shared history, he might be more inclined to see her point about Doyle's injustice. Toward both of them.

"How are Teresa and Connor and Megan?" she asked.

"Fine."

"Father Gus?"

"Fine."

Molly frowned. He was shutting down. What else could she use? "And Kathleen?"

He grimaced. "Finally quit the office."

"What was the last straw?"

"Don't know, but I heard they almost kissed at a church activity."

Molly shook her head without flinching. There was no way he could know Molly and Zachary had done the same thing when he was undercover as their priest. "Well, good on her for finally doin' the right thing. Quittin', I mean, of course."

She let another pause stretch in the conversation before she sighed. "When it comes down to it, Miles, do you think Doyle's goin' to make all this worth your while? I mean, if he's off doin' whatever he wants while we're here sweatin', what'll it be like when he doesn't need you?"

He maintained his aggravating calm. "Oh, Molly. It will definitely be worth it."

"And what will Doyle be doin' to make this drudgery up to you?"

"You know what? This really isn't your problem. Now, if you don't mind." He waved his magazine.

Molly sat back against the container wall. What on earth could a washed-up, mistried mobster on the fast track to jail offer to his last loyal lackey?

If she could only figure out how Miles was benefitting, she could find a way to appeal to him—and perhaps even save Zachary.

13

DOYLE HAD GIVEN UP on the first McDonald's with barely enough time to make it to Claire and Lizzie at Washington Park once her softball game was called for heat. Now he had the Caddy at a completely different McDonald's, though he hadn't risked the drive-thru this time.

Doyle glared at the gaggle of children in baseball uniforms swarming around a harried mom, changing their minds every minute about what they wanted while she attempted to order.

He had to get back, get somewhere secure enough for the Father to call him in time. The guy had to be out to Hometown. Probably set a new record from downtown to there, maybe using one of those little Kojak lights on the roof of his car.

He chuckled to himself. What he wouldn't give to see something like that. The Father scurrying around like hurrying would get her back faster, or keep her alive. Like anything he did would change the outcome of the day.

The Little League team in front of him finally paid and retreated to go find a table. But before Doyle reached the counter, his phone rang. He reached in his pocket—but no, that phone was off.

His emergency line. He grabbed the phone from his other pocket as it rang a second time. No caller ID on this one. They couldn't have traced this number to him. He'd never used it before. It was strictly for code-black, DEFCON-1 emergencies.

Whoever was calling was in major trouble—or was about to be.

"Hello?"

"Doyle?" His wife was calling the emergency phone.

He stepped out of line. "Claire? Are you okay?"

"Um, for the moment. I tried your other number, but you didn't answer."

He checked his pockets. Juggling too many phones today. "I don't know where it is."

"And where are you?"

"McDonald's. Claire, this number is for emergencies only," he growled. "Checking up on me doesn't qualify."

She hesitated. "Um . . . the bathroom sink flooded, and there's water all over the tile."

A code phrase. His skin turned cold. That meant authorities were snooping around. Not in his apartment yet. "How many tiles?"

"One or two, so far." Her voice quavered, either from fear or being unsure of the code, he couldn't tell. "Along the outside edge."

One or two Feds. Outside the building. "Anything we need to replace?"

"I—I'm not sure. Do you have any tools in your trunk?"

Goose bumps raised on his arms. "Has anybody checked?"

"No. Looked in the back seat. Now I'm just waiting for you."

She meant the agent had done those things. A warrant could be on its way. Shouldn't be anything that might trace them back to where Molly was. Nothing that might make the FBI think they had a strong enough case that the Father didn't have to do what Doyle asked—if the guy had gone to the Bureau at all.

"You sit tight," Doyle said. "If anybody comes to the apartment, don't you say a word. I'll be there in fifteen."

He hung up without waiting for her reply and strode out of the restaurant.

Zach's phone announced there was a thirteen-minute delay on his route to Hometown. Construction. This interstate had been under construction since before he'd moved here.

Zach pulled up his weather app: 99°. He couldn't look at the line that gave the heat index, but he knew it had to feel at least ten degrees hotter.

If you spent long enough in this heat, you'd have to be slowly baking. Actually, physically, baking.

He didn't dare try to find the stats on survivability. He couldn't bear to know.

The phone rang, interrupting the GPS's narration. He answered and hit the speakerphone icon. "Yeah?"

"Special Agent Saint?" a woman asked. His tech. Reyes.

"Yeah."

"We've got a couple things here. Let's see." She flipped through pages. "Update on that last phone number, the one that called you."

Doyle. Zach perked up. "Location?"

"Sorry, it's off. Burner cell."

Zach took the hit; another body blow today. How was he supposed to call Murphy when he got there if the man didn't have his phone on? "All right, keep an eye on that number. Should come on soon."

"There's a delay," the tech noted. "It can sometimes take half an hour or more to get a fix on a phone that's been switched on. Depending on the towers and that kind of stuff."

Wonderful. Zach tapped on the gas to keep up with the car ahead of him, then slowed to a stop again.

"Okay," Reyes continued. "We've also got a location on the first number—the one called Murphy. It's like ten miles from where it was before."

"You can stop tracking that one; Special Agent Mason and I found the phone."

Reyes took a second before she rebounded. "Well, then the lawyer's cell phone has gotten a bunch of calls. I guess it's not too surprising that most of the people calling him have a record."

Zach pinched the bridge of his nose. "Not really."

"Are we sure we're okay to be checking this? I mean, with privilege—"

"We're good."

Reyes hesitated. "If you're sure."

"I'm sure he was conspiring with his client, so yeah, we're good. Keep me posted." He thanked the tech again before hanging up.

Zach drummed on the steering wheel, adjusted the vents in the Cougar, tapped on the brake, rolled the car forward a foot.

He would not do what Doyle wanted him to. He couldn't.

Then why was he driving to Hometown?

He wasn't actually driving anywhere. He was sitting in the world's longest parking lot.

Zach let his head fall back against the headrest and started an inventory of his team. They'd called off searching Washington Park, most of the squad going back to double-check Murphy's minions' properties. Xavier was on his way to Doyle's. Jackson and Novak had talked to Sam Fahey and were supposed to track down Miles Hennessy next.

The last pair seemed most likely to have something to report. He dialed Jackson and Novak.

"Novak," he answered.

"Have you guys tracked down Miles Hennessy yet?"

The other agent sighed. "We're leaving his place. Nobody answered."

Nobody? Not his wife or kids? Miles himself could be home. Not like he had to work for a living.

Zach couldn't be sure whether this was a reason to be suspicious or not, but suddenly finding Hennessy felt urgent. "Let's put out a BOLO for Hennessy's car."

"You got it." Novak ended the call.

Traffic rolled forward—the first steady break they'd gotten. Maybe he'd be able to make it to Hometown. To the man Doyle wanted him to kill.

Was this the right way to get Molly back? So many right ways had gone wrong that he couldn't remember anymore.

Miles tossed the magazine aside. The feature article hadn't been interesting enough the first three times he'd started, and the heat made it worse. The fans weren't cooling much of anything, only stirring the steaming air, so thick you could taste it.

What, couldn't Doyle find a McDonald's—any McDonald's? He hadn't eaten since breakfast.

On the other hand, he'd go without food for a week if it made things go smoothly today. And so far, things were smoothest when Doyle was off doing whatever, even if that entailed guzzling whiskey sours at Brennan's.

He picked up the peach on the table. Molly was probably hungry, too. He could split it with her. He wasn't trying to make her suffer. Really, he wasn't a sadist.

"Can't you loosen these straps?" Molly called.

"Yeah." He rolled his eyes. "With scissors."

"Sounds good to me. Where am I goin', shackled to the bed?"

He leaned over the bigger fan. "If it's all the same to you, Molly,

I'm not taking any chances."

Molly visibly deflated. One good thing about the heat: it had steadily sapped her energy for trying to get under his skin.

"Miles," Molly said, quiet. "What is Doyle givin' you to do this?"

He wasn't about to take that bait.

"Even Doyle says he's on the way out. Fallen from the mob's good graces, you know yourself. The government must have frozen his assets, so he's not payin' you, and—"

"Give it a rest, Molly." He was too hot and too tired to play this game. "I'm helping Doyle and that's all you need to know."

She leaned forward, the chain on her ankle shackle clinking as she moved. "Maybe it's time for you to help yourself."

"And how, exactly, do you think I should do that? Turn myself in?"

"Well, it isn't too late."

Miles shifted in his chair, tilting his head at a sarcastic angle. "Oh? Is that what you're gonna tell your neighbor's kids? That it's not too late? Right."

"Please, Miles. Please. I'm askin'—" Her voice hitched. "I'm beggin' you."

He stared at the door. Did she really think this display was going to move him? Like he didn't know every little thing she said was calculated and weighed against her FBI training. Like he couldn't tell she was trying to use what little common past they had to build up his empathy.

"Think of Teresa. What would she say if she knew you were doin' this? How would you feel if someone took Megan on her weddin' day?

"Molly, shut up." He could only play the sympathetic ear so long. "Listen, all this isn't going to work for you. It isn't personal."

"How can you believe that? Of course it's personal."

Miles snorted. "To you, yeah. This is business to me. Haven't you learned in your line of work that you have to keep your personal feelings out of your job?"

"I've found that when I listen to my heart, I'm a better FBI agent. And a better person."

"Don't give me that crap. You think I care what you think of me? Like I don't know what other people think of us. Please."

After a long silence, he finally checked on her again. Molly wiped a tear on the shoulder of her T-shirt. He flinched mentally.

No. It didn't matter that she was crying, or that she was a woman, or that she'd always been kind to him. This was business, and no matter what this child thought, letting womanly emotions creep in would make him weak—and would ruin everything.

"Quit your crying and be quiet." He rolled the peach onto the table. She wouldn't get any of it now.

DOYLE WAS ALMOST TO HIS HOUSE when his emergency line rang again. If Claire was calling back, this definitely qualified. He grabbed the phone. "Yeah?"

"Doyle," Claire whispered. "They're in the hall."

Giving up on the code altogether? Didn't bode well. Doyle pulled into the first available parking lot: their church. "Stay calm. Act casual. Put me on speaker and put the phone in your pocket."

"When will you be here?"

He rubbed his temples. "Listen, Claire, I can't go in there."

"But this morning, you talked to them—"

"That was different."

"But—"

Doyle set his jaw. "That was this morning. Haven't you learned not to ask so many questions yet?"

"Sorry, Doyle," she murmured. She gasped. "They're knocking."

"Pocket."

The microphone of her cell rubbed against fabric. He could only hope Claire wouldn't do something stupid to accidentally end the call. Doyle muted his own mic and waited.

The door hinges creaked. "Can I help you?" Claire asked.

"We'd like to speak with Doyle Murphy," a man replied.

She hesitated, but when she spoke, her voice was stronger. "He's not home."

"Oh?" The man didn't believe her.

"No, he had another meeting with his lawyer."

"Uh huh. How often does he have to do that?"

Claire cleared her throat. "Well, you know, he has another trial coming up. They have a lot to plan."

"Hm." The man paused. "Exactly how many times a day do they have to meet?"

"I'm his wife, not his secretary." Despite her words, her note of defiance was fading. "I can't keep up with all his appointments."

"Well, then, can we wait for him here?"

"I don't think . . ."

"Do you have any ice water?" another woman broke in. "It's a scorcher out there."

"Uh, I can . . . I can get you a glass."

No, no way. A female Fed? Of course she'd get to Claire, get past her sorry excuse for defenses.

Twenty years of marriage still hadn't toughened up Claire the way she needed.

"Oh, thank you, I really appreciate it."

Doyle got to listen to the sounds of his wife in the kitchen: the clap of the cabinets, the crunch of the ice dispenser, the running of the water.

Just when Doyle was ready to give up on this call, the male Fed spoke again. "So, Mrs. Murphy, has your husband been home today?"

Great. All trace of Claire's brief streak of defiance from a few minutes before fled. "Of course he has. What are you trying to say?"

"We're trying to say that he's a person of interest."

Her voice held more defeat than usual. "He's always a person of interest. There's always somebody here to see him."

"Like who?"

She was silent long enough that Doyle checked his phone. "You and Father Tim were here this morning," she finally said. "You know that much."

"You know, actually," the female Fed spoke up, "we're here to talk to you."

Doyle didn't pray often, but he silently begged Claire to just. Shut. Up. "Me?" she said instead.

"That's right. Why did you and your husband switch cars today?"

"Um, well, I wanted the Audi. Lizzie wanted to drive after her softball game, and I don't like her driving the Cadillac."

Doyle reflexively glanced around the Caddy. He'd have to get rid of it. He pulled a U-turn to get out of the parking lot. Could he get the Audi under their noses?

"How'd you get the car?" the female Fed asked Claire.

"Doyle said to bring my keys, and we could leave as soon as we found it. Lizzie's game was called for the heat."

Silence fell for a few seconds, and Doyle strained to figure out what was going on. Cell phones weren't great for communicating body language. "Mrs. Murphy," the woman agent said, "we just need to talk to him."

Right. Obviously, he hadn't given Claire details about what he was up to today, but he had made it extremely clear that today was critically important.

"So where is your Cadillac, Mrs. Murphy?" the woman asked.

"Doyle has it."

"Thank you so much for the water, Mrs. Murphy. Could I possibly get some more ice?"

"Of course."

Doyle groaned and rubbed at his forehead. He wanted to hang up, to start making a new plan, but he had to see what these agents were after. These people never could cut to the chase.

The woman agent's thanks was warm. "So, Mrs. Murphy, is your Cadillac equipped with OnStar?"

No. No. He was *not* going down like this.

"Well, yes. But we don't pay for it—I mean, subscribe."

They still might be able to locate the Caddy. Doyle wiped the sweat beading on his neck even in the air-conditioning.

"That's okay," the female agent said. "Remind me again: do you know where your husband is?"

What was she getting at, repeating that question?

No reason carried across the phone line, until the female agent spoke again. "Would you like to know where he is?"

Claire's words almost didn't reach her own phone. "I'm scared to find out."

Oh, this again. Leave it to another woman to tap into Claire's chronic insecurity about Doyle cheating. As if the FBI had nothing better to do than track down his mistress.

The woman agent's voice dripped sympathy. "But wouldn't it be better to finally *know?*"

Doyle hung up and threw his phone across the car. No, no, NO.

He should have known better than to trust Claire to hold off the Feds. But he couldn't go in there and fix things now. It was too late to deny involvement. If he ran into the FBI now, he'd be out of luck. They'd take him, call off the Father, find Molly somehow—

No. That was his paranoia talking. Yeah, he should avoid the FBI, and yeah, he couldn't go into his apartment, but arresting him wouldn't automatically help them find Molly. She was secure—not even in one of his holdings. Hennessy had been smart enough to suggest that. The guy might go places if he kept that up.

The light finally changed to green and Doyle gunned it through the intersection. He couldn't afford to get pulled over, but he had to hurry if he was going to ditch this car before Claire dug up the necessary paperwork.

The next light—the last before their apartment—was red. Again. He needed to ditch this car, get another ride back to the warehouse, and he had to go and hit every red light on the way.

He hit his knuckles against the gearshift. He was lucky they hadn't already tracked him with this car. Did OnStar record where he'd been, or did they have to be subscribers?

Either way, it was a good thing he hadn't made it back to Miles and Molly in this car.

And then Claire had said they didn't pay for it—idiot woman. She made it sound like they were stealing an emergency service nobody needed these days anyway.

Her mistrust was going to ruin everything.

He pulled into their building's parking lot, scanning for the agents' backup. Didn't seem like anyone out of the ordinary was hanging around.

Doyle peered up at his windows. Claire was going to ask the FBI for his location, and they were going to figure out he was in the parking lot, or had just left.

He had to get out of here—but whose car? He couldn't trust his Audi. He'd left the keys with Lehrman's Cougar.

Teresa. Of course.

Zach had finally made it out to the suburb Doyle had sent him to. He stared at his target, the brick Cape Cod across the street. Of course Doyle Murphy wanted a hit on some dude in the suburbs.

And that meant Zach was supposed to open that car door, get out, walk across the street, and kill.

He didn't reach for the door.

He cast a glance down the peaceful, maple-lined street. A mother and a toddler played in their sprinklers. A mail carrier strolled down the sidewalk. An elderly woman waved to the postman as he approached her porch, and he called out in greeting.

The neighborhood seemed too good to be true. It could be hiding a dark underbelly, but the street felt like the kind of idyllic place he'd almost stopped believing in after six years with the FBI. The kind of place he and Molly would want to raise their children.

They weren't going to have children if he didn't get her back. And he wasn't going to get her back if he didn't go in there.

Zach found himself reliving every second of the day, trying to see what he could have done differently. Instead, he saw all the little things he'd done wrong today, a slippery slope trending steadily downward. He'd snapped at Reyes. He'd broken protocol to take Murphy's and then Lehrman's cars. He'd arrested Lehrman without much to go on and practically coerced a statement from him.

And now he was sitting here, thinking about going through with . . . this.

He couldn't. He wouldn't. It was every shade of wrong.

But he'd had dozens of FBI agents running at full throttle for over five hours and not a single thing they'd done had gotten him any closer to finding Molly.

What if this was the only way to save her life?

What kind of FBI agent was he if he even thought about doing this?

What kind of person was he if he considered *not* doing this?

There had to be another way. One that didn't involve this. Murder.

But the drive time and five minutes of sitting here, gawking at the house, hadn't produced any better ideas.

He was late to get to the house, late to call Murphy. But once he dialed, Zach was committing to this.

Unless he could come up with something else to do to save Molly.

Unless it was already too late. Zach dialed the last number he had for Murphy and braced himself.

It went straight to voicemail.

Zach's blood froze. Had he waited too long?

Molly shook her half-asleep leg to restart her circulation. Hennessy glowered at her again.

Perhaps it was the heat. Perhaps it was her attempts to forge a connection with him. Or perhaps something wasn't going well with Hennessy's scheme. Was Zachary on his way?

He couldn't be. If it were that bad, they wouldn't be sitting here. Hennessy would trundle her off somewhere. Or would he—?

She'd have to assume Zachary was nowhere close. But if Hennessy was this upset, everything was not going how he'd thought it would. Perhaps Doyle was backing out on a promise to Hennessy already. If Hennessy wasn't satisfied, then she had to risk another attempt.

But she couldn't do it while he was focusing his fury on her. She tried to make it seem like she was very interested in the wall, sneaking intermittent glances his way.

Hennessy pulled a multi-tool from a pouch at his belt. He unfolded it, pulled out a knife blade, and clenched the handle again.

A hollow feeling grew in the pit of her stomach. Now he had a knife. Was it too late for her to reason with him? Or maybe he was so angry with Doyle that he was going to cut her loose.

Sure now. The thin film of sweat on her back grew cold.

Hennessy nabbed the peach from the table and stuck the knife into its flesh. He sawed around the circumference, then wrenched the halves apart.

The residual fear in her stomach mingled with the rising nausea. Hennessy sliced a section of the peach and devoured it.

Warm saliva welled up in her mouth as he ate another piece of the peach. She looked up from the fruit to meet Hennessy's gaze.

He stared back with—not hate, and not quite pity.

She'd take it. "Miles?"

He raised an eyebrow, the anger slowly draining from his expression.

"Is everythin' all right?"

"Peachy."

Molly pursed her lips at the pun.

This was her chance. For whatever reason, he was the closest to her side he'd come all day. If she could push him, she could find out what he wanted from this situation and figure out how to leverage him or make him a better offer.

But she had to strike now.

Molly flexed her wrists. Pins and needles pricked her hands—they were losing circulation, falling asleep. "Miles?"

He grunted at her and started on the second half of his peach.

"He's left you out in the cold, hasn't he?"

Hennessy pressed two fingers to his temple.

"Doyle? He's not givin' you what he promised, is he?"

"What makes you think that?"

She moved her shoulders, trying to appear nonchalant over the pain shooting down her arms. "Somethin's the matter. And I know how Doyle and his ilk operate."

He snorted. "Oh, do you? What, the FBI let you read his profile, and you think you know how he 'operates'?"

"I haven't read his personal file, no, but I do know the general profile."

"Uh huh. You think you can predict what he's doing now from some psychobabble and my expression?"

This wasn't working. "I'm not sayin' I'm a mind reader. I'm only sayin' that people like Doyle aren't likely to keep their promises once they don't need you anymore."

He tore off another bite of the peach, ignoring her.

She leaned forward, the mattress creaking beneath her. "Think about it, Miles. He gets whatever it is he wants—out of his case, a payoff, anythin'—and suddenly he doesn't owe you anythin'. He doesn't need your help anymore, and he's movin' on to the next job."

"Yeah, right."

"Can't you see? How many jobs have you pulled for him, how many favors does he still owe you? How many times has he reneged, or never got around to the little things you've asked of him?"

Hennessy fixated on the wall.

"Aren't you gettin' tired of the broken promises? You've been playin' the same role for him for at least the last four years."

"Molly—"

"No matter what you do for him, you'll never get ahead. It's never made any difference before, and it won't make a bit of difference this time. He's not givin' you what he promised—he'll take whatever you're willin' to give him and leave you in the lurch. Where you are now."

He pinned her with a sarcastic look. "Are you finished?"

"Are you?"

Hennessy simply blinked at her in the silence. "Should I take that as a no?"

Molly sighed and let her gaze fall. He hadn't taken the bait even a little. Had she read him wrong?

She hadn't. Something was definitely the matter.

Was he that confident in Doyle coming through for him? She watched him again from the corner of her eye. Hennessy deliberately chomped on another slice of the peach, clenching his jaw as if he were grinding his teeth on each bite. He took the knife to the last quarter of the peach, peeling the skin from the flesh—glowering at her with extreme menace.

Not defeated. Confident. Calculating. Cocky.

Perhaps she couldn't convince Miles to let her go. Then she'd get herself out, if he'd only leave the container for a few minutes.

And his pride could be a good way to get him to do precisely that.

"Are you just an idiot, so?" she called.

He paused in peeling the peach. "Excuse me?"

"You are, aren't you? You think this time he's *really* comin' through for you. This time, you've finally proved your worth, and he'll make up for all those past disappointments with whatever he's promised you."

"You're like a dog with a bone here."

"And you're like an idiot."

A muscle in his temple throbbed. "You calling me stupid?"

She'd hit a nerve. Molly kept the same intense fixedness in her expression. "What, are you deaf, too? You're stupid for goin' along with this, you're stupid for thinkin' you could get away with this, and you're stupid for believin' Doyle for one minute."

"I'm stupid because I believed Doyle?" He snorted again.

"That's what I said. He's offered you somethin' you think is worthwhile, but you're wrong—dead wrong. You'll trust him right into an early grave, Miles. You'll never get out from under his thumb until you learn to think for yourself."

His knuckles around the knife turned white. "Think for myself," he repeated.

"Listen to yourself! Even now you can't think—you're only repeatin' everythin' I say. Use your brain, you dense idiot—do some thinkin' of your own for once. Just process what's happenin' right in front of your nose!"

"Like you know what's happening here," he said through clenched teeth.

Perfect. Not only had she struck a nerve, he was playing right into her hands. "I'm not too blind or too stupid to understand what you're doin' here. You're a pawn in Doyle Murphy's game—yet again. You're at the bottom of the food chain and you'll always be at the bottom of the food chain because you're too stupid and lazy to see that."

Hennessy rose to his feet and stabbed the knife into the wooden table next to him. Molly flinched, but didn't dare look away from Hennessy. "Stupid? A pawn?"

She steeled her voice to keep up her attack. "A peon, completely expendable brute force that Doyle is manipulatin' yet again to further his own ends—not yours. Oh, wait." She simpered. "I forgot. You haven't any ends. Those require original thought."

He strode across the room and pointed at her. "You don't know anything. You don't know anything about me."

He wasn't supposed to come toward her, but she couldn't let herself show fear. She leaned farther forward, setting her shoulders in defiance. "I know an idiot when I see one. And I'm lookin' at one. Biggest I've seen in years. Bein' led by Doyle Murphy like a dog on a chain."

"He is *not* the one in charge here." The muscle in his temple leapt with each word.

"You keep tellin' yourself that. You may believe it, too, if that's what makes you feel good. I'm sure Doyle likes you to believe you're the mastermind of the whole affair. Makes you easier to use."

"I *am* the mastermind!" He jabbed Molly in the collarbone. "You think Doyle Murphy is smart enough to come up with this? You think Doyle Murphy is the smart one?" He scoffed. "*I'm* the one that's come up with the big idea. *I'm* the one behind this."

She needed him to back up—now—but the tactic was working. She had to keep pushing him. "As I said, havin' you believe that must be awfully convenient for Doyle. I bet he even let you hold his mobile phone. Or perhaps his gun?"

"The gun is mine—the *plan* is mine! I'm the one letting him think he's in charge—why do you think I'm here and not him?"

"Because you're too stupid to figure out how to get out of peon-level guard duty."

He jabbed her collarbone again. "Now who's the stupid one? Now who can't figure out the 'master plan'?"

Molly laughed with a patronizing air, which wasn't hard, considering how petulant Hennessy sounded. "You're tellin' me you really believe you're the one pullin' the strings? You're really that obtuse?"

"Doyle didn't think of this. He couldn't possibly. Come on! We're talking about the guy who tried to blackmail an FBI agent—the guy who thought he could get away with that. He couldn't follow this plan if I drew him a map!"

She laughed again—until Hennessy slapped her.

She swallowed against the tang of blood, trying to focus on anything but the stripe of pain burning across her cheek. Finally, she raised her gaze to scowl up at him. "Violence. The first resort of small minds."

"You want to know what I'm getting out of this?" Hennessy drew in a seething breath. "I'm getting everything. The only idiot here is going to be out of the picture for good once the FBI catches up with him. First he blackmails one agent and gets caught, and now he kidnaps another? Sullivan will finally have to cut those last ties—and then there's going to be a vacancy. He'll see this plan, the way I've taken care of Doyle, the 'problem child,' and tied up all the loose ends—and he'll know he's got the right man for his second."

"And, what, Doyle went along with this because he believes you're his rightful successor? Because he knows he deserves to go to prison?"

Hennessy scoffed. "Doyle went along with this because I made him think it was his idea. He's so stupid he can't even figure out this wasn't his plan from the start. He thinks I'm in this to help him get what he wants—because I'm loyal—because I promised him I'd track down Cally Lonegan and cut his tongue out."

Impossible. Cally was in protection—they couldn't touch him, could they? "You don't really know where he is," she said, more out of hope than a bluff.

An evil grin split his face. "Now you're getting it."

The final implications of his plan dawned on her. Her thoughts halted. Did she dare to ask?

She had to. "And what about me? Amn't I a 'loose end'?"

"*That*'s why I'm here guarding you. While Doyle runs around and distracts the FBI, I'm here to keep you quiet. And once they catch him—" He held up the last quarter of peach flesh and squeezed it in his fist. "The one person left that can tie me to this won't be telling any tales."

Hennessy slung the pulverized peach onto the particleboard floor and retreated to the table. He yanked the knife free, plopped back down in his chair and gave her another menacing smile.

An invisible icicle dripped down her spinal cord and Molly shivered involuntarily. His grin was even colder than Doyle's.

ZACH TOSSED HIS PHONE ON THE PASSENGER SEAT in disgust.
Murphy wasn't going to answer. He was toying with him,
sending him out here to torment him. He wasn't going to give
Molly back even if Zach did go through with this.

But could he afford to gamble on that—with Molly's life?

He certainly couldn't afford to kill someone.

He'd mostly tuned out the radio, but the words "heat wave"
grabbed his attention and he turned up the volume.

"The latest reports have pegged the death toll at nearly one
hundred," the newscaster said. "And temperatures are still rising
today."

Zach snapped the radio dial to off. He grabbed his phone again
and tried Murphy's number one last time. Still no answer. He paged
through the numbers that had called him today until he found the
tech's number. There had to be something else she could check on.

"Agent Saint?" Reyes answered.

"Yeah, listen, I know you said you'd call when you had anything,
but I need to double-check a couple things. Did we find anything
suspicious in Lehrman's latest calls? I mean, other than the fact that
they're probably all criminals?"

"Nothing that I can see." Reyes's voice carried an apology. "Any
of these pop for you? We got Gerald Jensen, Regina Sanchez,
unknown, Michael Cutter, unknown, DeShawn Spencer, Doyle
Murphy of course, and Harry Palmer."

"Nothing." Other than Harry Palmer was the main character of

The Ipcress File, one of Molly's favorite '60s spy films.

"Let's see. We're still going through the Marshals to get ahold of Cally Lonegan."

There had to be something he was forgetting. "What about the other number that called Murphy this morning?"

The tech was quiet a moment and Zach could hear the rustle of shuffling papers. "Oh, yeah, Eddie and Laura Becker. Somebody around here is working on a background check on them. Do you want me to run it down and call you back?"

"Sure, why not?" Zach threw up his free hand in disgust. "Everything else is going wrong, let's see if we can add one more dead end to the map."

"Uh, okay, I'll get on that. The only other thing I have for you is that the phone is still off. Hasn't been half an hour yet, though."

"Yeah." He sighed and scanned the street again. A beat-up red Toyota a few houses down seemed . . . odd. Why did he notice that? He replayed the mental inventory of the street—the neighbors out on their lawns had all gone in because of the shady man strolling down the sidewalk. The shady man that was coming back up the other side of the street.

The shady man that had gotten out of this Toyota.

"Hold on a second." Zach switched to the camera app on his phone and zoomed in on the Toyota's license plate. "How fast can you trace a car's license number?" he asked Reyes.

"Illinois?"

He squinted. "Yep."

"About as fast as you can read it."

Zach rattled off the letters and numbers.

"One second." Reyes tapped away at her keyboard. "Anna Fahey."

That would be Mrs. Sam Fahey. Murphy's lackey. "Thanks." He hung up.

If Murphy called Fahey here, too, he had to be checking up on Zach. Making sure he went through with this.

He wasn't going through with it. Molly could be in danger because he was hesitating.

No, it was Murphy's fault his calls weren't getting through, not his. Zach looked up in time to catch the attention of the shady man across the street—this must be Sam Fahey. Sam stopped short and lifted his hand.

Crap. Zach reached for his gun. If Sam had it in for him, he was already dead.

Before he could draw fully, he saw what Sam was holding—a phone. Judging by the way he stood with his cell straight in front of him, he was either taking a selfie while sightseeing in suburbia or snapping a picture of Zach in the car.

Zach debated getting out to confront Sam or ignoring the man. If he talked to him, he might be able to find out why Murphy wanted his target dead.

Zach reached for the door handle—and his phone rang. Unfamiliar Chicago number. "Call off your thug."

"What?" Lucy asked. "What are you talking about?"

His little sister had terrible timing. Zach groaned inwardly. "I'm busy, Lucy."

"I know, I just wanted to see how you're doing."

"I will call you when I know something," he ground out. "Use your cell phone the next time you call me."

"It's dead because *somebody* made me unplug it at six a.m. to talk in the bathroom," she huffed. "Jerk."

She ended the call.

That had gone about as well as he'd expected. Zach paged through his phone history to try Doyle Murphy's most recent number one more time.

It rang. Twice. Not voicemail.

Murphy's phone was on, and he had to be expecting Zach's call.

If he wasn't going to kill this dude—and honestly, he had never really planned to kill him—what was he going to say to Doyle?

Doyle wiped his palms on his thighs. No sign of a blue Lincoln in their apartment building's parking lot. Where was Teresa? He leaned over for his phone and dialed her number.

"Hello?" she answered.

"Teresa, it's Doyle. Where are you?"

"Grocery shopping, but I'm almost done. Why? Isn't Claire home today?"

"I need your car."

She chuckled softly. "What are you going to do, drive two at once?"

"Listen, I'm doing something today, and I need to use your car. Please, Terry?"

"Of course, of course. How fast can you get to the Fairplay?"

"Two minutes." Doyle hung up and threw the car into gear. No time to celebrate. By the time the FBI tracked down the Cadillac, Teresa would have it back in the apartment parking lot. And if the FBI caught her, she'd definitely cover for him—and do a better job of it than Claire ever could.

As promised, two minutes after he got off the phone with Teresa, Doyle pulled into the Fairplay parking lot. Teresa was walking out from under the grocery store's red awning. She pointed Doyle in the general direction of her car, and he followed. The blue Lincoln was under the tree in the corner of the lot. There weren't any open spaces nearby, so Doyle pulled up to park behind her, blocking the aisle.

Everybody else could go around. It wasn't going to take that long.

Teresa knocked at his window. He popped the trunk and got out, but left the car running.

"What's this big job today? I don't think I've seen either of you work this much in years."

"We'll talk about it some other time, Terry." He reached for her waist, but Teresa swatted him away.

"Not here."

"What's so sacred about the Fairplay?" Doyle scoffed. Claire would never have dared to buck him like that. Another reason he liked Terry, though he wouldn't let her know how much he enjoyed her occasional challenge. Then she'd try it all the time.

"Are you both going to be tied up for the rest of the day?" she asked.

"Probably till at least five."

"And then you'll both be home?" Terry walked the cart back to the nearest return.

"Not sure," he said when she was close enough. "He might have to work late."

"Well, let me know if you finish up before Miles does."

Doyle winked. He held out his keys and took hers. "I'll see if I can make some time for you in a couple hours."

Terry flashed him half a sly smile and got in his car.

He unlocked the Lincoln as Terry pulled out. She waved at him.

He opened the door to let the heat out and cranked the air-conditioning. The shade from the tree hadn't done much to keep the interior of Terry's car cool.

The time on his phone read 11:43. Late, but not as bad as he'd thought. Maybe he hadn't missed the Father's callback yet. Or maybe he'd have to try again. Doyle switched on the phone and settled into the car to wait.

It took about thirty seconds for his phone to ring.

"Yeah?" Doyle answered. He hadn't missed the Father's call at all.

"All right, I'm here. What do you want me to do again?"

Doyle didn't buy that for a second. "You gotta pay more attention, Father. I thought you were supposed to be some sort of hotshot."

"And I thought we were doing this as a man-to-man kind of thing."

"What are you talking about?"

"Your little lackey."

Could he mean Miles? How could he know about Miles?

He couldn't. Time to bluff. "Listen, Father, it's his life or hers. Nobody else has anything to do with it. Nobody else is involved."

"Let me talk to her. None of this 'send a question through me' garbage. I have to hear her voice."

Doyle closed his eyes. Was he forgetting who was in charge here? "That's not the deal, kid. You don't get to set the terms. I have Molly, I call the shots."

"Uh huh. Then I'm going to have to call you back." The line went dead.

That idiot.

Miles stepped outside the container to answer the phone. Doyle's emergency line. "What?"

"The Father knows you're involved."

No way. The man wasn't clairvoyant, and they'd been beyond careful. "What did he say?"

"Told me to call off my lackey."

Miles couldn't help it: he laughed. Completely impossible. If Saint was smart enough to trace this back to him, then he was smart enough to figure out that Miles was no lackey these days.

"So, what, he's not going to do it?" Miles asked.

"He hung up on me."

Miles puffed out a breath. Now, that was something to worry

about. If Saint thought he could take control of the situation just like that, maybe he did know something more than he was letting on. "I gotta check on her." He hung up, then doubled back to the door to peek in. Molly sat on the bed, staring at the wall, her back to the door.

He stepped away again to dial Sam.

"I got a picture," Sam answered. "Stewing in his car."

"You got made, that's what you got."

Sam hesitated a beat. "Nah, no way."

"Yeah, he did."

"Well, what do you want me to do? Leave?"

"Be more subtle."

Sam coughed, though he seemed to be covering a more defiant response. "Fine. There had better be something big in it for me."

Miles hung up and resisted the urge to pitch the phone across the warehouse. Somehow, he'd let himself get to be the one waiting here with the hostage while everyone else tried to run the show—and screwed it up.

He strode through the door and threw himself into the chair. Molly opened her mouth to speak, but he leveled her with a glare. "Don't start with me."

They were ruining everything. His plan was foolproof, and the fools were trying to prove it. Really, they could ruin everything: lose Doyle's big fish, lose Saint. But as long as they didn't give Miles away, it could still work out. He'd given everyone else enough rope to hang themselves. He was here because Molly was the one loose end he couldn't afford to leave to anyone else.

But if Doyle and Sam didn't get their acts together, they were going to put even the safest parts of his plan at risk.

And stuck here, babysitting her, there wasn't anything he could do.

No. Things were not unraveling yet. It was going to work out. He was still in control.

16

FOR FAHEY'S BENEFIT, Zach tried to act calm and collected, watching the bay window of the brick house in front of him. Like he hadn't been watching the place already for—he checked the time on his phone. Only ten minutes? It had been too long since he'd been on surveillance if he'd already forgotten how slowly time passed in a car. Especially at—he checked the weather—102°.

If Doyle didn't have her somewhere with air-conditioning—

Sam Fahey hopped into his Toyota and sped off.

Zach rubbed his temples. Enough waffling. He had to make up his mind. Either he was going to get her back, or . . . he'd have to find another way to get her back.

They'd already tried everything and come up empty. He couldn't hang his only hope of seeing her again on getting permission to contact Cally Lonegan, or on Lonegan knowing anything that might help in the first place.

He had to do something. He could think on his feet. He opened the car door and stood, staring over the roof of the Cougar at the little brick house.

He'd call Doyle and do . . . something. Not this. Anything but this. Nothing in his life had ever felt more wrong—except his only other choice, letting Molly die.

If he did this, he wouldn't deserve Molly. But was his integrity more important than her life?

Maybe not—but murder was too high a price to ask.

Zach slumped into the driver's seat again. Ten minutes of

agonizing was too much. Even Doyle Murphy had given up on him, sending Sam Fahey packing because Zach clearly wasn't going to bow to his bidding. Maybe Doyle had already hurt Molly, or maybe—

Before he could finish his paranoid thought, a beat-up red Toyota rolled up the block behind him, into view of his side mirror.

Sam Fahey was back. Then it was still on. She was still okay. He could still get her back.

If he could find a way to get through this.

Zach's hand actually shook as he reached for his weapon. Would Molly be able to forgive him for risking her life—sacrificing her life?—for his morality, or was that worse than doing something so wrong to save her?

Either way, Molly should never forgive him.

There would have to be another way to catch Doyle. Zach pulled his car door shut and started the engine. She would have to find a way to forgive him.

And he would have to find her.

As he put the car into gear, his phone rang. He held his foot on the brake and answered his phone—the FBI tech. "Yeah?"

"Special Agent Saint?" The excitement in Reyes's nervous voice was audible. "I think I have something you're going to want to hear. Something big."

Zach clung to the phone like it was his last hope. Very well could be. "What is it?"

"I got the full background on Eddie and Laura Becker. You're not going to believe this."

"What?" he asked after a long pause.

"Eddie was a juror on Murphy's trial."

A member of the hung jury that was just dismissed—one who had a connection to Murphy after the trial.

Zach put the car in park again. "Did you check their bank records?"

"Nothing super unusual there—a bunch of deposits spread out in several places. But if you take them all together, it's almost twenty thousand dollars in separate accounts."

That was an impressive amount of work Reyes had pulled off. "Get me a current address."

"Got it right here." Shuffling papers carried over the line. "Oh, here it is. Kilkenny Lane—"

"Hometown, Illinois," Zach finished. "You're serious?"

"Of course."

"Good work, Reyes. This is a big find." He ended the call. He finally knew what he had to do.

Zach checked his weapon, climbed out of the car and dialed Doyle Murphy.

Doyle was halfway back to the warehouse when his phone rang. The Father's number. Was the FBI tracking this call? Just in case, he pulled over before answering. Couldn't risk revealing Molly's location. "Yeah?"

The Father didn't respond, only the sound of a hollow knock.

He was going through with it.

Something squeaked—door hinges, maybe. "FBI," the Father said. "You're coming with me."

"What? Why?" Eddie Becker's voice. Doyle grinned.

"I know everything. Let's go."

"I haven't done anything!" Hysteria forced his pitch an octave higher.

"Oh, I think you know. Our mutual friend—Doyle Murphy?"

"I don't know what you're talking about." Becker's words shook.

"You thought we wouldn't catch up with you? Come on—you

knew we caught him before. He's not smart enough to pull this off."

Doyle gritted his teeth, but kept quiet.

There was a long pause. Was Becker buying it?

"Come with me," the Father said.

Becker hesitated. "Please—I can't go to jail. Who will take care of Laura?"

"Not my problem. Let's go." A metallic clatter sounded, and then the ratchet of handcuffs.

The Father just happened to have handcuffs. As if Doyle needed any other evidence the man worked in law enforcement.

Two car doors slammed, then the engine roared to life.

He was really going through with it.

"Where are we going?" Becker asked, a whimper hiding in his words.

The Father didn't answer.

Becker waited a minute before he tried again. "Can you slow down?"

"No."

"Is there anything we can do about this? I really can't go to jail."

"Should have thought of that before you tangled with Doyle Murphy."

Doyle couldn't help a chuckle. Same went for the Father.

A yelp sounded. Probably Becker. Doyle hadn't asked for extra torment, but he definitely wouldn't turn it down.

"Careful, not like I can buckle up here."

The Father didn't respond, but another yelp from Becker seemed like answer enough.

"Please," Becker tried one more time.

Silence reigned for a long moment. And then a jangle—keys, maybe.

"Why are we stopping here?"

"Let's go." A car door slammed, then another.

"Wait," Becker pleaded. "Wait, please. What's—what are we

doing?"

A loud crunch of gravel, and Becker's begging reached a fever pitch.

Then two gunshots.

"Tell me where I get her," the Father demanded, now speaking directly into the phone.

"Give me twenty minutes and I'll call with the address."

"That's not our deal—"

Doyle ended the call, then allowed himself one moment to celebrate. He'd taken a chance letting the Father near Becker. But really, the Father couldn't have come within a mile of the courtroom while Doyle was on trial. He wouldn't know the jurors.

There was no backing out of it for the Father, and his career would be over if he ever dared to talk. One step closer. All he needed was the coup de grâce.

Doyle signaled and pulled into traffic. Everything was right on track.

Z ACH DROPPED TO HIS KNEES, ignoring the stabbing gravel. All
      that and he still didn't have Molly?

This couldn't be the end. Doyle could still call. They could
still track him down. Yes, this was a major setback, but he wouldn't
give up. He couldn't. Not yet.

"Please, whatever you want," Eddie Becker finally begged. "Just
don't kill me."

Zach rubbed his temples, then turned to him. "All right, Becker,"
he said. "Enough."

Eddie hesitated. "You're . . . not going to kill me?"

Zach cast a pointed look at the gun he'd just fired into the
ground. Obviously if he'd planned to kill Eddie, he'd already be dead.

"Do you work for Doyle Murphy?" Becker asked.

He couldn't even manage a humorless laugh. "No." And
pretending to, faking the phone call, losing Fahey in traffic—none of
it had helped. Zach climbed to his feet again. "But I really am taking
you to the FBI."

Eddie glanced down at the handcuffs, obviously not sure what
this meant for his future. "I can't go to jail."

"I suggest you start talking, then."

"I was on the jury at Murphy's trial. One of Doyle Murphy's guys
talked to Laura—found her at the hospital on a treatment day. She
told me about it during a family visit. We were close to bankruptcy
with the cancer." Eddie's voice grew pleading. "You've got to under-

stand."

Oh, Zach understood a thing or two about the lengths you'd go to for the person you loved. And even that hadn't been enough.

"So . . . can I go?"

This time, Zach did laugh. "I'm taking you downtown."

"You're still arresting me?"

Zach hauled Eddie to his feet—not that it was hard. The man couldn't weigh a hundred pounds. "Let's put it this way: I'm saving you. You do not want to see what happens if you make Doyle Murphy angry."

Eddie hung his head. "We needed the money—we needed the treatments. I could . . . I could still lose her."

Zach tried to ignore the sucker punch those words carried. He focused instead on the logistics of getting Eddie downtown. He still didn't want to mess with folding down the driver's seat of the Cougar to stuff Eddie in the back seat. He walked Eddie around the car to the passenger seat again.

"I don't understand," Eddie said. "Am I under arrest or not?"

"Well, I'm taking you in. But if you talk, you might be able to get a deal."

Hope sparked in Eddie's eyes. "You can give me a deal?"

"I'm not the one who makes deals. But I can guarantee that it's going to look a lot better for your case if you walk in to report what Murphy did." Zach settled Eddie in the passenger seat and walked around to the driver's side.

He'd come too close to the line this time, and he knew it. He should have talked to X, reported Murphy's demand, anything. And none of it had done Molly any good.

His phone buzzed in his pocket, and Zach pulled it out. Xavier calling.

Oh boy. "Hey."

"Do you have her?" X answered.

"No."

Xavier grunted, as if this was as much of a hit for him as for Zach. "Well," X said, "we're at Claire Murphy's, waiting on the OnStar location from her Cadillac. Heard anything from Reyes?"

Zach leaned against that gold-flecked paint job. "Yeah, we got something, but I'm not sure how much it's going to help us with Molly."

"Well?"

"Remember how Lehrman copped to something with a juror? We found the guy, and I'm bringing him in to throw himself on the mercy of the court."

Xavier gave a low whistle. "That's impressive—but not helpful for Molly, huh?"

"No. Oh, and I ran into Sam Fahey. Seems he's helping Murphy."

"Well, let's check out his assets, then."

"Bring him in, too." Zach's call-waiting beeped. He checked the number: Reyes. "Got another call."

"Murphy again?"

"No, the tech." Zach clicked over to the other call. "Yeah?"

"Agent Saint—let's see. We've got the background on Sam Fahey you wanted, the OnStar location and the cell phone location. What do you want first?"

Hopefully Doyle Murphy's phone and Claire Murphy's car would be at the same place. "Cell phone, OnStar, then Fahey."

"Okay, the cell phone we pinned down on or very close to I-57 in Washington Heights. You want the GPS coordinates?"

Doyle's neighborhood. Zach tapped his fist on his forehead. "Tell me the rest and I'll tell you what I need."

"Yeah, okay, uh, the OnStar location came back. The nearest big intersection is Western and 119th."

Claire Murphy's car was in the parking lot of her building or not too far away—and Doyle Murphy was either on his way there or leaving again. But not in Claire's car.

They'd missed him. Xavier and another agent were right there in his apartment and Doyle had ditched his car maybe twenty feet from his building without any of them knowing.

"And Sam Fahey was in prison until about six months ago. When he got out, his family moved across town. We don't have any hits on his rap sheet since then, not even a parking ticket."

If Fahey was trying to straighten his life out, helping Doyle Murphy with a hit shouldn't be on his agenda. "Great."

"So, which coordinates do you want?"

"None of them."

"Oh, okay." Before Zach ended the call, Reyes piped again. "Oh, there's one more thing."

"Yeah?"

"Permission came down from the Marshals, or whoever—you can call Cally Lonegan. But they want you to do it from here."

Zach pushed off the Cougar and opened his door. "I'll be there in ten."

Miles ignored Molly's unwavering glare, though he had to admit the heat of her stare did raise the temperature a few degrees.

He'd put her in her place soon.

His phone chimed with a message and Miles read the screen. A text from Sam Fahey.

Lost him in traffic, but heard the gunshots, the text read. Attached was a photo of Saint hauling Becker across the street in cuffs. Couldn't have staged it better.

He glanced back up at Molly. This ought to break her. He stood. "You want to know who's really in charge here?"

Molly sucked in air, but stayed cool. "Not interested."

"Oh, I think you will be." Miles crossed the room to hold his cell in front of her face.

She turned away, acting like she really wasn't interested.

She was worse than his teenager, and he didn't have to put up with any attitude from a woman in handcuffs. "Look or I'll make you look, if I have to break your neck."

Molly fixed a glower first on him and then the phone. He watched her for any response. The tiniest flicker of confusion—doubt—crossed her face.

She steeled herself and met Miles's eyes. "He arrested someone?" she said. Her tone said, *and your point is?*

"That what that looks like to you?"

"Obviously." Molly shifted away from him, making the bed frame protest loudly.

If she wasn't getting his message, he was going to drive the point home with a sledgehammer. "Hey, I tried to be nice to you," he started, totally reasonable. "You're the one that pushed me. I would've let you go along dreaming your happy little dreams that your knight in shining armor was coming to rescue you, and that you two would ride off into the sunset and live happily ever after. I would've let you die happy—I even tried to feed you—but no." He let his anger seep into his voice. "You had to push me, call me stupid, say I'm a pawn. Well, who's the pawn now?"

For only a second, Molly's gaze shifted back to the phone he was holding. She was doubting.

Time for the real blow. "I did you a favor," Miles repeated, towering over her. "You almost married him. Really dodged the bullet there. Unlike this guy."

She focused her attention on the corrugated wall. She had to understand what he meant, but he was going to relish explaining it anyway. "You know what happened next, right? You want to see the next photo? It's not pretty."

"I don't believe you."

"Want to talk to Sam Fahey? He was there."

She angled her head to peer at him from the corner of her eye, doubting him—but doubting herself, too.

It was definitely working. "Soon the whole Bureau's going to be after your fiancé. All I have to do is set it up to seem like he killed you, too."

Miles strolled back across the room and settled into his metal folding chair like it was a cozy recliner. His final, wordless message was loud and clear: *I'm not going anywhere.*

Zach left Eddie Becker to be questioned by agents from organized crime and sent the keys to the Cougar to impound before he headed down to Reyes's cubicle. On the way, he sent the latest coordinates for Murphy's phone to Xavier. He didn't mention that Doyle had ditched the car right under X's nose.

He stopped outside the lab. There had to be someone else out there with a stronger lead. Novak and Jackson were supposed to pick up Sam Fahey. Maybe he'd gotten back fast enough they'd caught up with him. He could check in with them.

Before he could find their number, his phone rang. Doyle Murphy calling.

He was actually going to give Molly back? "Where is she?" he answered.

"You know, I was thinking."

Uh oh.

"I need a little more proof that you did what I asked."

"What do you want, Becker's head?" Zach kicked himself. He shouldn't suggest something he absolutely could not deliver, and he wasn't supposed to know Eddie Becker's name.

"Eh, I'll settle for a hand."

"Look, I did it. You heard it. Where are we meeting?"

"Meeting?"

"Uh, yeah—remember, I do this for you, you give Molly back to me?"

Murphy laughed. "You're forgetting a couple steps here. We're only getting started."

His stomach tightened. It'd taken him too long to decide—and undecide—and decide what to do the last time. What more could he ask? "We had a deal. I want her back."

"Then do what I say."

"Without any proof she's alive since, what, nine? I killed a man for you—for her." He steeled himself and hung up the phone.

An analyst walking by whirled on him, wide-eyed. "Case," Zach gritted out.

The analyst backed away slowly, still staring at him.

Zach walked into the tech lab, second-guessing himself with every step.

Even if he wasn't going along with Murphy's demands, antagonizing the man who had Molly wasn't smart.

But pushing Murphy right might set him on edge enough to force his hand, or to force him to make a mistake.

Or so Zach hoped—and prayed.

He reached Reyes's cubicle as she lifted the phone. "Ready, Agent Saint?"

"Let's do this."

The tech dialed. "You know, rumor has it the SAC personally intervened to get this information without a court date pending."

"I doubt the Marshals are trying to make this difficult on purpose. Not like they want to keep us from saving our agent."

"Yeah, but there's all this red tape, and they have to 'evaluate the necessity,' and these things take—hello? One moment." She looked up at Zach. "It's for you."

He took the phone. "Cally?"

"Father—I mean, Special Agent Saint. You need something?"

"Not calling to check in, Cal."

"Yeah. Doyle giving you trouble?"

"He's taken—" How did saying this out loud still hurt after a lifetime of searching? Zach pressed past the pain. "—a hostage. Making demands."

"Well, I don't know what you want me to do. Not like I can talk him down or anything."

"No, but maybe there's something we missed. Somewhere he might be holding her?"

Cally was silent a moment. "You know, there was one thing that he was real particular about. Said I was the only one he trusted with it. I told the attorney, but she didn't ask about it at the trial."

"Think it got lost in the shuffle?" Or had Doyle Murphy gotten to the AUSA—Jill—too? Zach made the *gimme* gesture at Reyes for pen and paper.

"Dunno. It was called . . . oh, man . . . Romane Enterprises." He spelled it for Zach. "Only had a couple things under that shell. Said Miles Hennessy tipped him off to the properties, but he didn't want Miles to get a big head 'cause he followed his advice."

Zach gave the paper with the shell company name to Reyes. They should be able to find the properties—and maybe Reyes was familiar with how to trace shell companies back to their real owners. "Thanks, Cally. Anything else you can think of?"

"Not right off. Most everything else I got asked about at the trial. That one stuck out 'cause they didn't."

"Cally, you're a lifesaver. Really."

"Thanks, Father—Agent Saint."

"Thank *you*. Call your handlers if you remember anything else. That second—got it?"

"Got it. Take care."

"Agent Saint," Reyes called once he'd hung up, tapping her monitor. "We got two warehouses in the Near South Side."

"That's it?"

"Sorry. We can keep searching, check any other records for the names of the officers, you know."

"Sure." Zach pulled up the addresses on his phone: two warehouses half a block apart. They'd driven past that area half a dozen times today. It was maybe ten minutes from where they'd found the cell phone.

Had Murphy been running them in circles all day to taunt them once he finally revealed how close they'd come so many times?

Wouldn't put it past him.

But these warehouses were also less than half a mile from where he and Molly had arrested Grace Canavan. That could have been what her clue meant.

Zach turned to Reyes. "Great work—again. Keep it up."

She saluted and got right back to work on her computer.

On his way out, Zach texted the warehouse addresses to Walker and Roberts. They replied before he reached the garage: they were less than fifteen minutes away.

Zach could be there in ten.

And hopefully Molly would be there already.

D OYLE WAS STILL PRACTICALLY DANCING when he finally got his food at yet another McDonald's. Enough cheeseburgers to feed half a dozen teenage boys ought to make Miles happy.

It wasn't far back to the warehouse. He made the routine check of his rearview on the final approach. As he turned away from the mirror, he saw someone turn down the street behind him. A silver Subaru.

Middle of the day. On a weekday.

Could be someone coming back from lunch.

Doyle repeated that logic while sweat prickled down his neck. Was the Father this good?

Impossible.

But he did know Miles was working with him. The guy could have tracked down Miles's properties in the area.

Another car followed the first onto the street, this one a maroon SUV.

Doyle tried to drive "casual," passing the warehouse. The Subaru and the SUV followed him.

Even if it was him—and a posse—the Father couldn't know it was Doyle in Terry's Lincoln.

His palms slipped on the steering wheel as he made a right onto the street after the warehouse. If they weren't following him, they wouldn't take that right. He'd lose them, and he could swing around through the back alley behind the warehouse, safe.

The Subaru and the SUV didn't appear around the corner behind him. Doyle pulled into the alley behind the warehouses, still making the effort to appear totally casual. In case they actually were following him, he rolled down the narrow street until he reached the back of a warehouse half a block past Miles's, one neither of them owned. He pulled into an open garage bay and parked out of sight from the alley.

He shut his car door as quietly as possible and waited in the silence. Was it his imagination, or did he hear shouts of "FBI"?

Doyle slipped to the front of the warehouse to peer out the front windows. The building was set back from the sidewalk enough for him to see half a block down the street. The sedan and SUV he'd seen before were parked in front of the warehouse two buildings away. The opposite direction of Miles's. Two men were getting out of the SUV.

As he watched, a third car rolled up behind them, a white Hyundai. Two men and a woman got out—including the African-American agent who'd interrogated him that morning.

Finally, the driver of the Subaru got out.

The Father.

He really *was* that good.

Zach signaled for the other five agents to circle up. They obeyed, a couple still strapping on their vests.

"Doyle Murphy owns two properties on this block, this one—" He pointed to the squat, khaki warehouse at their end of the long block. "—and the other two buildings further down. We're entering armed, fast and *silent*." Kind of moot when they'd pulled up right on the street, but if Molly was in there, she was probably keeping them too busy to sit around staring out the window.

The mere thought that Molly could be right here was a shot of adrenaline to his heart—and his hopes. He barely managed not to grin as he doled out assignments for the first warehouse—not exactly easy without having seen the inside.

"Do not shoot until you confirm the target," he reiterated at the end of the instructions. "We have an agent in there."

And if he got her back now, they could still make it to their wedding.

If Molly was okay.

Of course she was. She had to be.

"Ready?" Zach asked.

The five agents nodded, splitting up into their groups for the entry.

"Let's go."

Molly jerked out of her heat-and-trauma-induced stupor when Doyle burst into the corrugated tin cell. "Miles, we've got company."

"Who?" Hennessy asked.

Doyle glanced at her. She leaned forward, hope filling her chest like helium.

Doyle lifted both eyebrows at Hennessy. As if she couldn't understand what that meant.

Hennessy snagged Doyle's sleeve and dragged him to the main warehouse.

In the thick hush that followed, Molly barely drew a breath—which was a reprieve from the musty sludge that passed for air in here. Could it be Zachary? Was she nearly free?

She could almost taste the relief, though her tongue filled her mouth like so much cotton. It was over. She could get water, food, a shower, air-conditioning. They might even make it to the temple in time.

Hope continued to expand inside her so fast it was nearly too much for her to bear after what she'd been through.

Could this really be over?

She forced herself to slow her breathing. Perhaps this ordeal was almost over. But she didn't have to sit here and wait for Zachary or anyone else to find her.

Miles was gone. This was her chance. She looked down at the safety pin on her drawstring. Time to get it.

Molly focused her attention on her arms. She couldn't move her hands anymore, and the circulation had slowed up to her elbows. Careful not to make the plastic straps scrape against her skin, she tried to rotate her wrists. The sweat between the bands and her skin made it easier to manipulate her arms, though they were mostly asleep.

The stress of twisting her wrists brought streaks of pain with the blood returning to her arms. Moving from her shoulders, she wriggled to help the circulation flow until she could wiggle her fingers.

Molly dug her fingernails into her palms as hard as she could, hoping the pain would stimulate her circulation more. It barely registered as pressure and pins and needles.

"Come on, come on," she murmured to herself, rocking from side to side on the mattress. Finally the numbness gave way to prickling that gave way to searing pain—and she had full control of her arms.

Now to get that safety pin.

Miles waited until they were well clear of the container door before he addressed Doyle. "You're overreacting. What, did you see some cars drive by?"

"No, not—"

He waved away the concern. "Then we're fine. Now where's our food?"

Doyle grabbed his shoulders and shook him. "Why are you thinking of food? *They are right outside.*" He pointed with fervor at the front of the building.

No. They couldn't really be here. He wasn't going to get caught. Right?

Miles shook off a nagging doubt along with Doyle's hands. He grabbed Doyle and started toward the front of the building. "Show me, then."

He obeyed, and Miles trailed behind.

Was Doyle this stupid? Not only had he led the FBI here—there was no other way they could have found them—but then he'd gone and announced it in front of Molly. That ham-fisted attempt to censor himself to keep Molly in the dark. As if she couldn't figure that much out?

He'd seen her eyes light up at the "veiled" message. Miles wanted to reach out and squelch that hope.

And he would, as soon as he walked back into that room. "They" couldn't be here. Wasn't like the FBI knew he was involved. Wasn't like they could track this place down that fast. It was held by a shell of a shell of a shell company. It'd take them days to dig that deep. Weeks.

Even if Doyle were a big enough idiot to lead them here, they couldn't know which building, right? "Tell me you didn't drive straight in with whoever it was following you."

"Give me a little credit. I went around the back and I parked in a warehouse down the block."

They reached the front windows, and Miles stood on tiptoe to see over the high ledge. Three cars lined the street, a few buildings down.

He should recognize almost any car brought in here. His men— his crew and those who would soon be his, anyway—owned most if not all of these buildings. And he didn't know these cars.

But it didn't take three carloads of FBI agents to search a vacant building. And it couldn't be them. "Doyle, it's three cars. It's nothing to worry about. Maybe they want to rent—"

"I saw him."

Miles made a valiant effort to ignore the sinking in his gut. "Who?" Like he really had to ask.

"The Father."

"Here." Again, no need to ask.

Doyle nodded.

Okay. Now it was time to worry.

MILES DIDN'T REALIZE HOW LONG HE'D BEEN STARING, clenching his teeth, when the agents emerged at last from the tan warehouse down the street, Saint bringing up the rear. He could finally release his jaw.

"See?" Doyle hissed.

Miles made a cutting motion across his throat. The six agents huddled together for a discussion.

Could they be coming to this building next?

No. He hadn't planned for that. Something he hadn't planned for? Outside the realm of possibility.

He'd been so careful. What had gone wrong?

"Did you turn off your phone?" Miles asked. In his peripheral vision, Miles saw Doyle nod. After a moment, Doyle pulled out his burner phone and offered it to Miles. Off. Battery out.

"Your other phone?"

"Off."

Miles frowned. "Doesn't Claire's car have OnStar?"

"Claire's car is at home."

"You know they could have put a tracker on your car."

Doyle waved, all too casual. "Not your concern."

Not his— Miles pinched the bridge of his nose, trying to allay the headache mushrooming behind his eyes. "I can't believe this." He fixed a steel glare on Doyle. "You led them right to us. They'll be here any second."

"It's got to be a coincidence. My car is clean."

Miles peered over the dusty ledge again. The FBI agents' huddle was breaking up. They were getting ready to move. He steeled him_self. If they came this way, there wasn't enough time to move his car and Doyle's. He glanced back—but Doyle's car wasn't anywhere in sight.

"We're going to have to do her now, aren't we?" Doyle murmured.

No way. Doyle didn't make that call—but he couldn't know that. "I thought you wanted to make the guy suffer. Make sure he really missed his wedding—reception too. Bring him as low as you could before you taunted him with that last hope."

"Yeah, but I don't think we have a whole lot of options here." Doyle leveled him with a sensible expression. "If everything else goes wrong, that's the one thing that has to go right."

He was right, of course. Miles couldn't leave a witness—someone who would identify him to Saint or anybody else. Doyle would keep his mouth shut—that was part of their deal. He thought he'd get enough information to hang Cally Lonegan.

But Molly—there wasn't anything he could give Molly to convince her not to mention him.

Other than a bullet to the head.

"We should get their attention." Doyle was already rising on his toes, as if ready to signal out the window. "We'll set the timetable, at least."

Miles grabbed Doyle's wrist to keep him from waving to the agents. "Oh, they'll come on our timetable," Miles murmured.

How was he going to get them out of this? How was he going to get *himself* away from here, safe?

The plan had to change.

The six agents started down the street—away from their building.

Miles relaxed a fraction. His plan was still intact. He was still in control.

"We gotta call them back." Doyle checked with Miles and the

SAINTS & SINNERS

street, back and forth, as if uncontrollably concerned that their one and only opportunity to get themselves killed was slipping through their fingers.

The realization hit Miles like a bag of cement. Although Saint had shot Doyle eighteen months ago, had killed a man for him today, Doyle still didn't comprehend the "Father" would kill him before he'd let Doyle harm Molly.

And a gun battle with six armed agents—all in bulletproof vests—couldn't end well for anyone in that room. Getting caught in the crossfire of Doyle's blaze of glory was not his idea of escaping the jail time that would surely follow kidnapping a federal agent.

"They'll come back. You think they're going to walk back to headquarters?"

Doyle accepted the logic, placated. Of course they'd come get their cars.

Miles swallowed an impatient sigh. How had this moron survived this long? He backed away from the window to pace and plot aloud. "All right, we need to think this through. If they're not here because they're tracking you, it seems like pretty long odds they'd come down to take in the sights."

"You think?" Doyle muttered something under his breath.

Sarcasm. Just what he needed from this idiot. Miles again tamped down his irritation. "Anything else that could've brought them here? Have you called anybody?"

"Only Claire and my lawyer, and those were mostly on an emergency line."

Oh great. "An emergency line? Doyle, they've got to be—"

"No, there's no way they can track this number. Out of state, registered in another name, burner phone, battery off, everything. Miles, I'm telling you, they're not tracking me."

Well, something certainly wasn't tracking. "Did you talk to anybody else who might own a warehouse down here?"

Doyle pulled up short. "No, I haven't talked to anybody. But . . ."

191

He peered out the window again. Miles looked in time to see the last agent disappear into a building half a block down.

"But what?"

"You know how you said this area was a great investment? Low traffic, easy access, off the beaten trail, but not too far?"

Miles nodded slowly. What had the idiot done?

"Well, I was thinking, I could use an extra property or two. You know, for storage."

He buried his face in his hands and finally released that waiting sigh. "You didn't."

"But—listen—they couldn't know. It's stashed real deep. Only one person knew about it."

"Who?"

"Cally."

Miles grabbed Doyle's shoulders. "You mean the rat that testified against you in your trial? Why didn't you tell me?" Miles shook the taller man as best he could.

"These places didn't come up at trial, Miles. They weren't in any of the papers or the filings. They were my only asset that wasn't frozen. The government didn't know then. They couldn't know, unless . . ."

"They talked to Cally," Miles finished.

"I want him dead."

Although Miles never had any intention of following through on that part of his promise, he silently echoed the sentiment. If Cally holding out on this one piece of information brought his brilliant plan to ruin, the rat would have to watch his back.

Molly stared at the safety pin. It still dangled at the end of the drawstring, taunting her.

With the feeling back in her fingers, every little movement reminded her that her wrists were already rubbed raw. Contorting herself to get at the drawstring was going to hurt.

She splayed her fingers and pressed the backs of her hands against her lower spine. She slowly leaned onto her back, trying to keep her hands in a usable position, and trying not to chafe her wrists on the plastic bands any more.

Molly pondered the ceiling a second to determine the best way to proceed. Rolling onto her left side, she maneuvered into a half-upright position. The contortions weren't comfortable by any stretch—or with any stretch—but they did let her pull her hands up around the right side of her waist.

The back of her left hand rested against the waistband of her pants, her palm and fingers free. She turned her wrist to get her fingers into the fabric at her waist—they tangled in the T-shirt.

Molly rested against the bed. Had she really thought she could reach all the way around to her drawstring?

If only the drawstring would naturally fall upward.

Or she could use gravity to her advantage. If she could roll over, she might be able to get her hands in the right spot underneath her waist. The drawstring might dangle down for her to catch.

She checked over her shoulder. There was enough room for her to roll over. The loose drawstring was long enough that it might get caught behind her if she attempted this, but she had to try.

Using her shoulders and her free foot as leverage, Molly flipped onto her other side—on top of her hand. Her waist landed on the box that connected the pair of PlastiCuffs, the straps cutting into her wrists. She could barely control her fingers through the pain, her weight on her wrists and the stress against the plastic bands.

And the drawstring hadn't whipped around far enough. The safety pin was resting on her high hip.

If she tried to maneuver her hands to the top again, she'd only jostle the pin off her hip, and then she'd have to start all over.

She managed an awkward shimmy to shake the safety pin off her hip. The drawstring swung down, the pin landing on the mattress—just out of reach.

No way. She was not giving up that easily, not now. Raising herself into the half-upright position again, Molly pushed her hands as far forward as she could. Her shoulders screamed against the movement, and she fell to the bed after only a second—but it was long enough. Far enough. She hooked one finger around the drawstring, pulled it into her fist.

The second it was secure, she flipped back onto her other side. Still holding the drawstring, she pushed up on an elbow to sit up.

Molly tilted her head back and blew out a breath. She rolled her shoulders and her wrists as much as she could without letting go of the string. The hard part was over. She hoped.

After allowing herself that brief rest, she pulled her hands back around to her waist so she could see what she was doing. She slid her hand down to the end of the drawstring, to the safety pin. It took her two—three attempts to open it.

She pulled the pin off the drawstring and passed the pin to her right hand. She couldn't possibly do this with her left.

Molly peered over her shoulder to guide her fingers. She laid the open safety pin against one of the yellow straps, the point toward the black plastic cube, the retaining block that held the ratcheting mechanism and connected the pair.

All she had to do was get the pin between the strap and the ratchet teeth—without dropping it. She pinched the straps with her other hand, pressed her right thumb against the spring of the safety pin and eased it toward the retaining block.

The tip of the pin met the first ratchet teeth and stopped.

Well, did she expect this to be easy? Angling her thumb to hold the pin with her nail, Molly pushed harder against the pin and tugged on the plastic strap to force the point into the right position.

Finally, it slid into the retaining block alongside the strap. She twisted her wrist and pulled against the strap—at last it pulled free.

She pulled her arms in front of her, flexed her wrists, circled her shoulders. Relief and elation washed over her. She was free. Zachary was here, somewhere, and if he wasn't, she could surely find a way to contact him.

Molly left the other plastic strap in place and glanced at the shackle on her ankle. Without keys or picks or a shim or a hairpin— handcuffs were one of the only locks that really were pickable with that makeshift tool—she wasn't going anywhere soon.

Perhaps she didn't have to free herself from that. If Doyle was right and Zachary was here, she only had to get far enough to make sure he could hear her from the street. Even in her present state, she could drag the bed that far; it couldn't be that heavy. It might even have wheels if it folded up.

If he was still here.

If he'd come at all.

Shaking off the thought, Molly stood on her free foot and reached for the head of the bed.

It didn't budge.

She dropped to the floor to find the problem. Bolts. The bed was bolted to the corrugated wall.

Molly scrabbled at the bolt heads. Perhaps if the nuts were on this side of the wall, she might have stood a chance of loosening them. But what was she going to use against the flat heads of these bolts? The PlastiCuffs?

Was she supposed to sit here and wait for Zachary, so?

195

Zach paused in searching the second warehouse. This would be the last corner of Doyle Murphy's last warehouse. There weren't any other places to check—no other leads. No other information.

Maybe no other hope.

And this corner held none of that for Zach. He watched Xavier scan the corner. They'd already identified that once again, no one was in the warehouse. Xavier was searching for anything, any place they might hide her. Or her body.

X turned back, signaling the all clear to Zach. Yet again, there was nothing—no trace evidence, no hair, no scrap of clothing, no blood trail and no Molly.

Zach clamped down on his frustration. What could they have done with her? Why couldn't he outdo them this time? He wiped the sweat from his brow—Molly had to be burning up in this heat—and wheeled away from Xavier.

"It's the last corner, Z." Was that resignation in Xavier's voice?

He was right. This was another dead end. Once again, their options were dwindling.

They couldn't give up, not now. Not yet. There was Sam Fahey. Miles Hennessy. She was still out there, she might still be waiting for them to rescue her—heck, she might have already escaped, just waiting for him to check his phone and come pick her up.

Xavier started for the door they'd come in.

Walker and Roberts joined them in front of the building. They stared up at the brick warehouse, squinting into the just-past-noon sun.

His best—and that of a dozen other agents and counting—still wasn't good enough to beat one mobster who was not that bright?

"We'll find something." Xavier clapped his shoulder.

Zach only nodded. He attempted to believe his boss, but that effort was failing as fast as his hope.

20

MOLLY STRAINED INTO THE SILENCE. Nothing. Nothing had changed for endless minutes.

She was alone, hands free, but still shackled to the bed. Doyle said they had company. But it had been quiet too long. No one was searching for her.

It was up to her.

Somehow, these seconds seemed longer than any others of the day. But still, after what felt like hours, no footsteps. No shouting.

No Zachary.

Was Doyle wrong, then? He'd never struck her as the oaf Hennessy seemed to think he was—though she would admit that his plans hadn't gone at all how he'd expected.

What if they'd been arrested, but refused to tell where she was?

Then Zachary would search for her. He'd scour every square foot of every kitchen, container and closet for a square mile before he'd give up.

But eventually, wouldn't he have to give up?

He wouldn't. Not until he was sure she was dead. She had another three—two and a half—days until he had to believe that. That was enough time to find her, especially if he'd been able to recruit help.

What was she saying? He was friends with the SAC. They could have half the Bureau on the case.

Despite her unwavering faith in Zachary, the image from

Hennessy's mobile phone again sprang to her mind. What was happening in that picture? It certainly appeared to be what Hennessy thought: some sort of less-than-legal arrest.

What if this was part of the ransom? Would he do that to get her back?

How could she face him again if he'd paid her ransom with his integrity?

Molly shook off the thought. That was a distraction. She had to focus on survival first. He had to be close.

And if he wasn't? She had to be prepared for that second possibility: that Hennessy would walk back through that door any second, his crisis averted.

Her hope squelched.

But eventually, their plan was to bring Zachary here—to kill her and then him.

She had to be prepared for that, too. Prepared to die—and prepared to find some way to exploit the situation to her advantage.

Once again, Molly scanned the corrugated metal enclosure. They would probably unshackle her. They didn't know her hands were free, so she could use the element of surprise. Where would they set this up, if they meant to kill her in the container? What could she use in that area?

She identified the most likely staging area, near the table in the middle of the room.

Molly tried to work through specific scenarios, but the lack of water—or the very real possibility that she wouldn't survive the day—seemed to be fogging her brain.

If she couldn't think clearly, she couldn't survive.

No one was here. Zachary wasn't coming to rescue her. She couldn't get out of this shackle. Her own faculties were failing her.

Impossible. Hennessy couldn't win. Zachary had to be here. She had to let him know she was here, too.

Shouting might not be enough, and it would only dehydrate her further. Hennessy and Doyle might not be coming back at all, and she had to survive as long as possible.

Molly lay back on the bed to pound a steady beat against the corrugated wall.

Help was coming.

She clung to that logic and that dying ember of hope as she methodically beat the metal wall with her foot.

They'd come eventually.

Miles again craned his neck to look out the window. The FBI agents were coming back down the street. To get back to their cars, they'd have to pass right in front of this building.

All he had to do was keep Doyle from screwing this up.

As if to test him already, Doyle began to raise an arm as if to flag the agents down again. Miles grabbed his sleeve. "No, don't."

"What?"

"We have to wait. We have to find the right time. The right way."

"Listen, Miles, if they're coming in here anyway, we need to make sure we have the upper hand."

Miles clamped down on a rising sense of outrage. Was Doyle seriously about to lecture *him* on strategy?

"If we get to set the terms, we're the ones who control the whole meeting. If we call *them* in, instead of letting them find us, then we'll control the whole interaction."

"Yeah," Miles cut off the rest of Doyle's "lesson." "But we didn't count on him having backup handy. Throws a major wrench in your plan?" He managed not to cringe at calling it "Doyle's" plan.

"I guess. . . ." Doyle peered out the window again.

"What are they doing?"

"They're almost to their cars."

Miles waited a beat. "Are they looking at any of the buildings?"

Doyle squinted. "Yeah, I think they're doing a visual check, but they're not coming—oh, wait."

Miles almost didn't dare to look, but he had to. He rose up on tiptoe for a better view.

They were coming. They'd already passed this building, but now the six FBI agents had doubled back and were coming down the sidewalk again, staring at the cement.

Tracking someone?

No, Miles and Doyle had always come in through the back, even when Miles was setting everything up over the last few weeks. And it wasn't like these agents would find an incriminating tire tread on the sidewalk.

What were they hunting for?

Now in the lead, Saint looked up—and straight at their window. Miles clamped onto Doyle's shoulder to keep him from shrinking back. "No sudden moves," he murmured. "He can't see us."

Yeah, that was a complete bluff, but he was sure about the no sudden moves—either of them ducking would be a flash of light or color that would be sure to draw Saint's attention.

Despite their efforts, Saint didn't lower his gaze. He picked up his pace.

The plan really was going to have to change.

Miles's heartbeat roared in his ears. He had to be ready for this. He had to control this situation to his advantage still.

Of course he could. Saint scanned the other side of the street. Miles took that split-second opportunity to pull Doyle out of sight.

If Saint was coming back, had he seen them or heard something?

No. Molly was quiet. They'd been whispering.

As if in response, a dull thud sounded from the warehouse. From the container.

They had to do something, or Saint was going to find them unprepared, out here, watching for him.

"Let's get to your car, Doyle. Now."

Doyle crouch-walked toward the garage bays at the back of the warehouse. He looked ridiculous—and slow. Wasn't like Saint could see in those high windows from down the street. Miles followed, swallowing a groan. "Hurry up."

Doyle led him out the back. They snuck down the block, careful not to be seen from the street, to the warehouse where Doyle had parked. Next door to the first warehouse the FBI agents searched.

Inside the warehouse, Miles followed Doyle around a corner and reached—his wife's car?

"Why do you have Teresa's car?"

"I needed another one."

Miles clenched his jaw. "And you picked my wife's?"

"She knew we were doing something today. I figured she wouldn't miss it."

"You mean you just took it from her?"

"Of course not. I gave her the Cadillac."

Miles pressed his fingertips to his temples. This was not the distraction he needed while his plan was in flux. "So she traded with you?"

"Yeah. Come on." Doyle pulled out his keys.

"Hang on. Give me my wife's keys." Miles held out a hand, and Doyle gave up the keys.

He still needed a plan. Something that would tie up all the loose ends and get himself away clean, no witnesses.

And suddenly he knew exactly what he was going to do.

Miles checked the front of the warehouse. A large open area, one garage door missing.

He turned back to Doyle. "You're carrying, right?"

Doyle shot him an *of course* look, lifting his shirt to show the gun at his hip.

Perfect. "Come on."

Zach shook his head as he rounded the back of his car. "Listen, Walker, I just don't see it." He stripped off his vest and tossed it in the trunk next to his wedding gift for Molly. This delay was the last thing he needed.

The other agent, tall and rail thin, groaned. "It's not like my badge wandered off."

He clenched his fists, then willed himself to calm down before he slammed the trunk shut. "If you want to keep looking for it, that's fine, but we really have to get back—"

Gunshot.

Zach immediately ran in the direction of the fading echo, already drawing his weapon. No need to check with the other agents—they were all going in.

But were they too late?

They came even with the first building they'd searched without success. Zach hesitated, slowing a few steps as he passed.

As if to answer his question, a second gunshot cracked the air. A little farther down the block. He picked up speed again, though he couldn't pinpoint the building from that the fading echo.

Two shots. Were they trying to torture her, or make sure she was dead, or—?

No. He couldn't go there. Not yet.

He reached the second building they'd searched—and stopped. Miles Hennessy was running out of the warehouse next door, toward the street, hands in the air. Zach lifted his weapon and Xavier and Walker, the first to join him, did, too.

"Don't shoot!" Miles thrust his hands higher. "Don't shoot!"

Xavier was the first to respond. "Hands on your head!"

Miles obeyed.

"Face down on the ground."

He glanced at the gravel scattered on the cement, hesitating.

"On the ground, now!" Xavier approached him, holding his gun more firmly.

Miles slowly knelt, lowered himself into a prone position and interlaced his fingers behind his head.

Zach joined Xavier standing over Miles. "Where is she?"

"Where's who?"

"Molly! Special Agent Malone! Where is she?"

Miles lifted his head. "I don't—I don't know."

"Then who were you shooting at?"

"Doyle." Miles gaped at him, like he still couldn't believe what had happened. Xavier dropped a knee onto his back and Miles grunted. "He was going to kill me!"

"You just shot at Doyle Murphy?" Zach nodded toward the warehouse. "In there?"

"Yeah."

"Is he armed?"

"No." Miles gasped for air. "He's dead."

21

IMPOSSIBLE. Zach ran into the warehouse, weapon at the ready just in case. The man who had Molly couldn't be dead— he had to meet him, he had to hand her over.

Once Zach was through the open door, the first thing he saw was blood. Doyle lay in a creeping pool of dark blood. A semi-automatic lay next to him.

Zach ran to Doyle's body. He kicked Doyle's gun away, dropped to his knees, dropped his own gun.

He should check vitals, administer CPR or first aid—do something to stop this.

Zach grabbed Doyle's shoulders. "Where is she?" he demanded. "Where's Molly?"

Doyle's eyelids slid open—and he focused on Zach. Zach still had a chance to find out where she was, to find her.

"Where is she?" He shook Doyle.

"Miles," he wheezed. He coughed. Bloody spittle sprayed onto Zach's face.

"Where is Molly?"

His eyes slipped from Zach's, lost their focus. He drew in another ragged, wheezing breath.

Zach spotted the wound, below his heart. He grabbed the front of Doyle's shirt and ripped it open, sending buttons skittering across the floor. He searched for something to use as a compress—what, cardboard?—before he pressed Doyle's tattered shirt over the gaping wound and clapped a hand on top.

"Stay with me, Doyle." He pushed against the wound and warm, slick blood oozed between his fingers.

That was good. Meant his heart was still beating.

But Doyle's ribs didn't rise or fall. Zach pressed two fingers to Doyle's neck and prayed.

Was that a thready pulse? Or was that his own heartbeat in his fingers?

"Doyle!" He shook one shoulder. "Tell me where she is!"

But his pupils were set. His chest was still. Nothing.

Slowly, Zach pulled his hand from the wound. No gush of blood followed. He sank back onto the floor.

Doyle was dead. And somehow, he'd still won. Zach tapped a fist against his forehead—and realized too late that he would leave a mark there in blood.

Doyle's blood. Because he was dead. And Molly would be, too, soon. If she wasn't already.

Zach willed himself to stand, to walk out of the warehouse, to return to where Xavier was hauling Miles, now handcuffed, to his feet. When the man saw Zach approaching, Miles scrabbled as if to get away.

"Whoa there." Xavier jerked Miles back to where he stood, two feet closer to Zach. "Do you understand these rights?"

Miles still stared at Zach. "I want a lawyer."

Too bad. "Why did you do this?"

"Z, man, he invoked."

"Why did you kill him?" Zach demanded.

Miles searched for Xavier behind him. X pushed him a step forward—toward Zach. "You gotta understand," Miles said. "He was going to kill me! He had a gun on me, said if I didn't cooperate, he'd shoot me. The man's crazy—off the deep end."

"What did he want you to cooperate with?"

"I don't know—something about kidnapping a Fed."

Zach leaned over the shorter man. "Where is he holding her?"

"I don't know, he wanted me to take him somewhere—somewhere—"

Zach wasn't buying it. "Where?"

"I don't know!"

"Is it here?" He was shouting, but his self-control died with Doyle.

"No, he made me drive here to talk, and then he said we'd go somewhere else—"

Zach clenched his teeth. "So help me, Miles, if you don't start talking, I will—"

"It was something-lawn. Lawn-something."

"Oak Lawn? Chicago Lawn? West Lawn?" What else was there? "Lawndale?"

"I don't know!" Miles cowered back a step.

"That's the best you can do?" This could cost Molly's life.

Panic sparked in Miles's eyes. "He had a gun on me! I wasn't exactly paying attention to the details! He said he was going to kill—"

Zach cut off Miles's protests with a right hook to the jaw. Caught off guard, Xavier didn't grab Miles in time and he fell to the ground.

Xavier knelt by the handcuffed man, glaring up at Zach.

He didn't have to put the rebuke into words. Police brutality, interrogating him after he'd invoked his right to counsel?

Xavier shook his head and called to Walker and Roberts to drag Miles back to his feet and escort him to their waiting cars. Kent followed, casting wary glances at Zach.

Xavier folded his arms and stood there in silence for a long time. "Doyle's dead?"

"Yeah."

X didn't have to say anything else. Zach had ruined any chance of prosecuting the only person they could hold responsible.

And none of this was even Miles's fault.

Everything inside Zach's chest felt like it was disintegrating, a supernova collapsing into a black hole. X was right—who else could bear the blame—and the punishment—for this?

Only Zach.

And he would. He was never going to see Molly again.

It had been so long since the gunshots that Molly was beginning to doubt she'd heard them. They were far away—but close enough that she knew this might be her chance to be rescued, if anyone called them in.

She kicked the metal wall of her prison again. Her thigh ached, and her heel throbbed from countless kicks, but she couldn't give up. Not yet. Not while the hope in her chest was so palpable that it was hard to breathe around it.

How long could it take for a first responder to get here? For shots fired, ten or perhaps fifteen minutes, unless some sort of local crime wave was tying up police, or that type of call was commonplace in this neighborhood.

And how long had it been? Molly pounded the wall again.

The area had seemed almost abandoned when they drove in last night. Of course, most industrial parks weren't exactly hotspots after business hours, but this neighborhood was eerily silent—a stillness not of a break for the night, but of long-undisturbed neglect.

No one was around to report the gunfire.

If anyone had, and anyone responded, they would have arrived already—or she'd at least be able to hear the sirens. And if they weren't coming—

They weren't coming.

Molly's kicking slowed to a stop.

Miles let an FBI agent place a hand on his head as she guided him into the back of the SUV. Still smeared with Doyle's blood, Saint walked up and nodded for the nearest FBI agent to step aside. The other agent hesitated, searching for her supervisor.

"Let me ask him something." Zach said.

"But—"

"Now."

The animal need for protection from Saint clawed at Miles's throat. He steeled himself to not change his expression. Sure, he didn't want to be the man's punching bag again, but more than that, he had to keep Saint from getting too close to the truth.

The FBI agent who was supposed to be shielding Miles stepped aside. "Your funeral," she muttered.

Saint turned his steely stare to Miles. This couldn't fall apart now. What could he ask?

"Why did it take you so long?"

"What?"

"We heard one shot and started running. We were two-thirds of the way there before we heard the second. That's an awful long time between shots."

Miles gave him a helpless look.

"What'd he do, shoot at you, miss and just stand there, waiting for you to hit him?"

"No. I shot first."

Disbelief etched into Saint's features. "Self-defense, you said?"

"It was! The man had a gun on me."

"Then why did he let you get off the first shot, if he was really so set on killing you?"

Miles made a noise between a scoff and a sarcastic laugh. "Yeah, he watched me as I drew and fired." He shook his shoulders, rattling the cuffs, and focused on the middle distance. All he had to do was play this cool. It was the one weakness in the plan—and he could bluff Saint.

"Then what happened?"

"He checked on you guys for a second, I drew, I fired."

"And the second shot?"

Miles looked up at Saint. "He tried to shoot me."

"And what, he missed?"

"He'd been shot. I'm not going to fault the man for having poor aim while dying of a chest wound."

Saint scowled at him. "So if the techs test him for gunshot residue, it'll be positive?"

"Of course."

Saint spun on his heel and waved to the other agent. She slammed the door shut. Miles focused on his knees, trying to master the broken slump of a man who'd just been forced to kill his friend and mentor.

His lips tried to curl into a smile—but not now. Not yet. They had to get out of here—get him a lawyer—get him out on bail—before he could smile.

Though this was a greater coup than anything he'd planned.

Now Doyle would never cause him any trouble. The moron couldn't roll on him sometime down the line when he figured out Cally Lonegan was still alive and well, or when it suited him. And he couldn't do anything stupid to bring them any more unwanted attention.

This was going to get Sullivan's notice.

And the hope that he'd seen in Molly's face before they left—the hope that flared his temper—was echoed in Saint's eyes. When Miles said he didn't know where Molly was, that light died, like he was rubbing out a cigarette's last ember.

As long as they didn't decide to search the whole block, everything would be just fine.

Zach returned to where Xavier waited by the crime scene. "I called it in," Xavier said.

"Everything?" Zach hoped X would catch the drift.

"Oh no. That's your job." Xavier started for the cars, brushing past him without another word.

Zach slowly sank to his knees on the cement.

He had lost. And Doyle was right—this wasn't a ball game. This wasn't even a test-your-wits-against-a-criminal-mastermind case. This was gambling with the life of the woman he wanted to spend the rest of forever with. The woman he'd been in love with for a year and a half, since before he had any hope they could ever be together.

Now, they never would be.

And it was his fault. He wasn't willing to do what Doyle asked. He wasn't willing to sink as low as Doyle. If he had, he never could have looked Molly in the eyes.

But he wasn't sure what principles were worth if it meant Molly died.

Now no one on earth knew where she was, whether she was alive or dead.

No. If Doyle was trying to get Miles to work with him and it had to do with Molly, she still had to be alive.

Unless Doyle needed help moving her body.

Whether she was dead or alive, how could they possibly search everywhere "something lawn" before Molly became too dehydrated or hot to survive? In this heat, she wouldn't even have the normal seventy-two hours of survival time without water.

She'd been missing for probably fourteen hours, and they were back at square one. By the time they found her—*if* they ever found her—

Time had already run out.

He'd lost her.

Zach stayed there for what felt like years, reeling from the pain.

He registered the footsteps behind him a split second before the hand clapped on his shoulder. Xavier stood behind him, holding out a paper napkin. "Clean yourself up."

"Huh?"

Xavier pointed to his forehead. "The blood."

Zach accepted the napkin, which proved to be wet, and then X's hand to make it to his feet. "Take a picture first, just in case."

Xavier grabbed his phone. He snapped shots of Zach's bloodied face and palm. Zach scrubbed at his forehead and cheeks.

He knew what X was trying to tell him: they weren't giving up. But investigating Doyle's death still felt like defeat.

By the time he got to cleaning his palm, the first Evidence Response Team techs arrived on the scene. Xavier directed them to Zach. He led them into the warehouse. "Semi-automatic." He pointed to the black gun a few feet from Doyle's body. "It was over here by Doyle—Murphy when I came in."

"You disturbed the crime scene?" The tech shot him an evil look, as if this kind of rampant stupidity was par for the course, and yet the bane of her existence.

Did this woman have any idea what had happened here? What this meant to Zach?

He tried to hold back the anger that would follow that line of thinking—but no flame of anger came.

It was too late for anger to do him any good. Taking it out on this kid wasn't going to find Molly. Or bring her back.

Zach wiped his palm with the now-pink napkin. "He was still alive when I came in. I had to make sure he was disarmed."

The tech turned back to Doyle's body. "Here?" She pointed to a streak of blood leading away from the pool.

"Yeah."

"So what do we know?"

"Miles Hennessy shot him. Says it was in self-defense." Zach silently scoffed at himself. Still in suspicion mode, still grasping at straws. Pathetic. Why else would Miles kill his boss here, now? "We have him in custody."

"So, one shot fired?"

"No." Zach swiped at his palm again. "Two shots. After he was hit, Doyle shot from the floor. Missed."

The tech nodded, her blonde bob bouncing. "GSR test, then. Did you take custody of the other gun?"

"No. He was unarmed."

"So it has to be here, or . . ."

Or Miles was lying.

And, what, he'd thrown the bullet at Doyle?

Yeah, right.

Still, if Miles was lying about that, he could be lying about everything. Zach immediately began scanning the area. Pathetic though it might be, he let himself hope Miles knew more than he was letting on.

Hope? Not likely. The black hole in his chest didn't budge, but he started the typical grid search pattern anyway, starting by Doyle. No telling the exact trajectory the shot had taken, but the bullet had obviously entered from the front, and Doyle had probably fallen where he stood. The three Evidence Response Team techs fanned out on their own paths.

Their measured footsteps echoed through the warehouse, a hollow clock counting the seconds. This might be his last chance.

But . . . if there was only one gun in the whole warehouse, then

Miles was lying about self-defense. That left the possibility that he knew exactly where Molly was, no matter what he'd—

"Got a gun," one of the techs called.

Zach barely glanced in the direction of the camera flash. Everything seeped from him in a sigh. It was a long shot, and he knew that. But it was the last one he had.

If they needed to know anything else, they could call him. He strode from the building.

22

ZACH WAS STILL WIPING HIS PALM when he reached his car, though the napkin and the last of the blood had dried out long ago.

Doyle's wasn't the only blood on his hands.

No. This wasn't his fault. It was Doyle Murphy's fault.

But still—if he'd just done . . . *something* better, wouldn't he have saved Molly?

Frowning at himself, Zach threw the nearly dry napkin into the front seat of his car. Walker and Roberts had already left with Miles, and Kent had gone to Claire Murphy's apartment to tell her, to escort her downtown.

He didn't need the official ruling to know when Doyle died. Too soon.

This was supposed to be his wedding day—not the day he would have to face two gruesome deaths. Soon to be three.

Or maybe he'd never have to face Molly's death. Maybe they'd never find her body, and he'd never know for sure what happened to her. Doyle could've left her with someone to take care of her. She could've escaped. What if she just had amnesia?

What did he think this was, *The Bourne Identity*? Zach sank into the driver's seat and hit his forehead against the steering wheel. She wasn't wandering around with amnesia. If Doyle had someone to take care of Molly, he wouldn't have tried to force Miles to help him.

Wherever she was, Molly was alone and dying. Or maybe already dead.

He finally acknowledged the deep, physical ache piercing his chest. He didn't know what else to do but press his fist to his ribs, as if direct pressure could help the pain.

Doyle Murphy wasn't the only one with a gaping chest wound.

Miles acted the part of the deferential, defeated enemy as they pulled into the parking lot. The agents pulled him from the car as if they were more afraid of hurting him than him getting away. Not that he could attempt something like that—way to raise their suspicions.

No, for now, he was going to have to act like the man who'd been forced to kill his best friend. Broken. Vanquished.

The agents took his arms to lead him into the building. He kept his head down during the entire processing procedure, except when ordered to face the camera for the mug shot.

That throbbing black eye coming on should look good there.

After fingerprinting, photographs and the usual rigmarole, he was taken straight to a caged interview room. His lawyer, Mr. Cyrus, was escorted in. The guard left, and Cyrus settled in at the metal table. "Please don't tell me if you're guilty."

Wasn't like Miles had never been arrested before. "But—"

The lawyer held up a hand. "You know the drill: I can't let you lie on the stand, and I can't knowingly argue something false, so it's better if we—"

"It was self-defense."

"Oh?" Cyrus paused like he had to recalibrate his spiel.

"Yeah. Didn't they tell you?"

"Apparently not," Cyrus muttered. "Okay, well, an affirmative defense is going to be a little different, then. Of course we'll want to get you on the stand." Cyrus launched into a plan for the defense—something about highlighting how frightened Miles was at the point of the gun, and how terrible a person Doyle was.

The jury would eat it up. There wouldn't be a doubt in their minds, even without all the mistakes Saint had made in the case.

And it would be an amazing work of fiction.

Miles let the scene replay in his mind. He'd asked Doyle if he had his gun. Doyle drew his chromed-out revolver.

"Fire a warning shot," Miles said. "Draw them down here. Then when they get here, we'll lead them back to Molly—we have the upper hand."

"Yeah, but—"

"Hurry up! They're going to leave!"

Miles covered his ears and Doyle fired into the air. The shot echoed through the warehouse. "Wipe it down," Miles instructed.

Apparently, he was in a following-orders mode. Doyle obeyed, grabbing a handkerchief from his pocket and rubbing off any fingerprints.

Doyle held out the cleaned gun wrapped in the handkerchief to Miles. "That good?"

"Yep." He slipped the gun in his pocket, then drew his own weapon.

"Miles," Doyle said in a warning tone. "We're not trying to start a gunfight. Might as well put that away."

Miles contemplated his semi-automatic. "I guess you're right." He raised the weapon and pulled the trigger. The casing bounced across the cement floor. It wasn't as hard as he thought it would be.

"Wha?" Doyle wheezed. He gaped at the blood seeping across his shirt. "Miles?" He staggered back a step.

"Gotta have the upper hand." He pulled the handkerchief from his pocket and rubbed the prints off his semi-auto. Doyle collapsed backward.

Miles stooped to collect the casing with his fingernails to keep the scorching metal from burning his skin. Before the blood could begin to pool, Miles placed his gun in Doyle's hand, carefully applying his fingerprints to the black plastic of the grip and the metal of the slide, and dropped the casing next to his body. Once they traced this gun, Petrowski's murder would be a closed case, too, tying that last loose end to anybody but Miles.

He grabbed Doyle's gleaming silver gun from his pocket, sure to leave his own prints on it before dropping it a few feet away.

"Why?" Doyle choked out.

Miles didn't look back as he jogged into the sunlight—toward the approaching FBI agents.

"So," Cyrus concluded. "We should have a pretty solid case."

"Sounds good."

"In the meantime, I've been doing a little legwork since I got the call." He checked his watch, then stood and helped Miles to his feet. "We have an appointment with Judge Grant in a couple minutes."

"A judge? Are we already going to try to exclude my statements after I asked for a lawyer?"

"No, no, we couldn't possibly get to that this quickly. But I have a couple friends in the courthouse, and they got us the fastest arraignment time in Chicago history."

Miles smirked. "A lot of lawyers eager to help out a mobster?"

"No, but a whole lot of people downtown are happy to help out a man who killed one of the most dangerous mobsters in the city in self-defense."

Miles finally allowed himself a full smile. Cyrus was worth every penny.

And everything was going according to plan, or even better.

Zach pulled out his phone and automatically pulled up the day's weather report. It hardly mattered that it was 105° if there was no chance of finding her.

Zach leaned back against the headrest. It would take hundreds of agents to search "something-lawn." He'd already come up with at least four suburbs or neighborhoods with lawn in them, just off the top. Plus surrounding areas . . .

And hope bloomed in his chest again, its desperate roots mingling with the angry black hole still seething there.

If they had every law enforcement officer in the greater Chicago area searching for her, they still might not get to her in time. Between exposure and dehydration, she would die painfully and slowly—but not slowly enough to give them time to find her.

His heart could hope all it wanted, but his mind knew the truth.

Even if he couldn't hope to find her alive, he couldn't give up on finding her altogether. He couldn't give up on Molly. If the search needed manpower, he knew how to get it.

Zach paged through his phone for the SAC's number and called him.

"Tell me you have good news," Evans answered.

"Not really. Doyle Murphy has been shot by one of his henchmen."

"Is Murphy talking?"

Zach braced himself to admit it, again, how close he'd come and how far they still were. "He's dead. But the henchman said Murphy was trying to get him to go to her, in 'something-lawn.'"

"Where's that?"

"He didn't know. Could be Oak Lawn, Chicago Lawn, West Lawn, or anything. Guess we should start tracking down everything we can find."

"Absolutely. I'll get Sellars and Inouye to direct the teams personally."

Zach waited for the relief to come—but it didn't. "Thanks, sir."

"Andrea and I are praying for you. Both of you."

"Thanks, President." Bringing up Evans's church title at work was always odd, but in this context it seemed appropriate, for once.

Zach ended the call and put the car into park.

The tiny tendril of hope still fighting its way through the reality crowding into his chest just felt . . . wrong. This wasn't happening.

She was gone.

Zach hauled himself to his feet and trudged back to the crime scene, where Xavier was supervising the ERT techs. Two of the techs were busily labeling and photographing, while the third was collecting the evidence they'd gathered so far. The only things that really seemed pertinent were the guns, a handkerchief and a single casing.

Did Miles or Doyle carry around a handkerchief? Maybe. But it was odd enough to attract his notice.

He approached one of the techs, a woman with a blonde bob. "What can you tell me about the guns?"

"Not a whole lot." The tech shrugged. She picked up the semi-auto in its plastic bag. "This is the one we found closest to the body, the one you kicked away. You don't want to know the model and maker, do you?"

"Not really. Is that all you know?"

"Almost all. It smells like it was fired recently. Pretty heavy, so it's got plenty of ammo left." She grabbed the bag with the casing. "Found it in the blood pool."

"That would explain why it's red."

The tech pursed her lips. "Uh, yeah. Nine mil." She dropped the plastic bags back into her evidence case and pulled out the second gun, a shiny stainless steel revolver. "All the chambers are full, but we can't tell how many of them have been fired without opening the cylinder. Also smells recently fired."

"Any fingerprints?"

"Oh, we'd take care of that in the lab."

"Then let's go."

She raised her eyebrows an inch. "You mean, now?"

"Yeah. Can't your friends handle the rest of the scene?"

The tech looked around. "Guys, how's it coming?"

"About a third of the way done with the grid."

She turned to Zach. "I can't leave yet."

He knelt next to her and checked the name badge on her vest. "Hey, Schuyler, we have an agent out there. She's been kidnapped on her wedding day, and there's a chance she might still be alive." He pointed to Doyle Murphy's body, being tended to by the coroner and his assistant. "That man over there was the only one who knew where she was being held, and he died before he could tell us."

She stared at the body for a moment and gulped. "Her wedding day?"

"*Our* wedding day. We have to know if there's anyone else we can tie this to. We have to know if anybody else was helping him."

"So you think printing his guns will do that?"

"Printing, tracing the registration numbers, anything. Look, I don't know. I don't trust Miles Hennessy, I'm out of options and I'm grasping at straws—take your pick."

Schuyler pointed to her coworkers. "What if they find something that'd break the case after we leave?"

"Then we have them call us."

She studied the cement floor for a moment. "Well, I guess it'd be all right." She closed her evidence box and stood. "Hey, guys!" she called. "I'm taking in the guns to start processing. We've got an agent kidnapped and she might still be alive, so let's put a rush on this, okay?"

The other two techs mumbled their okays, apparently engrossed in their photography, and Schuyler strode away. "Should I drive?"

"I can." This time, however, he didn't allow hope to break through the armor around his heart.

23

MILES'S LAWYER SIGNALED FOR HIM TO STAND just before the bailiff called the next docket number—*People v. Hennessy.* The court officer escorted Miles from the pen, and Cyrus joined him behind the defendant's table as they read the charges: second-degree murder and manslaughter.

"That's good," Cyrus murmured. "They're hedging their bets. They aren't sure they can win this."

"Do you have a plea, Mr. Hennessy?" Judge Grant asked.

"Not guilty by reason of self-defense." Miles angled his chin to better display his injury—his black eye must be starting to purple up.

"Miss Hardt?" the judge called.

The Assistant US Attorney flipped through her file folder. "Sorry, Your Honor." Ms. Hardt flashed him a smile calculated to wring out his last drop of sympathy. "They're really rushing this one through."

"Because my client deserves to be free."

Ms. Hardt finished scanning a page and looked up. "The prosecution requests remand."

Cyrus guffawed. "And I'm sure we'd all like ice water, Miss Hardt."

"Your Honor, the defendant is part of a criminal organization responsible for thousands of crimes in the last—"

"Your Honor, my client has never so much as been questioned in any previous proceedings. He has a perfectly clean record."

A little bit of a stretch, but his rap sheet was empty, at least.

The AUSA was undeterred. "He's related to a number of convicted or admitted mobsters by blood and marriage."

"So sue him for marrying for love." Cyrus paused and gave the lawyer a second glance. "On second thought—don't. You seem the malicious-prosecution type."

"Mr. Cyrus," Judge Grant warned. "Can the *ad hominem* and give me a reason, will you?"

"Certainly. My client shot a man who was holding him at gunpoint, trying to get him to be party to kidnapping a federal agent." His tone was calm and reasonable, as if he and the judge had a rapport. "Incidentally, this man was a prominent mobster who was recently mistried, and who has terrorized the South Side for at least a decade."

"Is that what your file says, Miss Hardt?"

"Well, yes, but—"

The judge gave Miss Hardt a look that said *really, lady?* "And you seriously asked me to withhold bail? Fifty thousand dollars, cash or bond."

"We'll be posting now, Your Honor," Cyrus called over the tap of the gavel. The judge gave a dismissive nod. Cyrus shook Miles's hand. "Almost done."

Molly tried to wet her sandpaper tongue. Could dehydration set in this quickly? Or had it been building all day and only now, in the silence, she was noticing?

The electric fans buzzed on the other side of the room, but the air around her felt as still as death.

Would these be her last thoughts? Was this how she was supposed to die—alone, overheated, desiccated? Her body to remain undiscovered until Hennessy confessed or . . .

Or perhaps it would never be discovered. And everyone would be left to wonder, left to hope in a distant corner of their minds that maybe she was really all right somewhere, maybe she'd survived and was safe, and maybe she'd make her way back.

And maybe, in a distant corner of her own mind, she held that same hope.

But they weren't coming. It had to have been an hour since the gunshots. No sirens, no shouting, no searching.

Then she was somewhere where gunfire wouldn't bring police attention. Then this could also be somewhere no one came unless they absolutely had to.

Then she'd have to save herself. That had always been the plan, hadn't it?

Molly steeled herself to start again. Her reach was greater now that she was free from the cuffs. Perhaps something on this dusty, neglected floor could help. She slipped off the bed, grateful for the distraction from her dry mouth.

The column of sunlight streaming in the door had grown steadily shorter. It must be well past noon. The bare lamp at the far end of the container was now the main source of light, throwing deep shadows across the chaotic mixed wood grain of the floor.

She'd already searched there and come up empty, but with the raking angle of the light, she could see that the floor must have already been cleaned.

Miles had thought of everything.

She didn't imagine his plan included gunshots. He could be dead for all she knew. But enough of his plan had worked that she might join him.

Molly glanced at the dusty cardboard boxes he'd left lining the walls. Could there be anything in there to help her?

Crawling as far as she could with the shackle, she could barely reach the closest box. She pinched the corner of the cardboard and pulled it back toward her, dragging it until she could sit on the edge of the bed with the box in front of her.

The flaps of the box weren't taped down. She flipped them open, sending up a cloud of stale dust. Molly reared back, but still choked down a bit of the dust. Just before she released the box flaps to cover her sneeze, she caught a glimpse inside the box. Paperback books. Some of the covers even looked familiar—classic pulp spy covers.

Sniffling, she rubbed at her nose and tried to blink the dust from her eyes. Paperbacks? In a shipping container? They'd dealt with boxes of donated books regularly at the parish office, and once in a while they'd found a few rare pulp spy novels—but a whole box of them, here, now?

Perhaps it was a tender mercy, something to take her mind off her imminent death and how alone she'd be in those last moments. Molly opened the box flaps more carefully this time and reached in. She pulled out . . . packing peanuts.

But—she'd seen—she was sure— She threw the flaps open as wide as they'd go, ignoring the dust, and dug through the white Styrofoam peanuts. No books. Nothing at all other than the peanuts.

Slowly, she sat up on the bed and pushed the box away with her foot.

She was imagining things. She was so dehydrated she really was losing her mind.

Her imminent death indeed. Her skin grew cold and Molly shivered.

She didn't bother trying to focus on the corrugated metal above her as she gazed straight up. Despite her best efforts, panic flickered at the edges of her conscious, and she had to fight that.

Panic wouldn't help her. It'd only bring the end more quickly as she used up whatever water stores she might have left.

Molly tried to swallow, but, as usual, nothing really happened.

She slid her hand along her back. Was she still sweating? If she was, she had water in her system, enough to survive. Enough to hope.

She pulled back a clammy hand. Was that good or bad?

Perhaps she'd die of heatstroke first. She racked her brain for the symptoms—but all she could remember was that the body's core temperature had to be dangerously high.

This room's temperature was dangerously high. Was she close? Over? Was her mind shutting down because of the panic, or was she losing the ability to think and function because she was dying?

It didn't matter. She would not sit here and give up.

Surely she would think of something.

If she could only think.

Zach pulled back into the FBI parking garage once again. This day kept going in circles.

Circling the drain.

And yet here he was, going through the motions still. Though he knew there was no chance of saving Molly.

Next to him, the ERT tech cleared her throat. "You need a minute?"

"No." Zach tried to ignore the dash clock and killed the engine, but he still saw the time—1:46.

They were supposed to leave her apartment for the temple in an hour. No doubt their families would be leaving soon, too.

He got out of the car, locked it, and followed Schuyler up to her lab.

Time to call their families. Time to admit the truth—he'd lost Molly and all of his efforts, the best of his abilities, hadn't been enough to save her. When it came down to it, he wasn't enough to crack the one case that had mattered most to him in his career and his life.

He wasn't enough, and Molly had paid the price.

Schuyler busied herself getting to work as soon as they reached her lab, leaving Zach to pace the floor. And on top of dealing with losing Molly, he'd have to tell his family, her sister, her parents. That everything he'd tried—well beyond his capacity—had brought him not one inch closer to saving her.

That they might never find her body, and that they would all live in suspended motion, wondering if or when she might return to their lives, hoping that she was safe somewhere. Worrying—and wishing—they'd find the evidence to close her case one day, and they'd finally have a body to bury.

"Have you ever gotten a fingerprint off a shell casing?" Schuyler broke into his thoughts.

Zach took a second to ground himself in the lab again. "What?"

Schuyler held up a container of coating powder and the spent shell from Doyle's gun. "Ever gotten a fingerprint off a shell casing?" she repeated.

Still reeling, he could only shake his head.

"Have to use special powder."

For a long moment, Zach simply stared at her. Why was she doing this?

"Seemed like you could use a distraction." Schuyler tried for a sympathetic smile.

Was it that obvious?

Schuyler continued with her distraction. "Fingerprints rarely adhere to metal surfaces on guns and bullets."

He glanced at the guns waiting on the counter in their plastic bags.

"Maybe eight to ten percent of the time, we can get something useable off a gun. Until the last couple years, that is. Ever see *The Dark Knight*?"

Zach racked his brain for the scene she was referencing, but no matches came up. "Yeah, but . . ."

She waved away the topic. "The technique works best for spent shells. Easier to run a current through something that size, as opposed to a gun, and the heat from firing actually develops the print better."

He finally approached her workstation. "Even if he wiped it off?"

She shot him a look that said *we're way smarter than that*. "Even if he used soap. But who washes bullets after loading them?" She took the casing to a machine that would have fit in a photography lab. After positioning it on the plate, she flipped the switch on the microscope-looking thing hanging over it. "It can tell where the fingerprint was because the residual oils would inhibit the conductivity, as compared to the adjacent surfaces."

Zach had no idea what that meant, but Schuyler didn't notice. "The drawback, of course, is that it'll take at least a couple hours to develop the full print."

"A couple hours?" The argument that Molly couldn't wait that long died in his throat. For all he knew, they were already too late, even if they had some clue where to search.

That was when it finally sank in: he'd already given up the search. Now he was just trying to convict her killer—an accessory— anybody.

"I said we'll see what we can do." Schuyler nailed him with a pointed look. "You're the one that wanted to come back with this evidence—I'm trying to get as much as possible from what we have." She turned back to the counter and pulled out Miles's shiny revolver. She gingerly painted the bright blue magnetic powder over the gun's chromed surfaces.

"What's with the blue?"

Schuyler stayed focused on her work. "Would you be able to see black fingerprint powder on a black gun?"

"The gun's stainless steel." And with the high-shine finish, a very flashy choice.

"Yeah, but the grip is black." She finally met his gaze. "Are you going to question everything I do, or let me do my job?"

"Sorry." Zach held up defensive palms.

She hesitated a second. "No, *I'm* sorry. I'm not used to talking while I'm working. But I can." She turned to the gun, stroking the powder over the barrel. "Hm. You'd expect a gun that's all chromed out to have a ton of fingerprints. I mean, in high school band, I was constantly having to scrub fingerprints off my flute."

Zach opted for silence as Schuyler moved on to the grip and trigger. The bright blue finally adhered to something on the barrel near the cylinder—but would it be enough to be a usable print?

Schuyler lifted the revolver to examine the powder at an angle. "How do you get prints there, like that?" She offered it to Zach.

Without touching it, he mimed how he'd have to hold the gun to align his fingers with the prints. The prints were right along the barrel and cylinder, as if Miles held it along the top. "Maybe tucking it in a waistband?"

She set it down again to continue brushing the powder down the grip, but nothing came up. She flipped the gun over to brush near the hammer—and another blue oval appeared. "Somebody's pretty lucky today."

Not him. Definitely not Molly. "Only if they tell us something we don't already know."

Schuyler photographed the prints to record their location on the gun before lifting them with a tape. "It's a start, right?"

"Sure."

She picked up Miles's revolver and held the release to swing the cylinder out. "One spent shell in here, the other five chambers full and unfired." With a gloved fingertip, she pried the spent casing out of its chamber and pulled out the coating powder again.

"I thought you said it would be hours before the other one was finished."

"It will be. This one can be next in line."

In a couple hours. Even Zach's frustration was losing steam. He couldn't make the technology run any faster by yelling at her. He'd already flown off the handle too many times today. It was too late to do any good.

Schuyler pushed the cylinder back into the revolver and slipped Miles's gun into its evidence bag. She opened up Doyle's semi-automatic next, using hot pink powder this time. Which, Zach had to admit, *would* make any fingerprints stand out.

But if they only had a one in ten or twelve probability of getting fingerprints off a gun, hadn't they already used their chance?

"Now," Schuyler began her narration as she worked on the barrel, "with a plastic-bodied gun, we have a little bit worse chance to lift prints. The grip and trigger have this 'stippled' texture molded into them, like they want to make my job harder." She lifted the gun to show it to Zach—but considering it was almost identical to his service weapon, he didn't need the anatomy lesson.

"It's to keep the gun from slipping in our hands."

"Oh. Right." She laid the gun down and dusted down one side of the grip. "But," she said as she turned the gun over, "there is one place we can sometimes get a good print." She pointed to the slide above the trigger. "If someone's dumb enough to put their thumb on there, since it's not slick metal."

"Nitridized." Zach watched as she brushed the powder over the slide—and a hot pink print appeared.

"Hey, streak of luck number two. Good things come in threes, you know." Schuyler reached for her camera.

"Let's hope so," he muttered. "Don't forget to brush the whole slide—maybe the guy racked it."

E VENTUALLY, SCHUYLER'S EFFORTS to keep Zach distracted petered out. Zach silently watched the machine work while Schuyler herself was busy somewhere else. He had no idea what the results meant.

Or what he could say to Katie Malone if—no, when he called to tell her.

He had to call her—she deserved to know the truth. That Zach had failed her, her whole family, his whole family—and most of all, Molly. That she was never coming home.

Could he admit that out loud?

He didn't have a choice. He pulled out his phone and scrolled through his call history. All the calls to and from Doyle, his one hope of getting her back. And now nothing.

Zach found a quiet corner of the lab and pulled up Colm and Katie's number. He was going to have to hit the icon to call. He was going to have to tell them. He was going to have to admit he hadn't been able to save their daughter.

Zach braced himself and tapped the icon to call.

The phone rang three times before Katie answered, breathless. "Zachary? Where are you? Where's Molly? You're both terribly late, young man."

"Katie, I have to tell you something."

He was answered with silence. "Can you sit down?" he asked.

"All right." The caution in her voice almost made him prolong the lie about Molly translating in Joliet.

"I don't think Molly's going to be able to make the wedding."

"Oh, Zachary." Her pity was for him? "I'm so sorry, love. Are you sure you can't push the ceremony back? I'm sure they'll have to let her go soon, won't they?"

"Katie." He put on his best modulated, measured voice. The one he'd use to break bad news to any civilian. "They won't be letting Molly go anytime soon."

She hesitated a beat. "Why do you say it that way, Zachary? I thought you were friends with the Special Agent in Charge. Get him to call off the assignment."

"It's not that simple."

"I thought he was invited to your ceremony." Sarcasm seeped into her words. "Heaven knows I certainly amn't, but your boss, yes, of course he is—but really, you're not so close to him that you can't ask him to get your fiancée to the church on time—"

"Katie. It's not up to us now. It's out of our control."

She snorted. "What, they're using her as a bargainin' chip in their diplomatic negotiations? Traffic jam in Joliet?"

"She's not in Joliet, and she's not on assignment."

Katie let several seconds pass, as if she was sitting there blinking in stunned silence. "Dear God," she murmured, a prayer. "What's happened?"

"Stay calm."

"Where is she, Zachary?" she demanded

Zach glanced around the lab, but no one was paying attention to him. "Don't panic, that's not going to help anything."

"Not panic? Tell me she's all right and I'll not panic."

He said nothing.

She scoffed. "You call me to tell me my daughter is heaven only knows where, and you haven't the slightest clue whether she's all right, and you want me to remain calm?"

"Katie."

"Is that how you're handlin' this? Remainin' calm?"

"Katie." The comforting shifted to a cautioning tone.

"Are you lookin' for her? Or are you too calm to care?"

"Katie," he cut her off. "I have been searching for her personally since six o'clock this morning."

That cowed her into a half second of silence. "Are you sure she hasn't got cold feet, or some last-minute errands?"

"Don't you think she would have mentioned something to you?"

"But she did say that somethin' was botherin' her—a feelin' somethin' would go wrong with the weddin'."

Guilt kicked at his gut. He'd told her not to worry. "Well, she was right."

Katie paused again before speaking. "Zachary." She sounded like a field officer marshaling troops—and Zach was suddenly reminded that she'd been an undercover operative, too. "You find her. You do whatever's necessary—and take as long as you need. We'll handle everythin'."

"Thanks," he murmured.

He should have said more, but the words couldn't take shape in his brain.

He had to let Katie believe Molly was still alive. At least a little while longer. For her sake.

Who was he kidding? It was completely for his sake—so he didn't have to tell her, so he didn't have to admit it aloud. So it wasn't real.

"The second you need anythin'," Katie continued, "you let us know. And if there's anythin'—absolutely anythin'—we can do to help find her, you call immediately. Got it?"

"Yes, ma'am."

"Good. I'm sure you're doin' all you can. We expect to hear all the news, so."

Zach assured her he would call with regular updates and ended the call as quickly as he could.

Zach sank back against the wall of the lab. He was a liar. And a coward. He could only give Katie a shred of the truth, protecting himself more than her feelings.

She had it right at the beginning. He hadn't done enough to look for Molly. He hadn't handled it like he should have. Katie was about to trust him with her daughter, and he'd failed in the worst way.

And now he'd get to tell his family.

His phone rang—and it was Lucy. His little sister had the worst timing.

He could tell Lucy, the only member of his family with some clue what was going on, and the only one who knew he was a covert operative for the FBI. But he couldn't ask her to explain this for him.

He hit the icon to ignore the call, but the call connected anyway. Of course.

"Zach?" Lucy asked.

"Yeah," he said on a sigh.

"Have you seen the news this afternoon?"

That was slightly better than bringing up Paul. "Been a little busy."

"I know—sorry—but—is Doyle Murphy actually dead?"

He almost wanted to laugh. Lucy couldn't be as naïve as she pretended to be, if she could call him now and deliver a roundhouse kick to the ribs like that. "Yes," he said. Very. Distinctly.

"You already knew?"

He was not going there now. Probably not ever. "Are you with Mom?"

"Um, yeah?"

"Let me talk to her."

He had to tell his parents. He steeled himself.

He'd have to find a way to explain how he knew all this without telling the whole truth.

"Zachary," she answered, her annoyance tempered with understanding. "Where are you?"

"Hey, Mom."

"Please tell me you're on your way to the temple."

For one second of brilliant pain, his heart went supernova again. He'd almost forgotten how little he'd told his mom. His phone beeped, telling him another call was coming. He checked the number—he knew that number.

Half a second of adrenaline spiked in his system before his brain caught up. It wasn't Doyle Murphy calling—it wasn't even Doyle's number, just another number he'd seen too many times today.

Zach sent the call to voicemail and held the phone to his ear, Mom still in the midst of her drawling fuss. "I know how you like to cut things close with your schedule, but this is getting ridiculous. Your father and I have to leave in—"

"About that, Mom—you don't need to leave quite yet."

"What did you forget now?" Once again, her tone turned him into a naughty little boy.

"I—I didn't. I mean—"

"Huh." Schuyler's single syllable echoed through the lab.

Zach looked up. Schuyler squinted at the computer screen, frantically waving for Zach to come over.

"I'm sorry, Mom, I gotta go. Work."

"Zachary—"

He ended the call and headed over to Schuyler.

"We're absolutely sure this casing came from the semi-automatic?" she asked.

"Didn't come from the revolver." Unless Doyle happened to bleed out on someone else's bullet casing, while his went missing.

"Huh," Schuyler repeated.

"Why?"

A crease formed between her eyebrows. Schuyler walked over to where the hot pink and bright blue fingerprints waited. She held them out to Zach. "Notice anything?"

He took the cards and glanced at them. "No."

She walked him over to the computer monitor showing less than a third of a fingerprint. "How about now?"

He shrugged and shot her a helpless look. Schuyler plucked the pink fingerprint card from his grasp and slapped it against the monitor.

Zach's eyes jumped between the card and the screen. The hot pink prints, he remembered, went to Doyle's semi-automatic. The same gun that had ejected the casing, where they'd found the fingerprint displayed on the screen. What was this about?

"Not seeing it," he finally admitted.

With a sigh, Schuyler took the card down and dug up a jeweler's loupe. She returned the pink card to him and he took a closer look, then peered at the computer screen again.

"Okay, I'm not a trained fingerprint tech," he said, "but that doesn't seem like the same pattern."

Schuyler smiled. "It's not." She pointed to the bottom of a semicircle on the monitor. "We only see complete rings at the bottom of prints on the whorl pattern. Everything else has some straight features to each ridge."

"But what if we have it upside down and that's not the bottom of the print? I mean, how can you tell?"

She traced the straight, broken lines below the semicircles. "All prints, and especially the whorl, show increased curvature toward the end of the digit." She checked to make sure he was still following her and added, "They're only flat at the bottom."

"Okay, so this print came from a different finger than this one." He held up the card.

"That's possible." The tech nodded an acknowledgment. "We can have different pattern types on different fingers. However, the whorl pattern is most common on the ring finger and the thumb. Which of those are you going to use to handle a bullet or the back of the gun, Agent Saint?"

Good point.

As much as he wanted all this to be true, he couldn't afford to trust his burned-out suspicion meter. He had to be sure. "But if this came from Doyle's semi-auto—" He waved the hot pink print again. "—how can we be sure it's a thumbprint?"

"Educated guess." Schuyler held up her left hand as an imaginary gun. She grabbed the "slide" of her finger gun as if to rack it. "The fingers would be all together; the thumb is a solitary print. Also—" She pointed to a spot above the trigger. "On the weapon, there's a divot here. Conceivable to put the thumb there, but not a great idea while firing."

The energy began building in his system, ready to run away with him. But that had gotten him nowhere today. With an educated guess, half a print and statistics, they were saying the thumbprint on the outside of Doyle's gun didn't match the one on the casing it had supposedly fired.

Any reason to suspect Miles could still help him find Molly was a straw worth grasping. But Zach's luck had run out a long time ago.

Schuyler frowned at Zach, like she was angry that he was either this obstinate or this slow. "I checked IAFIS against Doyle Murphy's prints, by the way."

The fingerprint database didn't match either? "Wait, which one—the gun or the casing?"

"And then there's this." Schuyler didn't answer him, grabbing the other fingerprint card. She handed it to Zach and he examined the bright blue prints. The set of three didn't seem remarkable, but as he peered at the fourth, a solitary print, everything suddenly made sense.

A circular whorl pattern.

"How common is the whorl pattern?" he asked.

"Fairly common in Asians," the tech informed him. "Fairly uncommon among Caucasians."

"And do the prints we have on file for Doyle Murphy have a whorl?"

Schuyler leaned back against the counter, smug. "Nope."

The pink prints—from Doyle's semi-automatic—matched Doyle.

The blue prints—the prints from Miles's revolver, the ones with a whorl—matched the prints from the casing that was supposed to have come from Doyle's gun.

Unless Doyle Murphy had his underling load his gun for him, something was seriously wrong with this picture.

Zach turned to Schuyler. "Looks like we need to talk to Miles Hennessy."

Schuyler gave him a slow grin. "Nail him to the wall."

Zach was halfway to the jail when his phone rang again. The same number that had called while he was talking to his mom. "Hello?" he answered.

"Saint, this is Novak. Disregard my message."

Bad news, then? "Okay."

"Fahey changed his mind."

"Wait, what? Start over."

"We picked up Fahey like you said. He invoked, but we finally got his lawyer here. Says he doesn't know anything about a kidnapping, just took pictures as a favor to Miles Hennessy."

Hennessy. Again.

"Great work," Zach said.

"What do we do with him?"

"Up to the AUSA." Zach got off the call as fast as he could.

He needed to see Hennessy. Now.

Zach made it to the jail in record time and requested to see Hennessy in the holding cell.

The reedy officer behind the desk lifted his chin proudly. "We put a real rush on him."

"What?" Zach grabbed the desk between them. This could not mean what he thought it meant.

He was supposed to be getting information out of Hennessy. His very last chance.

"Yeah, we all knew it wouldn't be right to keep him here long—I mean, the man did a public service."

"What?" Zach asked more loudly this time.

The corrections officer glanced around at his buddies. "I mean, he killed Doyle Murphy. Do you *know* who Doyle Murphy is?"

He scoffed. "Of cour—I—where is he now?"

"Who, Hennessy?"

"No, Doyle Murphy." Zach rolled his eyes.

"Oh, the morgue. He *is* dead—"

"I meant Hennessy."

The officer registered his mistake. He cleared his throat, composing himself, and read his computer screen. "Not sure. He and his lawyer left a while ago. Headed for the courthouse."

Zach wheeled away. Ridiculous. That was what they got for turning Hennessy over to local authorities for a few hours.

Did he go to the courthouse to try to catch Hennessy? He checked the wall clock. 2:02.

He didn't even have the watch Molly gave him yesterday. She'd been so completely cut out of his life.

But there was still time to fight for her. Maybe he could call in a favor. Maybe he'd already cashed in that particular favor—maybe she'd never owed him anything in the first place—but it was all Zach could do to hope Jill would help.

Miles knocked on his own apartment door. Cyrus had driven him home—though he was sure to pay for that later, literally—and he could relax. Molly was completely secure, and they were clearly never going to search two buildings over from the crime scene—or even be close enough to hear her if she wasted her energy screaming inside the container.

All he had to do was wait. Give her two or three days, tops, and she'd be easy to handle. Not a pretty sight, most likely, but he'd be able to lock up the container and dispose of her body. Somewhere where, if they did find it, they wouldn't be able to trace it to him.

Everything was working out even better than his plans. Now he wouldn't have to babysit her constantly, and he wouldn't have to go through the mess of shooting her.

Miles tapped his foot. What was taking Teresa so long?

Finally, she pulled the door open. A rush of a spicy floral scent greeted him before his wife could. "Miles." Her enthusiasm seemed forced. "You're home early."

"I guess." He eyed her as he stepped into the apartment. Her red, wavy hair was disheveled; she ran her fingers through it with one hand and tugged on the bottom of her blouse with the other.

A middle button of her blouse was undone. Teresa wasn't huge into appearances, but she would notice something like that.

"Babe." He furrowed his brow and pointed to her shirt.

"Oh," she laughed, and turned away to fix the button. "Sorry about that."

He drew her close. "You don't have to apologize."

She laughed again, again sounding fake, and pulled away.

"What smells so good, babe?"

Teresa made a vague gesture toward the kitchen counter. "A candle."

"Since when do you burn candles—and in the middle of July?"

"It's new. I just picked it up today, and I wanted to see what it smelled like."

Miles nodded slowly. What was going on? Why was Teresa acting so skittish?

She opened the fridge. "How did your, uh, thing go today?"

"How did you know I had a 'thing' today?"

"You must've told me."

Like he'd tell her that. Like any of them would ever allude to

242

what they were doing—or that they were doing anything. "Pretty sure I didn't." And suddenly, it came rushing back. Doyle had told her—Doyle had taken her car. With her permission. "Did . . . Doyle tell you?"

"Doyle? No, I—uh—why would I, I mean—"

He pulled her away from the fridge and closed the door. "Teresa?"

"What?" The innocent act wasn't working. Maybe another day, when he was too busy with his plans. But today—when he'd spent all day watching other people and plotting—

Today he was getting paranoid. He shook off the rising jealousy. "Doyle told me you switched cars."

"Oh, yeah, we did. He needed it." She waved a hand like she was wiping the subject away. "So, um, did he have to 'work' late?"

Miles chuckled softly. "No, Doyle's resting now."

In her first expression that resembled a true reaction, Teresa cocked her head. "What? What do you mean?"

"Doyle's . . . not coming home."

The line between her eyebrows grew deeper. "Miles, what are you saying?"

"Doyle Murphy is dead." The relief those four words brought was so sweet he could almost taste it. Never again would Doyle do something stupid to embarrass Sullivan or the organization. Never again would Doyle bring them unwanted attention.

And he was free to take Doyle's place—and Sullivan would surely see that.

"What—what happened?" Teresa gasped, her back now to him.

Though they had spousal privilege, Miles didn't dare deviate from his story. "He tried to kill me, Teresa. I had to shoot him. I had to."

He placed a hand on her shoulder, but Teresa pulled away. She ventured to the living room. As she turned around to sink into the couch, he could finally see the horror and the pain on her face.

An expression he'd already dealt with enough today.

But he wasn't about to take out his frustration with Molly on Teresa. He crossed the room to sit next to her, put an arm around her shoulders. "It's okay, babe. I'm here—I'm okay."

She jerked to look at him, bewilderment flashing in her eyes. Then she pulled away. Again. "You killed Doyle?" she whispered.

"I had to, Teresa."

"Because of us?"

Now Miles was the bewildered one. "What? What do we have to do with—" He stopped short when Teresa raised her gaze to his, her head again cocked in confusion.

"Us" didn't mean him and Teresa.

"Us" meant Teresa and Doyle.

Time slowed down, and their conversation from the time he'd walked in replayed itself in double time in his mind. She'd been expecting Doyle. She'd been burning a candle—or a dozen candles. She'd just changed her clothes.

Miles shot to his feet. "You and Doyle?" he shouted.

"You didn't know?"

"How—how could you? I have been a *prince* to you! Not once have I even considered—and everyone else, everyone else—but you—and Doyle?" Not Teresa. Not Doyle. He didn't expect much loyalty from Doyle, but his wife?

He didn't know which was worse—Teresa cheating on him, or Doyle pulling one over on him for this long. Miles pressed his fingers to his temples, his headache back with a vengeance. This couldn't be happening.

"We didn't mean for it to happen. We didn't want you to find out this way."

He made a chopping motion, cutting off her rationalization. "Save it." He stalked back to their bedroom.

But even here wasn't safe. Had she . . . ? He couldn't think it.

Miles opened the third drawer of his dresser. Beneath his pants, he found his revolver.

Teresa—no. He wasn't really going to hurt his wife. Like he could do that, no matter what she'd done.

But there was someone else—and he could make sure Molly didn't do anything to steal his victory away, either. He marched back through the apartment and grabbed the keys on the counter.

The keys to Doyle's Cadillac. Miles clenched the keys tighter and slammed the door behind him.

He might not feel right taking his frustrations about Molly out on Teresa—but he wouldn't have any qualms about using Molly as a stand-in to exact his revenge.

AS SOON AS HE WAS THROUGH THE GLASS FRONT DOORS, Zach tapped the icon to call. The phone rang, and he held his breath.

"Agent Saint?" AUSA Jill Hardt answered with surprise. "Tell me you have more good news."

"Sorry. Can you find out whether Miles Hennessy was arraigned today?"

"Oh, I can tell you how that went." She swore. "My luck to catch arraignments this afternoon. Just finished for the week, so I can't complain, but they go and ram this case down my throat at the last second—and you know, if it'd been up to me, I would've busted him over to the DA or *nolle pros*'ed him."

He should probably know what that meant, and would have, if he could've been more involved in prosecuting his cases. Zach didn't bother to ask, pushing the conversation forward. "Did he get remanded?"

"No. His lawyer gave me attitude about requesting it, too."

"Did he post bail?"

She sighed. "Yeah. I mean, yeah, he did us all a favor—I certainly didn't want to have to go through another trial like Murphy's last one, did you?—but fifty grand for murder two? What a joke."

"How long ago was this?"

"I just finished up, so . . . maybe twenty or thirty minutes ago. Forty-five on the outside."

He could be anywhere. Zach reached his car and climbed in, not sure where to go.

"So," Jill continued after a pause. "Any thoughts on what to do with the lawyer?"

"Your call. And I think they've got another of Murphy's guys for you to go check on."

"Hey, remind me when your wedding is?"

"Thanks, Jill," Zach avoided the question and ended the call. Obviously, she didn't know about Molly.

But Miles Hennessy just might.

Hennessy had been at the courthouse within the last hour. That was enough time to possibly make it back to his apartment. Or the airport, if he had half a brain.

The crime scene and Hennessy's apartment were both to the south. He could start that way and figure out where to go while he was on the road.

Once he was on the long on-ramp to the interstate, Zach called Xavier, who was still at the crime scene as far as he knew. "Do we have Hennessy's car in the impound?" Zach asked as soon as X answered.

"Yeah, a Lincoln in his wife's name, out back of the warehouse. They towed it away."

"I need to track him down, and apparently he's already posted bail."

"What?" Xavier sounded even more surprised than Zach.

"Think he took the bus home?"

X thought a minute. "His lawyer might've taken him. We're done here, so I can get over to his building."

"Great. Anybody already down that way?"

"Just sent Kent to talk to the grieving widow."

"Thanks."

Kent didn't bother with a greeting when he answered the phone. "There was a goldish Cadillac somewhere in the mess of cars today, right?" he said.

"Yeah." Zach mentally reviewed the long list of vehicles they'd had to follow that day. Was Claire Murphy's Cadillac a priority now? "Did you get ahold of Claire Murphy?"

"Uh huh. Didn't take it well."

He wasn't going to take it well if this didn't pan out, either. "Today's Cadillac was hers."

"And we're sure Doyle Murphy is dead?"

Zach voice grew tighter. "Yeah, I was with him when he died. Why?"

"Unless Mrs. Murphy's a man, I don't think she's driving this Caddy."

Wait a minute. "You have eyes on the Cadillac? Can you read me the plate?"

Kent rattled off the letters and numbers. Zach hadn't memorized her plates, so he couldn't be sure, but it sounded familiar.

No. He didn't dare hope at this point. He'd been disappointed too many times today to believe something might actually go his way. "Where's he going?"

"We're headed inbound on I-90/94."

They were coming straight for Zach. He glanced out the window. The last major landmark was the other interstate. Where they'd chased Lehrman driving Murphy's car. "I'm headed toward you, just past I-55." Zach asked.

"We're maybe three miles away. Wait—the Caddy is exiting at 47th Street," Kent announced.

Zach scanned the road signs. Speeding toward Hennessy and Kent, he had to be ready to get off the interstate on short notice.

"He's heading left under the freeway. You on your way?"

"Yep. Passing the 35th Street exit."

Anybody could be driving that car. Claire Murphy might be having the worst day of her life, with grand theft auto to compound her grief.

But what if the driver was Miles?

He had to run this down.

He could go down to 47th Street and try to follow them, or he could get off at the next exit and move to intercept.

Zach signaled to exit.

Kent kept up a running commentary on which cross streets he and the Caddy passed. Zach trailed them in parallel eight blocks to the north, catching up faster when Kent hit a construction bottleneck.

"He's turning on Patoka Avenue," Kent said. "Heading north."

Toward Zach. For once, something was going his way. Zach glanced up at the sign for the next cross street: Patoka.

Maybe two things. He signaled left and managed to make the light before the yellow expired."I'm on Patoka, coming your way."

Kent crowed with victory, but after another minute or two, he groaned. "Uh oh."

"What do you mean, 'uh oh'?"

"He's made me."

Zach sucked in a breath. "Are you sure?"

"He adjusted his mirror and did a double take, and now he's flooring it."

"Hang back, but watch him." How could this guy make Kent?

The traffic light in front of Zach changed to red, and he came to a quick stop. "Sitting at the light at Riverbend Drive," he told Kent. He willed himself not to look at a particular warehouse at this corner.

"I'm there. Three cars back, right lane."

They'd already met up? Zach grabbed his binoculars from the center console, scanning the cars across the intersection to catch a glimpse of Kent or the Caddy.

And then Kent swore. "He's getting in the left turn lane—we're losing him."

A red Mitsubishi turned off the road, and the champagne Cadillac pulled up to the line in the turn lane on the other side of the intersection.

Zach peered through the binoculars. "Eyes on," Zach announced. "It's Miles Hennessy driving." He didn't even try to keep the triumph out of his voice.

Until Hennessy pulled him back into the present—he made the left. Zach checked the lanes around him. They were all full, and he would have to get across three lanes to follow Hennessy.

"You've got to be kidding me," he muttered. Zach panned with his binoculars to follow Miles as far as he could. Not far.

Why would he be driving the car of the widow of the man he'd just killed unless it was something important? They were this close—and they were losing him.

He rubbed his eyes, then his eyebrows, then forehead. "Not possible," he muttered. "Not possible."

Wait. That was Claire Murphy's car—a Caddy. OnStar.

Zach lifted his phone again, back to Kent. "I've got a backup plan. You see the DontRain warehouse on the corner?"

"Yep."

"Let's meet up there. See you in a minute."

"Good luck."

Zach thanked him and hung up. Before the light finally turned green, he pulled up the phone number for Reyes, the tech.

"Agent Saint?" The timidity was almost gone from her greeting.

"I hear you have some OnStar tracking info for me?"

"Uh . . . well, I did a while ago."

"Let's get it back then. And hurry."

She said nothing, but the tapping of her keyboard was enough for Zach. As he waited, he pulled into the half-empty DontRain parking lot.

It had only been four months since Molly had come here to save him. He might actually have a chance to return the favor today.

"Okay," Reyes said. "One minute, we have to open up the police access channel to their system again, and then they're going to locate the car and feed it back to us."

After another minute or two of silence, Kent pulled into a spot next to him.

And they waited.

Every option exhausted, Molly lay in the stifling silence and simply breathed.

Could she live without a foot? Dancing would never be the same. Nothing about life would. But she'd get used to it.

Could she survive amputating her own foot? That was the harder question. She'd heard stories of people who were trapped who had to cut off a limb to survive. She'd never imagined she'd be in the same situation.

The alternative was even less appealing.

What if she couldn't do it? How on earth could she break her bones? She stared up at the corrugated metal above her. Was she ready to die?

Nothing unresolved sprang to mind. Other than not marrying Zachary, of course. And that might have been her own fault. If she hadn't been so adamant that she didn't mean to marry anytime soon, perhaps they'd already be married.

Aside from the regret gnawing at her, Molly felt . . . at peace. Surprisingly so. Relieved, almost. Not relieved that she'd ruined their wedding—their lives—but the tension and fear that had been building throughout the day had dissipated.

Perhaps she really was prepared to die.

She inhaled the calm and let it flow through her. Perhaps they'd find her, perhaps they wouldn't—and she'd be all right either way.

Until she heard footsteps echo outside the door. Her eyes snapped open. Were they here? She could feel her heartbeat in every extremity, as if she were one giant exposed nerve.

But it might not be Zachary. She tied an iron band around the hope trying to run amok in her mind. It could well be Hennessy and Doyle come to taunt her further—or to carry out their endgame with or without Zachary.

Molly pushed herself up to a sitting position. Her vision went black. Her nausea and vertigo threatened to send her back down to the mattress. She managed to stay upright as her vision faded to a dull red, but she was still reeling when the door swung open. Against her better judgment—she didn't need to pass out—Molly held her breath and pulled her arms behind her, hiding her freed hands.

Hennessy. Was it the red still coloring her eyesight, or was his jaw set and the muscle in his temple throbbing in fury?

"Okay, we got GPS coordinates," Reyes said. "Let me get these on a map." She read off an approximate address—half a block from where they'd arrested Miles.

Then running into Miles and Doyle wasn't a coincidence or timing or anything. Miles was at the warehouse with Doyle because—

Because they were holding Molly down the street?

Zach put his car in gear. Somehow, he managed to thank Reyes, end the call and shout their destination to Kent all at once before he pulled into traffic.

And this time, he didn't bother to stop the hope welling up in his chest.

He texted the address to Xavier, who he hoped hadn't made it far from the original crime scene half a block away.

That GPS position had to be exact. He swung onto the right road—the one they'd already driven down once that day and come up empty.

They had to find her this time.

Zach mentally winced. He'd driven—maybe even walked—right by her. Shouldn't he have—?

No, no way could he have known.

Zach slammed on the brakes in front of a warehouse. One they'd walked by before.

Xavier pulled up behind his car as Zach was strapping on his vest. "Is this it?" X called, hopping out of his car, already wearing his vest.

"Only one way to be sure."

They drew their weapons and made their way around to the door—locked with a padlock.

"We don't have time for this," Xavier muttered. "Your picks in the car?"

Zach held his gun by the barrel, stood clear of the line of fire, and whacked the lock in the middle of the shackle. Once, twice—and the lock popped open.

"Now *that's* skill." Xavier, his weapon already at the ready, led the way in.

This was the right place. Zach could sense it as he crept in behind Xavier. Now he had to pray they weren't too late.

Molly blinked away the tint in her vision, but Hennessy's rage was only dimmed by his evil grin and an angry purple streak over his cheekbone. "Oh, good." His sinister sneer spread. "You're still here."

"Thought I might stick around."

He sighed. "Well, Molly. It's been fun, you know, but all good things must come to an end."

"Oh, must they?" If this was the end, it was coming more quickly than she'd expected. "I thought we were supposed to have an audience."

"Unfortunately, all our guests are busy."

She spent far too long trying to parse his statement. Was he saying something and she was too dehydrated to read between the lines? "What happened to Doyle?"

Hennessy flushed a deep crimson. "Who cares what happened to Doyle?" he shouted.

Molly pulled back. "I thought he'd want to be here for his grand triumph."

"Well, he's a little too *dead* to make it."

She watched him fume for a few seconds. He couldn't be serious. "What?"

"Doyle Murphy is dead."

Had that been Hennessy's plan all along? It certainly hadn't seemed that way when he was roaring at her earlier. He'd intended to get out without Zachary seeing him.

The plans had changed. And Miles Hennessy meant to kill her. Now.

She'd run through the possible scenarios for an execution: where he might position her, where she might stand. All her plans flashed through her mind, too fast for her to grasp any single one.

She'd have to take him by surprise. She couldn't let him see her hands were free. Not yet. All she had to do was get him in range. And hope he had something on him she could use to get out of the shackle. Unless he took it off to move her to a better staging area first.

"Yeah." Hennessy's voice carried to her as if from far away, she was so lost in her own thoughts. "Your boyfriend isn't going to get that engraved invitation like we promised. Sorry."

Though her mind raced, panic didn't come. Not even when Hennessy pulled out the gun—not the same one he'd had last night.

He didn't have to undo her shackle or move her to a better spot. He could shoot her where he stood.

If she wanted to get out of here, she needed him to come closer.

"Ah, I should've known." She tsked.

He glowered at her again. "What?"

Molly nodded toward his revolver. "That you'd use that."

"Uh, yeah? Why wouldn't I?"

Now her pulse picked up. This was her chance. He thought he was better and smarter than them all—and that was his weakness. "Well, for starters, because even someone so stupid as you could figure out that leavin' a mess like this would be traced back to you in a millisecond."

"Excuse me?"

"And because you obviously aren't enough of a man to do the job yourself."

Scowling, he raised the weapon. "Oh, I'll do it myself. Like I did it for Doyle."

Molly hesitated a heartbeat. *He* had killed Doyle? "And you did it with a gun, of course. Like a coward."

"What?" he demanded.

"You're a coward, usin' that. You aren't enough of a man to kill Doyle yourself, and you're not enough of a man to kill me with your own two hands."

Every muscle was etched into his neck. "You think I can't kill you myself?" He slammed the revolver onto the wooden table across the room.

She struggled to stand on the bed. "I'd stake my life on it."

"We'll see who's the stupid one, then." He stalked across the room.

Molly thrust her neck out, daring him to touch her as he

approached. He came close enough that she could see his flared nostrils and the swelling at his cheek, close enough for him to reach out and grab her. He started to raise his arms—and Molly jerked her head up. She stared over his shoulder and let her jaw drop. "Zachary," she breathed.

Hennessy whirled around.

Molly struck.

ACH AND XAVIER CREPT THROUGH THE WAREHOUSE, quiet
enough to fixate on the whisper pulsating through the place,
and the distant hum of something electric.

Somebody was in here, and the whole block had felt deserted
when they'd searched near here an hour ago.

Zach cleared the last aisle of empty, derelict racks—nothing. Then
where was that sound coming from?

Xavier whistled for his attention, and Zach turned to him. His
boss signaled to the other end of the building. Zach ran to see.

A car. The garage door behind it was open and he shielded the
sunlight to make out the silver Mazda. Not one of the cars they'd seen
so far today, but any sign of someone here meant they might be in
the right place.

Zach nodded toward that end of the building, and they hurried
down the empty aisle. As they cleared the last rack of crumbling
cardboard boxes, a series of shipping containers came into view.

One of them stood with its doors open, light spilling into the
shadows nearby. Zach took off at a dead run.

He barreled through the open doors, Xavier right behind him.

"FBI!" they both shouted, sweeping the inside of the container
with their weapons.

Miles Hennessy stood at the other end of the container. Zach and
Xavier fixed their weapons on him. His face red and his eyes bulging,
Hennessy strained his fingers for them.

"Hands in the air," Xavier shouted.

Hennessy reached for his neck—for the yellow plastic band there. He choked for air.

Not again. They couldn't come this close only to have the prime suspect die on them again.

Hennessy fell to his knees, and someone tackled him from behind. Someone with dark curly hair.

Molly.

For a full second, he couldn't believe what he saw. She was here. She was alive. She was safe.

Zach pushed Xavier's gun to aim at the floor. Molly struggled to her knees, her gaze still fixed on Hennessy in front of her. He moved as if to push up. Molly planted a knee in the middle of his back, pulling on the choke strap hard enough to force Hennessy's back to arch.

Well, she had a handle on the situation. But then, Zach wasn't exactly surprised. It was Molly, after all.

Xavier looked to Zach. "She's going to kill him."

"You better believe it."

X gave him a *what's wrong with you, man?* face.

Oh, right. Zach raced to her. He slid an arm around her waist, ready to lift her off Hennessy. Molly tried to jerk away from him, but he held her tighter.

Xavier finally approached to take custody of Hennessy from her. He and Zach both reached down to pull Molly's hands from the yellow plastic strap—a pair of PlastiCuffs still secured on one of her wrists.

She threw an elbow that caught Zach in the middle of the chest before she looked up, knocking the wind out of him.

"Zachary?" She wriggled out of his grasp, skittering back onto a low metal bed behind her.

Zach recovered, Hennessy coughing and sputtering enough for both of them. Xavier took Molly's position kneeling on Hennessy's back and forced his arm behind him.

Zach stepped over Hennessy's feet to the bed. He held out his hands like he was trying to calm a frightened animal, then sat on the edge of the mattress.

She backed up. "It's not real," she muttered. "Not real, not real, not real."

"Me? Of course I'm real."

He got his first good look at her face, deathly pale. She did *not* believe him. He took her hand, grazing his fingers over the raw stripe around her wrist. Molly flinched and grabbed his hand, flipping it over. He'd missed a streak of dried blood somehow.

She met his gaze, beyond stunned. Horrified.

"It's Doyle's," he hurried to reassure her.

"Is that better?"

Huh? "Than what?"

From the floor, Hennessy protested, incoherent and loud. "It's not supposed to go this way!"

"Miles Hennessy," Xavier said, "you are under arrest. And this time you're going to stay that way. You've got the right to remain silent—use it." He launched into the rest of the standard *Miranda* warning, hauling Hennessy to his feet.

Zach tried to make his voice as soothing as possible, but with Hennessy's loud sputtering, he was almost shouting to be heard. "Molly, look at me." He slid his hands up to cradle her neck and the back of her head.

He pulled her close and leaned down to whisper in her ear. "Molly, it's me. You're safe now. You're safe. I promise."

He could feel her back moving with each shallow, panicked gasp, but as he repeated that phrase over and over, her breathing began to slow. He rubbed her back.

Her shirt was nearly dry. He was sweating from five minutes in this heat. This was bad.

He'd finally found her. He was not about to lose her again.

Molly filled her lungs at last and finally, slowly, pulled back to look at Zach. Trepidation still hung in her deep blue eyes, and she searched his face as if she expected him to disappear or turn into someone else.

"You came," she said.

"Of course I came."

She threw her arms around him. He held her and ran his hand over her dark curls. "It's okay. I got you."

"And I can't see how you're goin' to get rid of me this time."

Zach barely managed to smile at her joke. "Did they hurt you? Feed you? Give you water?"

"They didn't."

Zach felt her forehead: hot as a fever.

They'd found her, but she wasn't safe yet.

"We need to get you out of here." He stood, helping her to her feet.

"Wait." She pulled free and pointed at the handcuff still around her ankle.

Zach patted his pockets, although he knew very well he'd left his key in the car. "Anybody got handcuff keys?"

"Um." Xavier pulled the same searching routine as Zach. Neither of them worked in a capacity where they were arresting criminals every day.

"Check Hennessy's pockets," Molly said.

Xavier followed Molly's suggestion and came up with a wristwatch on the first try.

"Wait a second." Zach squinted at the silver watch. He couldn't be sure from here, but it looked like—

"It's yours," Molly supplied.

Xavier found handcuff keys in Hennessy's other pocket. He tossed them to Zach, who unlocked the cuffs.

"Zachary?"

He looked up. It was so good to hear her say his name.

"Take me out of here."

"Yes, ma'am." He scooped her into his arms and carried her out of the container, pausing only to grab his watch before taking Molly to get more help.

She was free. Molly pressed her cheek against Zachary's shoulder, reveling in the feeling of safety: Zachary's arms around her again. And also because the vertigo was nearly unbearable.

Was her head spinning and her stomach rollicking because of the dehydration or the shock of being saved just when she thought her life was at an end?

Sunlight turned her vision bright red. She squinted harder against the light, willing herself not to remember who she'd seen through her last red vision.

A furious Hennessy come to kill her.

Molly snapped her eyes open and scanned the area. Xavier was a few feet ahead of them, taking Hennessy to a tan Chevrolet parked behind Zachary's silver Subaru. Zachary reached his car and set her down on the curb. She immediately gripped his car to keep from pitching over.

Zachary picked her right back up again and carried her a few more meters to Kent's car.

"What are you doin' here?" she asked once he'd hopped out of the car.

"I was in the neighborhood." Kent's grim expression didn't match his joke. He opened his passenger door, and Zachary set her on the seat. The air-conditioning blasted her face.

It was heavenly.

"Do you have anything to drink?" Zachary asked Kent.

"Diet Pepsi?"

"No, no soda—water, Gatorade, anything else."

Kent scanned the interior of his car while Zachary ran off, hopefully in search of water. Molly turned to the cup holder and popped the lid off Kent's fountain drink to fish out an ice cube.

She almost felt bad for sticking her fingers in his drink, but guilt could wait until she was all right. She popped the ice cube into her mouth and stole another to rub on her face.

Zachary reappeared with two half-full water bottles. "From our last run." He opened one and gave it to her.

She gulped down the hot water in both bottles.

"Go slow," he said.

The water reached her stomach and immediately threatened to turn right back around.

Zachary watched her as if waiting for her to vomit, but Molly breathed through the nausea.

"I'll check my trunk." Zachary dashed away again. Molly swiped another ice cube before he returned with a mostly empty bottle of Gatorade.

Everything he was doing for her, and all she could focus on was the dark stain on his hand. "Why do you have Doyle's blood on you?"

Zachary traded her empty water bottle for the Gatorade. "He's dead."

That wasn't an answer to her question. Before Molly could ask again, a surge of nausea overtook her. She wasn't sure whether it was the dehydration or the sight of blood.

First the photograph, now actual blood on his hands?

"Hang on." Zachary stood to talk to Kent over the roof of the car. "Have you called 9-1-1?"

Molly didn't hear his response, but Zachary didn't pull out his mobile to call, so she assumed Kent had either handled it or was about to.

"I don't need an ambulance," she murmured.

Zachary crouched down next to her again. "You're running a fever, love."

That didn't make sense. Did it?

When she had no response, Zachary added, "Heatstroke can kill you, and you're dehydrated."

She held up the empty Gatorade bottle as a protest. He took it, again flashing the stripe of blood on the side of his palm.

Zachary was even wearing the same gray William & Mary T-shirt as in Hennessy's photograph. But, then, he wore the same thing at least once a week for their morning run. "Have you been lookin' for me all day?"

"Since six this morning, when I pulled up to your place and found the squad cars."

"Squad cars? For Mr. Petrowski?"

Zachary frowned. "He didn't make it, Moll."

She clutched at her shirt. Miles Hennessy had murdered Mr. Petrowski because of her. This—all of this was her fault.

Including anything Zachary had done in a desperate attempt to get her back. She picked up Zachary's bloodstained hand. "What happened?"

"Hennessy shot Doyle. He said self-defense; evidence might say otherwise. I got there right before he died." His voice dropped to a murmur. "Too late to save him."

The gunshots. Zachary *had* been there when she thought he was about to save her. "Miles showed me a picture of you arrestin' someone today?"

"Doyle sent me on an errand."

She quirked an eyebrow.

"A hit," Zachary finished. He turned her hand over, fidgeting with her fingers, his gaze focused there too. "I faked it for Doyle and took the guy—a juror he'd bribed to fix his mistrial—into custody."

She couldn't tell if he was lying—Zachary was a good liar, sure, but after being fed so many lies today, her trained ability to read people was as off-kilter as her equilibrium. But avoiding her gaze wasn't a good sign. Molly disentangled her hand from his and tilted his chin up. "Then why won't you look me in the eyes?"

He shook his head. "There wasn't a right answer. I couldn't kill the guy, but . . . not killing him could have meant killing you."

She watched him for a long moment. He still couldn't meet her eyes. Not because he was lying—because he was ashamed.

Molly patted his free hand. "I think you made the right choice."

"Well, it worked out."

"Even if you had, Doyle wouldn't have given me up. His plan was to kill us both."

Zach offered her a weak smile. "I never could've looked you in the eyes again. Wouldn't deserve to."

As if to prove his point, he finally met her gaze, tucking a curl behind her ear.

Molly finally registered the approaching siren, not far away, rendering any argument from her moot. Not that she really had the energy to be fighting off an EMT. "What about the ceremony?" she managed.

"You . . . want to make the wedding?"

"What time is it?"

Zachary pulled the watch she'd given him out of his pants pocket. "Half past two."

"We can at least try. If we get there too late, then we can re-schedule."

A short man in a blue uniform stepped up behind Zachary. "Who's got the emergency?" he asked.

Zachary gave him a quick rundown of the pertinent facts—all mention of kidnapping conspicuously absent.

"Can you walk?" the EMT asked Molly.

"I can." With help from Zachary and the EMT, she climbed from the car and made it the few feet to the ambulance. She barely managed to climb up the high step and settle on the gurney.

A second EMT, waiting in the ambulance, took her temperature and read it off: 102°.

"That's bad, huh?" Zachary asked.

The first medic waffled. "Two degrees from heatstroke, three and a half degrees from normal." He adjusted a small fan to blow directly on her face and chest, and both paramedics pulled out instant ice packs, cracking them to start the chemical cooling reaction.

"How much have you had to drink today?" The second paramedic tucked an ice pack behind her neck, while the first took her blood pressure.

"I don't know . . . five or six ounces."

Molly thought she saw the EMTs exchange a look, but the next thing she knew, they were swabbing her other arm to start an IV.

"Oh, please, I don't—"

"You're dehydrated and getting close to heatstroke," the second EMT pointed out, echoing Zachary's own logic. "This is the fastest way to fix both problems."

"And then we'll get you to the hospital—"

"No!" Molly sucked in a little breath, stunned by her own shout. "You can't. I'll sign a release, only—I have to get to my weddin'."

This time, the paramedics definitely exchanged a look. "Do you know what day it is?"

Molly scowled. Did they think she'd lost her mind? "Friday, July twenty-first."

"It *is* our wedding day," Zachary confirmed from the foot of the gurney. "Supposed to be."

The medics gaped at one another and back at him.

"Would you believe . . . bachelorette party gone wrong?" Zachary's spurious explanation sounded like a total guess.

"No," the first EMT said, his tone flat.

Zachary shrugged. "Worth a shot."

What were the paramedics going to do, kidnap her—again? If she refused treatment, their hands were tied. "We can do the IV here," Molly interrupted. "And then I'll sign the release and you can go."

"If your temperature gets low enough," the second EMT said. The first medic fixed him with an irritated look.

"If it doesn't," the first EMT added, "straight to the hospital, got it? And we have to give you a full unit." He held up the IV bag.

"Deal." Molly shook each of their hands and then held out her arm for the needle.

Once the cool liquid was flowing, the EMTs let Zachary hold cold packs to her cheek and palm—and finally cut her free from the last PlastiCuff.

"I guess I owe you an apology," Zachary said.

Molly jerked around to look at him, but the sudden movement sent a jolt of pain searing through her skull. "An apology?" she managed.

"Yeah. The other night, when you told me you just knew something was going to go wrong today?"

She groaned softly. "Zachary, I've never been so sorry to be right."

"And I'm sorry I said you worry too much."

Xavier and Kent knocked on the open ambulance door. "Looks like a party," Kent said.

"Every minute," one medic grumbled. He took her temperature again: 100°

What did they consider low enough?

"You gonna make it?" Xavier asked.

"To the ceremony?" she replied.

Xavier laughed, and then stopped, looking back and forth between her and Zachary, neither of them smiling. "You're serious?"

"If she cools off enough," the first EMT insisted.

Zachary squeezed her hand, and his message was clear: *you will.* "Can she give you a statement now?" he asked his boss.

"I . . . guess so?"

Molly gave a quick retelling of the events of the night and day to the voice recorder on Xavier's mobile, making sure to include Mr. Petrowski's murder and the information she'd collected about the mistrial—and enough to put Hennessy away for at least a couple decades.

"We good?" Zachary asked as soon as she finished.

Xavier shrugged. "Gonna have a lot of paperwork." He eyed Zachary for a moment. "And I guess I'll take care of it. Didn't have time to pick up a present anyway."

Molly nearly hopped up to hug him, but remembered the IV in time. She glanced up at the bag. Nearly finished. But the simple fact that she felt as though she *could* get up and hug him spoke volumes. "Thank you, X."

Xavier gave them a salute. "See you at the reception."

"Good luck," Kent added.

"Thanks, guys," Zachary called.

"Sounds like you've had a busy day," the first EMT murmured. He checked her pulse and then her temperature again. "Ninety-eight point nine." His tone said he was begrudgingly giving her clearance.

Molly took a deep breath. Instead of feeling like she'd been sealed inside a roaster, it was merely a hot day. Instead of feeling too flushed to even think of food, she was famished. Instead of feeling like her mind was slipping, she felt sharp.

Amazing what a little water and electrolytes could do for a body.

"How are you doing?" Zachary asked.

"Best I've felt all day." No one pointed out that this was a very low bar. "Where's that release?"

The second EMT handed her a clipboard with a form and an information sheet. The first paramedic removed the IV, then handed her two bottles labeled Oral Rehydration Solution. "Drink these within the next hour, and at least that much water every hour after until midnight. You need to stay out of the heat today, and for a couple weeks at least." He fixed her with a look more pointed than the IV needle. "Including pictures."

"Mum will love that," she muttered.

"She'll just love the fact that you're safe."

Molly drew a deep breath of cool air. She was really, truly, finally safe.

And in two hours, they would be married. Zachary helped her out of the ambulance, but she could walk the twenty feet to his car under her own power.

"Sure you want to try for this?" he asked.

"Zachary," she said, "I have spent the last fortnight worryin' night and day that somethin' would happen today. Somethin' did happen, but I, for one, refuse to let Miles Hennessy win and ruin our weddin'." He squeezed her arm, and she gave him a nod of finality. "Now, drive."

B Y THE TIME THEY REACHED THE CURB by her building thirteen minutes later, Molly had already finished her first bottle from the EMTs. She'd also informed her mum—her ears were still ringing from Mum's squeal of delight as soon as she'd said hello—and Lucy that she was safe. Already in the car on the way to the temple, Lucy conveyed the message to Zachary's mum, Debbie, except she substituted "now finished with work" for "safe."

Debbie, Lucy, and her mum had all vowed to be at her flat as fast as they could. All Molly had to do was go upstairs and wait for them while Zachary went home to get ready himself.

And she sat frozen in the passenger seat, her hand glued to the door handle.

After a moment, Zachary touched her shoulder. "Molly?"

"I know."

He started to speak again, but paused. "Sorry," he finally said. "Should've understood sooner." Zachary put the car in gear. Before Molly could wonder where he was taking her, he pulled into the underground car park below her building.

Where Mr. Petrowski was murdered. Because of her. She let go of Zachary to bury her face in her hands. He rubbed her back gently as he drove.

After a moment of winding through the basement, the car stopped. Zachary switched it off and pulled his keys from the ignition. "It's okay, Molly. You can look."

"Crime scene cleanup can't have—"

"I parked on a different level."

Molly lowered her hands, but the concrete walls and pillars of every level looked the same. Zachary got out and walked around the car to help her out. She might have had EMTs to cool her down and rehydrate her, but that and three swallows of the case of Nutella Zachary had gotten for her wedding present was hardly enough to fully recover from her ordeal today. He walked her to the elevator.

Not the one closest to her apartment. Not the one she'd ridden with Hennessy. But when the car arrived, the linoleum tiling and the faux wood paneling felt the same as the other two elevators in the building. A vise tightened around her ribs. Zachary urged her forward.

"Molly," he reassured her. "You don't have to do this today. We could reschedule."

"Sure, but I mean to do it today. And we can't show up lookin'—and smellin'—like we do now, you know yourself." She gestured down at her T-shirt and yoga capris, and his ratty William & Mary T-shirt and track pants.

Zachary saluted her. "Yes, ma'am."

She gripped his fingers and stepped onto the elevator. The doors slid shut behind them, and Molly exhaled. Zachary kept an arm around her, as if he were afraid she might disappear again.

At her flat, he pulled out his keys and slid one into her lock.

"You have my keys?"

"Um, not your keys, exactly." He pulled the key out a few millimeters, twisted it to the side and held it with one finger, and grabbed his wallet to smack the key. The key flipped in the lock. He turned it the rest of the way and unlocked her door.

"Bump key," she noted. They'd watched that episode of *Burn Notice* only last week.

He shrugged sheepishly. "It's why I've been guarding my keys—so you can't check out the groove pattern."

"Worried I'll outdo you, so?"

Zachary laughed. "Oh, I'm counting on it. Just trying to keep you from humiliating me." He tilted her chin up to give her a gentle kiss.

"Ah, but you wouldn't have it any other way," she codded him.

He tickled her waist. "You got me there. Now, let's get you some food." He escorted her to the couch, and left her there a moment to retrieve water and a pear from the kitchen.

Molly leaned her forehead against his prickly jaw as he settled in next to her. He needed to shave, and to get ready. Her hair was surely a frizzy mess. But she couldn't stomach the thought of walking away from him.

Of being left alone again.

"Oh," Zachary said. "I haven't told you about the infamous Saint family pre-wedding lecture yet."

"Shouldn't you be goin'?" she asked between bites, trying to ignore the vise tightening around her shoulders at the thought of him leaving her.

"I can wait."

Molly pinned him with a skeptical look. Zachary patted her knee. "Listen, I don't want to leave you alone any more than you want me to."

"All right."

"Dad starts off with this, 'We need to talk, man-to-man,' kind of speech, basically to let Mom and Lucy know they need to go in the other room—but it's like he thinks we're having 'The Talk' again."

A knock at the door saved Molly from sharing Zachary's cringe-worthy fate. He stood to answer the door.

"I knew you could do it!" Mum declared as soon as he let her in. She hugged Zachary, planted a huge kiss on his cheek, then pushed him aside to rush to Molly, the skirt of her green dress fluttering out behind her. "Are you all right, love?"

"I am, for the most part." She'd hold off on telling her about limiting the photos out of doors, though.

Her da, in a suit for perhaps the third time in his life, stepped into her flat to shake Zachary's hand. "Fair play." Da clapped him on the shoulder.

"Oh, absolutely," Mum piped up. "Deadly job, Zachary."

"We need to keep Molly out of the heat."

"I can tell my own parents," Molly chided him. "You go and close the door."

Zachary went to obey, but before he could, a voice from the hallway called, "Wait!"

Lucy and Zachary's parents, Debbie and Jim, filed in as well. They were also ready for the wedding, his parents in royal blue, and Lucy in a filmy dress in the color she'd picked.

Molly's sister Bridie brought up the rear. "Fionn's keepin' the kids entertained." She glanced at Lucy's blush pink dress and spun around to cast a look at Molly that was more sour than any lemon.

Molly, who'd carped at Bridie's ugly, discordant pink-and-green wedding eight years ago.

"Now it's a party," Zachary murmured, and closed the door at last.

"All right." Molly raised her voice to address the assembled crowd. Zachary wove his way through the family to help her to her feet. She was steady enough to stand on her own, thank you, but she opted to hold his hand. "Obviously we're very far behind schedule."

Debbie squinted at her, then at Zachary, her blonde bouffant bobbing as she swiveled between them. "Is that what you two wear to work?"

She double-checked what she was wearing. Tatty pajamas still.

Mum adjusted her glasses—green frames today—and scanned her up and down again. "What on earth happened to you? What are all those marks, love?"

Molly held up her hands, noticing the chafing on her wrists. The bandage from the IV and the marks on her ankle certainly weren't helping either. "Long story—suffice to say, we both need to take showers, and I'm goin' to need a little help gettin' ready."

"Actually, we've got it covered." Lucy held up a cosmetic bag. "Go hop in the shower already!"

Zachary turned to his mum. "Mom, can I get a key to your hotel room?"

Debbie nodded, again jiggling her hair, as she searched through her purse. "Here you go, hon."

"Thanks, Mom. Told you getting a room near Molly was a good idea."

"Come on, Zach." Lucy waved away his faulty reasoning. "You know we stayed there because we like her better than you."

Molly caught Zachary's gaze for the briefest second. They both knew Lucy had begged to stay on this side of town because it was farther from Paul's apartment.

Lucy took Molly's elbow. "Let's hurry up so we actually make you part of this family—before you change your mind."

Molly laughed and headed toward her room. "Come on, Bridie."

As her sister followed, she could hear Zachary's instructions to their mothers. "Make sure she eats something—she skipped lunch and breakfast—and gets plenty of water."

Lucy escorted Molly into her bedroom, making straight for her closet. "You know what you're wearing to the temple, right?"

"I do."

"Can't believe you'd let her wear pink," Bridie muttered. "After the stink you made—"

"Oh, whisht." Molly waved away her older sister's argument.

Bridie eyed the closet where Lucy was searching for the right dress. "She's the one with the bad breakup, so?" Bridie murmured.

"She is."

Bridie's scowl finally softened. "I'll go make you somethin' real to eat, Molly girl." She squeezed Molly's shoulders and ducked out.

Molly gave her room a once-over. Nothing had changed. Her dress, her shoes, her suitcase. Even the sheets were kicked aside as she'd left them.

Before Miles had come.

It felt like a lifetime ago.

It felt like it could happen again this very second.

Molly closed her bedroom door and leaned against it.

Lucy poked her head out of the closet. "Are you okay? What happened today?"

Molly forced a smile. "We'll talk about it later."

And she would. She was weak and still recovering, but she would make it through the rest of this day, and then she could really rest.

Lucy tossed Molly's favorite emerald green dress onto her bed. "Okay, you hop in the shower, and I'll go—"

"Could you wait in here, perhaps, please?" Try as she might to hide her feelings, panic pushed the pitch of her voice past asking and into pleading.

"Oh. Sure." Lucy settled on the bed and plugged her phone into the charger on Molly's nightstand.

Where her ring should have been. Molly whirled around and whipped the bedroom door open. "Zachary!" she called down the hallway.

The front door to her apartment was open, and it swung shut halfway to reveal Zachary on his way out. "Yeah?"

"Tell me you know where my ring is."

He flashed her a calculatedly guilty grin and ducked out.

"Now will you get in the shower already?" Lucy chided.

She sighed at Zachary's antics, though she didn't really mean it. Before she closed her bedroom door again, Molly pivoted back. "Da? I need one more thing before I start gettin' ready."

Zach was out of the shower in his parents' hotel room when he realized his change of plans hadn't accounted for one thing—his tux. It was now across town, hanging neatly in his living room. Mocking him from afar. Just getting there and back would take more than an hour, let alone changing and driving to the temple.

What was he going to do, wear his dirty clothes for the photos? Granted, nobody would be looking at him—he'd seen Molly in her dress; she was gorgeous—but somehow he didn't think she'd appreciate the extra help in making her look good.

There had to be a place he could get a tux nearby in an extreme rush. Zach grabbed his phone to search for one, but got sidetracked by a waiting message.

Congrats was all it said. From Paul.

Thanks, man, Zach tapped out. He drew a deep breath and blew it out slowly. Lucy had expressly forbidden them from sending an invitation to her ex—although she and Paul were still dating when Zach and Molly set the date, so the guy already knew today was the day.

Wish I could be there to tell you in person, came a second message. *I'll have to mail my gift.*

Zach steeled himself and tapped out one more message.

Lucy would kill him. Mostly because she was still in love with Paul.

He hit send anyway. Then he deleted the conversation. And Paul from his phone for good measure.

He pulled up a search for tuxedo rentals nearby, but before he dug into the results, a knock came at the door. He peered through the peephole, though no way was he opening the door in a towel. He'd definitely hung the Do Not Disturb sign.

Peering back at the peephole on the other side of the door stood Colm Malone. Molly's dad. What was he doing here?

And then he saw it: in each hand, Colm held a hanger.

There were certainly worse things than his soon-to-be father-in-law seeing him in a towel. He tucked it tighter around his waist and pulled the door open. "How'd you get these?" He took the hangers from Colm—his tuxedo and a suit to wear to and from the temple. Zach hung them on the pole behind the door and turned back to his almost-father-in-law.

"Someone needs a tan," Colm deadpanned.

"Yeah, and I doubt two weeks in Ireland is going to fix that."

Colm picked up a shopping bag from the floor. Zach's shoes and socks.

Molly must have given her dad a list of everything he'd need.

Sudden movement down the hall made Zach jump—and reach for his gun. His shoes dropped to the floor, but fortunately his towel didn't. He didn't wear a holster with a towel anyway.

Down the hall, his own dad approached, with a messenger bag and a suitcase rolling behind him . One Zach always carried to the temple, and the other was packed for his honeymoon.

"Thought you might need this, too." His dad handed over his bags. "And I've got your other suitcase in the trunk."

"Thanks so much, Dad, Colm."

"See you there." His dad and his almost-father-in-law both nodded and pivoted for the door.

"Colm," Zach called him back. "How did you get in my apartment?"

Colm held up a gray key. Zach took it—a perfect copy of his key, only plastic. Like from a two-part epoxy. Like she'd gotten his key, made an impression, and cast this herself. Like he hadn't spent the past two months guarding his keys from her. "Huh."

Colm raised an eyebrow above his wire-rimmed glasses. "Didn't you know Molly had it?"

"Oh, right. I forgot I gave it to her. Thanks again."

"No bother." He started away, but turned back, his face solemn. "Zachary?"

Great, another "man-to-man discussion." And this time he was going to have to listen to the lecture in a towel.

"Cherish my little *wan*."

Zach relaxed. "Of course. Always." Colm walked away and Zach shut the door behind him. He consulted the clock radio on the nightstand between the beds. 3:59. They were supposed to be at the temple any minute. He could only hope someone had thought to call to say they were running late. He'd settle for arriving in time to change clothes before the ceremony. They were at least half an hour away.

Except it was a Friday, and rush hour had already begun.

Crap.

Zach threw on his suit and grabbed his tux and temple bag. Was there any way they could beat the traffic?

No. By now, the roads had to be packed. They were going to have to reschedule—did temples do that on the fly?—and that was going to ruin Katie's timed-to-the-minute photo session and reception.

Unless . . . Zach grabbed his phone, paged through his recent calls and dialed.

"Agent Mason called," Evans answered. "I heard you have good news."

"Great news. We found her, she's okay—mostly—and we're getting ready to leave for the temple."

"To leave? Where are you?"

Zach gave the address to the hotel.

"You'll never make it with rush hour traffic. You know what? Stay put. Let me call a friend."

"Thank you, sir." Zach ended the call. He hadn't dared to expect the SAC could do anything—really, he would've settled for magnetic flashing lights—but something told him this was going to work out after all.

A knock at the door pulled him from his little victory. He threw it open. There was Molly, her knuckles poised to knock again. She was dressed, styled and gorgeous as always. The ruddy tint to her skin had faded to a blush that highlighted her freckles and deep blue eyes.

The front part of her hair was swept back, but the rest of her dark curls hung loose—not what she said she was going to do with it, but how he loved it. She held a water bottle in one hand and the last two bites of a sandwich in the other.

She really was okay. The nightmare was over.

It was really happening. They were getting married. Finally.

They weren't getting married. Molly couldn't bear to tell him. She took in Zachary in the doorway, his hair still damp and tousled, his top two buttons undone, his tie slung around his neck. She bit her lip, then reminded herself she mustn't smudge her lipstick.

This was why she never wore lipstick in the first place.

"Have your recommend?" Zachary asked.

"And the marriage license. You?"

He patted his back pocket. "Yep." He fetched his tuxedo and bags from the room. "You look amazing," he whispered as he stepped into the hallway.

She smiled and traced her thumb across his forehead as if to smooth out a furrow in his brow. "You look stressed."

"Thanks a lot. How are you feeling?"

"Better and better."

He brushed a kiss against her lips. "Good."

Molly rubbed the lipstick off his lips. She polished off her sandwich, and they started down the corridor, Zachary busily raking his fingers through his hair.

"Your hair is fine," she reassured him. "Lovely."

"Exactly what I was going for." Zachary fished in his pocket and pulled out his wristwatch and a key. A gray plastic key. The copy she'd made of the key to his flat.

"I was waitin' for the right time."

"I think you found it." He slipped the key back into his pocket. "You win this round."

"What's that? Four in a row?" They stopped at the elevators, and Molly finger-combed his light brown hair into place while he fastened on his watch. He smiled, his azure blue eyes lit with that same hidden truth she'd always loved. She traced her fingertips down his now-smooth cheek.

All this effort for nothing. She'd called the temple, and while the sweet, shaky-voiced secretary was sympathetic, her options were limited. Apparently, this weekend was a popular time for weddings. She said she'd check for an opening tomorrow, but didn't sound hopeful.

The elevator chimed its arrival, and they stepped into the car. "You know, Zachary," she began once they were on the way down. "Perhaps we shouldn't go racin' off. I mean, we're not goin' to be able to make our sealin', so maybe we should just have . . . another rehearsal dinner, you know yourself. Let our parents get to know one another better."

He snorted. "You mean give your mom another chance to warm up to mine?"

"Apparently they've been bondin' today."

Zach cringed. "I don't like the sound of that."

"Definitely dangerous," Molly agreed after another sip of water. "But again, there's no reason for us to rush, so."

"Sometimes, Molly," he said, "you have to take a leap of faith."

"I'm all for faith, Zachary, love, but unless God's goin' to part the Red Sea of I-90 . . ." The elevator chimed as it reached the ground floor.

The doors slid open, they stepped into the lobby—and she heard the sirens.

"Oh, good," Zachary said. "Our ride is here."

Her jaw nearly hit the floor. "What?"

"Well, more like our escort."

She couldn't help a little gasp. They might actually make it? Tears pricked at her eyes.

She was recovering. They had a chance of making their wedding in time. Her heart felt so full, her chest couldn't contain it.

Zachary shifted his parcels around and held out her ring to her. "Marry me, Molly?"

She was beginning to get used to everything about their relationship being out of the ordinary—but this had to be the first time lights and sirens would accompany a couple to the beginning of eternity. "Promise me not every day of our life together will be like this."

"Not every day. But probably every other."

Though it might well be true, Molly laughed until he kissed her. "I love you," she murmured.

"So marry me."

She pretended to acquiesce with a patient sigh. "All right, you win."

"I certainly do." He beamed at her and slid her ring on her finger. "Oh, and I love you, too."

Zachary kissed her again, sweet and tender, and they started out to greet the sirens.

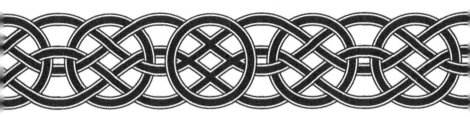

Dear Reader,

Thank you so much for reading *Saints & Sinners*! This book completes the Saints & Spies series, releasing ten years to the day after I came up with the initial idea for the first book. I finished the first draft of this book exactly one year later. Obviously, this book was nine years in the making. For a while I didn't think it would ever get to you, but now I'm really happy to share this story! I hope you enjoyed it as much as I enjoyed writing it and sharing it with you.

I've worked tirelessly to make this book enjoyable for you. Can I ask a quick favor? If you'd be willing to review this book online, it would help me secure advertising spots and spread the word about this book. Additionally, if you send me a link to your review, I'll send you an invitation to join my review team and get a preview copy of my next novel. You can email me your link (or for any other reason! I love hearing from readers!) here: Jordan@JordanMcCollum.com.

Looking for more to read? Check out my previous series, Spy Another Day, if you haven't already. If you join my reader's group, you'll get a free ebook to get you started in the series! You can join me here: http://jordanmccollum.com/read/

Thank you again, and I hope to entertain you again soon!

Jordan McCollum

P.S. Want even more happily ever after? Be sure to join my readers' group to get an extra short story about Lucy & Paul! Join here: http://jordanmccollum.com/read/

Acknowledgments

I WAS SURE THE FIRST BOOK in this series would be the longest I'd
ever take from writing a book until its final publication, but each
successive book has taken even longer. After nine years and two
major rewrites, I'm so glad to finally get this novel out to you.

Publishing is a very demanding job, and I couldn't do it without
the love and support of many people, most of all, my family. My
husband, Ryan, and our children, Hayden, Rebecca, Rachel, Hazel and
Benjamin, are all very patient while Mom tried to sneak in just
another page or two of work. My support network extends back, too,
with my parents, Ben and Diana Franklin. They helped me to love
reading and writing from a young age, and they were my first
(demanding!) editors. My sisters, Jaime, Brooke and Jasmine, and my
grandparents, Dale and Phyllis Harmon, are my biggest cheerleaders.

Since this book has been sitting on my hard drive(s) for nearly a
decade, a crazy number of people have read part or all of it. Once
again, Sarah Anderson was invaluable as an alpha reader, although I
only gave her the first draft of the first chapter during the writing
process. She was the first to read the finished first draft as well, and
continues to cheer me on as much today as all those years ago.

After her, more feedback on the early chapters came from
Christine (C.K.) Bryant, Donald J. Carey, Raquel Hert, Pendragon
Inman and C. Michelle Jefferies. Skip ahead a couple years, and
Kierstin Marquet helped me polish the first chapter further.

More recently, I received invaluable feedback and encouragement
from Raneé S. Clark, Heather Baird, and Ben Franklin (AKA Dad).

After their kind words, I found that I was actually quite proud of this story! Naturally, Sarah Anderson gave it one last read-through—and two thumbs up—before it was ready for you. My review team were also instrumental in some final refinements. Thank you!

In addition to critiques and readers, I also had a lot of help and support from other sources. My ever-patient accountability group, the Society of Agile Writers, was immensely helpful. They listened to me complain about editing this book nearly every day and encouraged me to keep moving forward. Best of all, they were there with me to celebrate the triumphs of finishing each stage! So many thanks go to Donald J. Carey and Shallee McArthur.

I want to again thank Sarah M. Eden for fantastic advice on writing an Irish character. As with the other books in this series, Aisling Doonan of RubySasha Designs kindly read this book and helped with my Irish phraseology and culture from a native's perspective. Rebecca Blevins provided editorial feedback, but any errors left here are all mine.

Additional research help came from FBI Special Agent Mark Roberts, who graciously answered my plot questions and helped me find the right ways to handle some elements. Procedural errors, however, are mine. And poetic license, let's say. Yeah, sounds good. (For example, the whorl fingerprint pattern isn't all that rare, but it is the only one you can differentiate from the bottom of the print. Sorry!)

A special editorial shout-out goes to my mother, Diana Franklin, and special pep talk shout-outs to Sarah Anderson, Diana Franklin, Jaime Wilkins, Brooke Anderson, Jasmine Bennion and Raneé S. Clark, for last-minute help to get this book out into the world.

Special thanks also goes to my mother's book club, especially my old friends (and family) Aunt Melony, Auntie Ros, Sally, Becci, Barb, and new friend Karla.

As always, the source of all inspiration, talent, time and effort is my Heavenly Father, and I'm eternally grateful to Him for these blessings.

About the Author

PHOTO BY JAREN WILKEY

AN AWARD-WINNING AUTHOR, JORDAN MCCOLLUM can't resist a story where good defeats evil and true love conquers all. Her first four novels, the Spy Another Day series, were all voted as finalists for the Whitney Awards, a juried prize. In her day job, she coerces people to do things they don't want to, elicits information and generally manipulates the people she loves most—she's a mom.

Jordan holds a degree in American Studies and Linguistics from Brigham Young University. When she catches a spare minute, her hobbies include reading, knitting and music. She lives with her husband and five children in Utah.

Made in the USA
Las Vegas, NV
16 June 2023

73471162R00162